Kingdom Keeper

THE REMARKABLE ADVENTURES OF ODEMOG OF MAZGAMOR

BY

R.A. DUNNE

To the extent that the image or images on the cover of this book depict a person or persons, such person or persons are merely models and are not intended to portray any character or characters featured in the book.

KINGDOM KEEPER
The Remarkable Adventures of Odemog of Mazgamor

Copyright © 2025 by R.A. Dunne

All rights reserved. No part of this book may be reproduced in any form or by any means without the prior written consent of the author and publisher, excepting brief quotes used in reviews.

Editing & Proofreading: Donna Millar, donnamillarinspirations.ca

ISBN- paperback		978-1-0698253-0-8

First Paperback Edition December 2025
Electronic Edition December 2025

*Dedicated to
my cherished eleven.
You are loved.*

"With great power comes great responsibility."
Stan Lee

The Gathering

High above the crashing waves of the northeast coast of Mazgamor, members of The Circle were seated, sharing news of the Kingdom. In a room resplendent with tapestries telling the stories of Gatherings past, King Magnus, as this Gathering's acting prefect, hosted the leadership circle. Warmed by fires on three sides, the Circle sat listening to one another's point of view.

"I have reminded you before, my fellow Circle Members, this is a dangerous man." Piralius emphasized his point, bringing a clenched fist down on the table at which they sat.

"There is no need to raise your voice, Piralius; you are not alone in your thinking." Magnus, seated to his left, put his hand on his old friend's shoulder.

"Then why do we wait to act?"

"It is true Magnus," said Morlog. "While we sit here he slinks about, or his men for him, and who knows when he will next strike. You, of all of us, know most recently the extent of what he is capable." Morlog looked to Magnus with empathy. He referred to the incident of the Nineteenth Gathering, when Constantia Glen was practically burned to the ground on command of the one to whom they referred.

"Morlog makes a solid reference," Kasreya added, knowing from her own village's early experience, thanks to the actions of the predecessor of their current nemesis.

"It is simple. He moves about, in and out of the shadows, watching our every move and plotting against us. Whether it is Thane-Ra himself or his raiders, there is always a sense of someone or something lurking. Even the sight of a riderless horgle flying overhead gives one pause and can be cause for concern." Morlog shook his head. "I cannot say he has been in Sweetbrooke Wren, but I can say I pay attention when branches move in the wind or a log creaks or twigs break. It's—" he paused and leaned sideways looking discreetly around a bowl on the table. "It's like a creature looking for his quarry. He edges out, pulls back, creeps forward, looks around, and—" BAM! Morlog brought his hand down hard, his palm slapping the table with full strength. A squirrel sprang up in the air from behind a large wooden bowl, bushy gray tail twitching in shock as it came back down to land, staring in fear at Morlog. Caught!

"SKEETER! What in burning flames are you doing here?"

"Uh, gabelnuts?"

"Someone get this creature a gabelnut and clear him from this chamber," Morlog shouted.

While the others at table sat frowning, Kasreya leaned forward and plucked the largest gabelnut from a bowl of fruit and nuts and gently passed it to the squirrel. She winked at Skeeter, who smiled, twitched his tail, and without looking back, raced down the edge of the table, jumped away, and scurried under the door.

All at table looked at one another as Morlog finished, "We cannot even know our own safety in this great hall." He raised both arms in a broad gesture. "None of us knows who Thane-Ra befriends to act against us."

"I agree," MaginTor said. "You have my vote, Morlog—I say 'nay' to his membership; Thane-Ra should not continue as one of our Circle. As to his being welcome at Gatherings, I say 'nay' to that also. He must not know of our defenses, and attendance gives a window to our strength when observing the combative games. If you agree, though I do not, he may remain at Gatherings; still, I say, he must at very least secede from the Circle."

"A vote then?" called King Magnus. Four more 'nay' votes and Thane-Ra's place in The Circle was eliminated. The message this censure communicated was strong.

Voting at table were six members, representing six of the seven villages or provinces of the Kingdom. Thane-Ra, as the seventh, had declined a formal invitation warning him of this vote. His absence simply communicating his disdain for all.

In attendance, from the very north was Piralius of Aureopiscis, a very stubborn, independent man of means whose family had fished the northern coast for generations. To the Circle, he represented prosperity through hard work. To his east, in Dragho Point, the home where they journeyed to unite for each Gathering, lived the overseer of the Point and all that made the Gathering what it was. MaginTor was only one of two of this generation known to mix any magic arts with his training. MaginTor was a renowned educator of history, sciences, and healing amongst other illuminating subjects. To the Circle he represented knowledge and healing.

From the distant southwest came the rough trader, Thorandal, who preferred being at sea to setting foot on land. A tough sea dog, he was appreciated in Trader's Peninsula for his vast knowledge of trade, the oceans, and lands most present would never imagine seeing. Although an amiable man, it behooves one not to cross him for his temper would tell another story. In his absence it seemed that Trader's Peninsula ran itself. Justice would be administered when he returned from each voyage and this, in itself, proved a source of caution for those who reside in Trader's Peninsula and entertainment for those who planned visits and trade at the Peninsula. Thorandal represented fair trade to The Circle. While Thorandal was a fairly good rider, he still preferred his ship, *Venusia,* over a horse. Each year, Thorandal's arrival by ship seemed a natural signal of the commencement of the Gathering.

In the lively village of Siwa, located across the Dragon Bay from MaginTor and his people, lived Mistress Kasreya of the Clan Tsesiwa who, in this time, was the only female member of The Circle. To The Circle, she represented the games and skills of combat. Reya, as she was affectionately known, led a matriarchal village whose gift was the precision of archery. Many opted out of the archery competitions held at the Gathering for they were dominated by the Tsesiwan women. Every year a few younger, braver souls new to the Gathering (one was required to be of age to participate) would be set in their place quickly by a defeating Tsesiwan arrow scoring the point that set these women apart.

West of Siwa, and the only village in the Kingdom that did not border on the ocean, lay the farming community of Sweetbrooke Wren. It was there that Teller Morlog resided. A storyteller and the Master Teller of the Kingdom, Morlog lived a singular life encouraging others to tell their stories. Well respected, he represented Tellers within the Circle. Morlog was a great teacher of tellers but few studied long with him for he was a perfectionist at his craft. The need for patience on the part of both student and teacher was great. Few lasted but for one young man. Morlog took great pleasure in his fondest pursuit as uncle and teacher to a young farmer and trader by the name of Odemog.

King Magnus of Constantia Glen, the most southern province of Mazgamor, represented leadership and compassion to the Circle and both of these he offered well and fairly. As a father and a King, Magnus brought great care to his role. Perhaps his gentle ways were too carefree and this was what made him such an easy target for Thane-Ra. Although known only to Queen Madelina, he still grieved the pain he felt his carefree defense of Constantia had brought upon his people by Thane-Ra's attack. United with his fellow Circle members, Magnus hoped to convey a strong message to Thane-Ra that enough is enough. No one would tolerate or bear his advances on their territory any longer.

With the decision made to restrict Thane-Ra from membership in the Circle, he would no longer be privy to information of arms men and women, tactics, knowledge, or skills shared amongst the Circle and at the Gatherings. Perhaps this action baited a hook as Thane-Ra already seemed to care little for his absence. It had only amplified his opportunity to move on villages with lesser defensive forces during a Gathering. Time would be the only measure by which they would know these answers.

And so, with this matter attended to, the continued business of the Circle and events of the twenty-second Gathering would commence. Already in the courtyard below, musicians could be heard to play the cheery welcoming tunes that brought neighbours from far and wide in the Kingdom. This event would celebrate healers, teachers, tellers, warriors, and leaders of all kinds. The Gathering is a time of acknowledgement, show, and most definitely tell.

Once a little one came of age, having passed eighteen cycles of the dozen circle moons, as the elders described it, he or she would be welcome to compete with others in the various games and performances. The youth acknowledged the excitement of turning eighteen and the great honour of attending the next Gathering. They would begin practicing their chosen skill with great enthusiasm.

For Magnus and Queen Madelina, this would be a special year. Their eldest, the Princess Annabella, had just turned eighteen; this would be her first Gathering.

The Queen and Princess stood at the marble rail of the upper plaza looking down at the festivities. Annabella wore a deep red velvet gown with a high collar connected to a silk-lined lace panel down the front of the bodice, her long hair cascading over her shoulders. Her mother, regally dressed, stood elegant in a cerulean blue velvet gown with long bell-shaped sleeves that folded back to show a cream silk lining. The bodice of this striking gown was finished with a high neckline, yet still showed off her neck and flawless features.

"Daughter, what story shall you captivate us with this night?" the Queen asked as she adjusted the colorful ribbons in Annabella's long blonde hair.

"I have not yet decided, Mother. I am fascinated by the Sweetbrooke Waters tale. Still, I think the story of how you and Father met is quite amusing and could win hearts in my favour."

"Don't be cheeky, child. That is not a story for tellers! You will keep any stories of Magnus and me to yourself, lass. Perhaps you should tell the tale of The Meadows?"

"What a lovely suggestion! I shall start with that. If I win, then next I shall tell your story!" Annabella laughed as her mother took her by the shoulders and feigned a rigorous shake.

* * *

With the music calling them out of chambers, the Circle Members adjourned their conference for the day and went their separate ways, each to open a different event. Kasreya was first out of the room with Thorandal not far behind for he would assist her in this task as there was no event for trade. They were off to opening ceremonies for the combat games. There, too, Amara, Kasreya's young cousin, would be competing in an archery demonstration emphasizing height and flame.

Trickling from the chamber slowly, others listened to the conversation of Magnus and Piralius.

"Piralius, we do not see one another enough. I know you would travel long and hard but I invite you to my castle following this Gathering."

"You know I cannot bear the thought of such lengthy travel, and so close to Khordrya. But for you, I shall give it serious thought."

"We shall welcome you with open arms, my friend," said Magnus as he thumped Piralius on the back.

The two stepped out into the sunlight and were greeted by well-wishers visiting from all about the Kingdom. The Twenty-second Gathering was underway.

* * *

Samezog reached down, hand extended to Deronezog. They grasped one another, hand at forearm, and Sam pulled his friend from the ground. Dero bowed graciously to Sam, acknowledging his defeat.

"The victor, Samezog of Sweetbrooke Wren," called the adjudicator from the side. "Next match: pairs, the victor Samezog, with Odemog of Sweetbrooke Wren. This will bring today's game to a close. Today's finalist will compete with the Eastern finalist who will be decided in the early morning heats commencing at sunrise."

A pair of eyes watched from high behind a stack of hay and waited. Sam stood patiently waiting for his opponent to come to the centre field. Minutes passed and soon the announcer called again, "Last call for Odemog of Sweetbrooke Wren—last call."

Sam looked around the combat field and then stood with his sword tip in the earth, both hands on the hilt, and stared at the ground. From behind the haystack emerged a giant of 6' 8½ inches in height. He stared across the field as he walked forward. Sensing something, Samezog looked up. Setting his eyes firmly on the giant, a smile slowly crept across his face. The giant stopped at legal distance and set right hand upon the hilt of his left draped sword.

"Sam." Odemog spoke firmly.

"Odemog."

"Be prepared to fall."

"On your mark," Sam murmured. He kicked the tip of his sword up seeing Odemog's grasp tighten to draw sword from sheath. With 18 inches difference in height, Odemog clearly had the advantage in battle. Still, Sam was quick and raised his sword swinging. The first defensive move went to Odemog. The two parried for some time—advantage Odemog for height; advantage Sam for fleet of foot. In the stands sat King Magnus, Morlog, and the other members of the Circle cheering both swordsmen back and forth favouring both, favouring neither.

As Sam tired, for he would only tire in this battle because of the amount of footwork required to stay ahead of one so much bigger than he, his sword became heavy. Round after round they fought until Odemog kicked Sam's foot out, knocking him to the ground. He plunged his blade into the earth beside Sam's right ear.

"Bit close there, chum," a startled Sam declared.

"Not by a long shot, Sam, not by a long shot!" Odemog reached down quickly and pulled his friend from the ground as the audience cheered heartily for him. Odemog bowed his head forward and gestured sideways to Sam—a further roar erupted from the crowd. It was well known that whoever would make it to the last fight with Odemog would fight a delirious battle and lose to the giant, but what an entertaining battle it would be. In fairness, Sam was the winner when compared to all other combatants but in regulation, it was in fact Odemog who won. He could not help his size and above all he was a truly fair competitor and this could not be taken away from him.

Circle members, the audience, and the swordsmen stood together celebrating the Western sword combat finals. Few noticed a rider enter the gates and pause. On seeing the King, the rider turned and approached. Kasell observed the rider and dispatched sentries, their spears crossed diagonally in front of the horse, blocking his path.

"Identify yourself," demanded a sentry.

"Yarman, messenger from Constantia. I bring urgent news to the King."

When away on such a trip, the make-up of the arms men at the palace, save for a few most trusted men remaining with the Royal Family, was comprised of newer members. None recognized Yarman but called him forward as his colors and presentation were all correct to those of a Constantia messenger. Kasell approached to take the message.

"And what brought you today, soldier?" asked Kasell.

"I bring word, as you shall verify," he revealed a scroll and passed it to Kasell who promptly broke its seal, "that the twin princesses are gravely ill. It is thought they will not survive long. I am to await a reply and return immediately."

Nearby, the King overheard the exchange of the substance of the message.

"Kasell, what news have you?"

"Majesty, it appears that Princesses Lily and Tulip have grave symptoms. This is word from Healer Lord Forthrumal. You are asked to return without delay."

"My darlings!" Greatly distressed by this news, the King looked around considering his options. "I cannot. The Queen shall go to them. I cannot leave a Gathering in progress."

"I shall be away then, to take word back to the Castle of the Queen's imminent departure," Yarman offered.

"Stay, rest your horse. It is a two-day ride for you. You may exchange your horse for one here and join the return party," Kasell commanded.

"As you wish." The rider dismounted and followed a sentry to gain refreshment, passing his horse off to a stable boy who attended to his mount.

Kasell watched the man as he walked away. Something inside did not feel quite right about him. Although he made it a point to welcome all new arms men, Kasell did not recognize this one. It was rare for him to miss a new recruit. Still, his presentation was well in form.

In such distress for her twin girls, the Queen bade the King to leave immediately. But, as leader of the Gathering, the King could not depart early.

"Magnus, you must come at once; our daughters' health takes precedent," Queen Madelina pleaded with the King.

"These are our daughters and I love and care for them deeply, my love, but the Kingdom requires me here first. On closing, I will follow immediately."

The argument was brief as both knew to argue long wasted valuable travel time.

The travel party, consisting of the Queen, Princess Annabella, and a full escort, prepared with a grave sense of urgency and was ready to leave within an hour. Yarman, the messenger, was to return with the party but as neither he nor his mount could be located when all were ready to depart, they were away without him.

And so, Queen Madelina, accompanied by Princess Annabella, who wished to remain at her mother's side, departed on the two-day journey back to Constantia Glen.

* * *

The Circle Members were meeting informally in a grounds tent as they discussed an official vote to close the Gathering and enable King Magnus to rejoin his family. Heads turned as a voice rang out: "Rider!"

Arms men of Constantia ran to the gated archway to stop the runaway horse. A wounded rider returned, slumped over his horse. The King's first arms man, Kasell, raced to catch the man as he slipped from his saddle. The rider uttered his last words: "Sir, the Queen…"

* * *

The Gathering closed with neither a vote nor a traditional ceremony; there was no blessing of water for healers or graduation of tellers. Such an occurrence had not taken place since the Nineteenth Gathering. On this occasion, as before, it simply closed as word of the dying rider spread through Dragho Point. There had been no time for formal declarations. Those who camped left their tents and gear to the care of the keepers of the Point. Riders took to mordagha and horse at once, flying and riding out from the Point fortress and encampment. Following the route known to have been taken by the Queen and her party, all headed south and west where they would cross the River Constantia, follow parts of Sweet Brook, and pass through The Meadow before veering southeast toward Constantia Glen.

The first party of riders to find any sign of the Queen's escort was a flight of Master Riders of Sweetbrooke Wren, Odemog among them. While a mordagha typically flies in leisurely fashion, it would still travel more ground than a horse. (Often a source of argument between the two species of beast…but that is another story.) And so, they flew ahead of the ground riders. In fact, they had not travelled long when the signs were observed. Flying past the hill people, a small nest of cottages in the hills above the village of Aureopiscis, they had reached the place in the Kingdom known as the convergence, where the borders of Sweetbrooke Wren, Siwa and Aureopiscis all converged. It was here they found an overturned coach, pale yellow in colour (the Queen's favourite). The Master Riders directed their mordaghas to land. Odemog, on Nassir, was sent back to inform the King and other searching parties of their discovery and location.

Seeing Nassir flying above, Kasell addressed the King and gestured skyward. Looking up, the King felt hope for a moment but was quickly overcome by a profound feeling of darkness.

Too soon, this cannot be a good sign, he thought. *Too soon.*

"Majesty," called Odemog, as Nassir closed in to land. "Queen Madelina's coach was found at the convergence. Regretfully, it was found overturned and neither she nor the Princess Annabella are there."

"Show us the way," called the King.

Nassir turned and lifted himself and Odemog to air quickly and at a speed of flight that could be followed by horse and rider, showed them the best trails to follow in order to reach the coach before they lost too much light.

Those who remained with the coach searched the forests and fields around the convergence. There they found many a fallen rider. A hard fight had been fought here. No sign of the Queen, the Princess, their first arms man, or who or what had fought these riders. They had simply disappeared. No creature remaining had survived. Both rider and mount perished. In a kingdom where beasts, creatures, and human, understand each other's language, not one was left alive to tell their story. This saddened both man and beast as they surveyed the loss. The question on all their minds was: if they were not left behind with those who perished, were they somewhere alive? Above them, Odemog, on Nassir, circled the location as the King's party drew closer.

The closer the King came to the site, the darker the feeling in his heart became. On seeing the fallen, he was overcome. In silent agony he dismounted his horse. With Kasell by his side, King Magnus walked the forest floor, pausing over each lost arms man, remembering them for their service. By now, others had righted the overturned coach. The King walked a circle around the coach looking for a sign. Of what he did not know. Still, he looked the coach up and down. He reached for the handle. Kasell stepped ahead of him and quickly opened the door for the King to climb up and into the coach. Once he was inside, Kasell quietly closed the door out of respect for his King and gestured for others to back away. He, too, stepped back to give the King privacy in the coach.

Magnus sat quietly within for some time. He thought of his wife, his twins and his dearest daughter, Annabella, who had accompanied them to the Gathering for the first time. He placed his hand over his heart, feeling almost as if it were slowly breaking.

"Kasell!" He shouted. "We must away, immediately. I must see the twins and princes. We must return to Constantia without delay. Have a follow party bring the coach. The Queen will need it." In a quiet place within, Magnus remained hopeful.

Loyal and efficient, Kasell was at the door of the coach before the King had finished calling his name. He gestured to the arms men who encircled the coach, quickly checking to ensure it would travel well. The King emerged, going straight to his mount. Then, he stopped.

We must be quick, he thought. *I must fly.* Not a master rider himself, he was rather unsure of the great mordaghas. He looked over at Odemog, staring intently for a moment.

"Odemog, it would ease my heart greatly to get home with speed of flight. Do you see a way to it?"

"King Magnus, it would be the honour of any master rider to be able to escort you home," replied Odemog. In a matter of moments, two smaller master riders leapt from their mordaghas crossed over and double mounted with another, freeing up saddles for both King Magnus and Kasell. Kasell gave instructions to those who would travel by land: wait for the next search party to catch up; continue the search travelling south together to be safe. Although unsure, the two Constantian horse riders, now astride mordaghas, Kasell and the King, soon left earth, taking to air in flight with Odemog and the others who flew in tight formation for reassurance. The flight took south with Odemog in the lead. To get them home as quickly as possible, Odemog would lead the flight through Volcanic Valley, shortening the passage back to the King's home. As they flew, the King silently prepared himself for what he would find at home and how he would tell his children what had become of their mother and sister, when even he knew not what had become of them or if they were even alive. Although his trip home was short, it was the longest journey this King had ever made.

In his great distress, it was not the King who observed the twin princesses playing in the orchid garden when they arrived at the Castle; rather it was Kasell who saw them first. Magnus's pain lifted somewhat and he was happy to be united with his family. But he did not notice that they were surprisingly healthy with no sign of fever at all. Kasell noticed. He went to work immediately to learn just who had dispatched such an urgent and false message to call the Queen home.

Odemog

"Skeeter, you must come down from there at once," Odemog growled as he leaned back in the saddle atop his mordagha. He shielded his eyes from the glare of the sun as he watched Skeeter leap gingerly from branch to branch as if descending a staircase. From the last shaking branch, Skeeter leapt through the air and landed on Odemog's shoulder. Odemog shook his head and made a clicking sound through his cheek. "Clk - clk. Away then, Nassir."

Skeeter took hold of Odemog's ear and held on for his life as the winged mordagha took flight. A mordagha is a difficult creature to learn to ride. It terrified Skeeter to ride with Odemog although the title of Master Rider had been bestowed upon him moons ago. When a mordagha takes flight, it happens very quickly. Storytellers say that the challenge of the mordagha is the mental barrier the rider can experience. When one thinks too much about the appearance and stature of a mordagha, it seems quite impossible to ride—or for that matter, fly. Some say it is because there are no reins like those used for efficiency and coordination with a horse. However, one directs a mordagha verbally as they are very good conversationalists and strategize well with their riders. There are no foolish mordaghas, only brave ones.

A mordagha looks like a rhinoceros to some, an elephant to others. They have a short horn centered on the forehead that resembles the legendary horn of unicorns although not as long, a stub at six inches in length. It is a generations-old argument, from where they descend. But all arguments aside, they are a round-bellied, winged creature that should not be able to fly, simply by laws of physics. This explains how difficult they are to ride. When a mordagha takes flight, they first bounce their hind quarters, as if to sit, and then push up, as if to jump. They flap their wings—themselves, deceivingly small, yet powerful and lift their front legs last. It would be like a bucking horse, were it not for their wings and belly. What always appears last to lift is their round belly—so round that all who ride are seated in a side saddle for comfort. And when that belly lifts it seems to dance left, then right, then left again. One might think that the creature first tries to throw the rider off forward, then backward and then a last effort is in the attempt to ditch the master by left or right side. Still, this is not so, as the mordagha is a gentle creature that feeds on vegetables and greens and prefers juicy water plants. It is an observant, playful creature with unusually good humour. It is said that some in the Kingdom never learned to ride because of these deceptive moves, but those of the Clan of Odem in the Wren that surrounds Sweet Brook were all known to become master riders.

Airborne, and gliding toward home, Skeeter relaxed his grip on Odemog's ear. The marks from where his claws had clenched were red because he had held on so tightly. He clambered down the front of Odemog's chainmail and curled up in the space between the horn of the saddle and the crook of the mordagha's neck. This was a favourite cozy wide spot between the shoulders of the beast that afforded much comfort on the long journey home to Sweetbrooke Wren. Skeeter, a silver-grey squirrel, closed his eyes and wrapped his bushy tail around himself to stop the rushing air. He was very proud of his tail.

A minute into his slumber, a rumble brought him back to listen to a familiar tune that Odemog had begun to sing. The mordagha, named Nassir, pressed his ears back against his head to block out the chanting for it was always at least a half-note off-key.

We fly, we fly
To Sweetbrooke Wren,
Home at last our journey's end.
Nay foe but friend we always find
Homes filled w' love and family kind.

This is our treasured Sweetbrooke
Flow waters gaily through
Swe-et-brooke, they freshen life as nothing can,
The brook 'tis life so sweet for man.
Swe-et-brooke, Swe-et-brooke,
The brook 'tis life so sweet for man.

Odemog finished his song and continued to hum the tune as he leaned back, carefree in the saddle atop Nassir. Through the sky they flew for some time, Odemog watching as the valleys and fields below rushed past them as if racing in the opposite direction. He stopped humming long enough to hear Skeeter snore rhythmically, curled up in a little ball near his right hip in front of the saddle. The air was warm and the sky blue as a robin's egg. There was not a cloud to be seen for miles in any direction as they flew north, returning from Trader's Peninsula.

With not a worry in the world, Odemog stopped thinking long enough that he began to sense hunger, realizing he had not eaten a thing since his porridge, cornbread, eggplant dish, creamed corn, applesauce, and hot, hot green tea at dawn. And so, as would be the habit of any extremely large man or beast, he began to ponder his next meal. Today, he thought, is the perfect day to feast on roast rabboo with vegetables such as turnips and yams and carrots, of course eggplant and, well, any hearty vegetables—oh, and Brussels sprouts. LOTS of Brussels sprouts, slathered with creamy, fresh butter. He had learned long ago to perfect the cooking of his favourite food—yes, a Brussels sprout. He knew one must tenderly cut them from the stalk and gently poke a knife twice in the bottom of the sprout to form an "X". Brussels sprouts, when harvested fresh from their stalks and cooked to perfection, would absorb the broth in which they were cooking. Then, slathered with fresh, creamy butter, he could almost taste them as he imagined popping them in his mouth one morsel at a time; a crunch to break them in half and they melted on the tongue—delightfully delicious! As Odemog contemplated cooking his meal, his mouth began to salivate. Best of all, he knew that in the root cellar was a very large rabboo caught just that morning by chance before he left to trade.

When wanderers and visitors would first meet Odemog in Sweetbrooke Wren, or while he was on his travels, they would know just by looking at him that he loved food and had a very big appetite. For Odemog, 6'8½ inches tall to be precise, meant that meals digested very quickly in his belly. In the Kingdom of Mazgamor, most of the citizens never reached more than five feet in height. Although, strangely, there were some female citizens, particularly of the Clan Tsesiwa in the village of Siwa nearest the North Dragho Ocean, who would grow as tall as five and a half feet in height.

Odemog would be home within the hour and knew that Mega, his mother, would have at least in part, dressed the rabboo to welcome him home. With this knowledge, his hunger grew.

When Odemog left that morning, Nassir was put to work. They were on their weekly adventure to Trader's Peninsula to trade vegetables from the village. Many thought the vegetables, particularly the carrots, were sweeter than any other in the land. Of course, this was due to whatever magic was in the waters of Sweet Brook itself. Fields upon fields were irrigated with water straight from the brook. Vegetables, grains and greens, fruits and nuts grew large, strong, plump, and very tasty in their respective seasons. Mostly, the people of the north were vegetarian, but that rascally rabboo was a treat that could not be turned down at table. After this day of trade, Odemog returned with his satchels filled with blades and tools from the visiting traders and brightly coloured fabrics and silks from other distant Kingdoms. As he pondered the day and continued his flight home, he leaned forward on his elbow and patted Nassir's shoulder.

"Take us lower, Nassir, over the water," he said.

Nassir raised wings up, brought them in and stretched his neck out and down. They dropped quickly in the sky but a foot, causing Skeeter to lift from his resting spot. Odemog caught him with his palm like bouncing a ball and, still curled up wrapped in his tail, the squirrel settled back down in the crook of the saddle between Nassir's shoulders. He stirred not a muscle. This caused Odemog to snort a small laugh because he knew that, had Skeeter known what had just happened, there would have been much—about nothing—well, almost nothing.

Just a few feet above the trees, Odemog watched as they now followed Sweet Brook, wending their way north, opposite the direction of the brook. *It should be called a river,* he thought, *it's certainly big enough.* He watched the trout jumping in the water and turquoise bullfrogs leaping into the water as Nassir's shadow passed over them. Ahead he saw an eagle close wings and drop from the sky, diving to catch supper up from the brook. It reminded his stomach of his hunger. Reaching back, he drew a bundle of carrots from the satchel. Holding them by the greens, Odemog ate them one by one in three easy bites. Dangling the greens over Skeeter, he tickled him, then leaned forward and fed the greens to Nassir, who quietly wished a carrot had been left attached for he felt his hunger creep up as well.

Having just been tickled, Skeeter brushed his paws across his furry face to Odemog's further amusement. Stirring and stretching, Skeeter rose from his sleep. Lifting his head high, he felt the breeze on his face and thought to curl back up again to stay warm. Instead, he turned and smiled up at Odemog. Climbing up the chainmail, Skeeter hunkered down on his friend's left shoulder in much the same way as Odemog rested on the back of his mordagha, Nassir. With his right paw, Skeeter loosely held Odemog's ear as he reclined, belly protruding, leaning on his left paw. His tail blew to his side, prompting him to wrap it round his exposed back feet. The three continued their gaze over the fields and Sweet Brook as they journeyed northward.

The light began to change in the sky; the day was moving on as it was now long past noon, perhaps even closer to half past the third hour. Temperatures would soon start to change to cooling and shadows would continue to grow. From the sky, the trees that lined the brook looked like tufted vegetables poking up from a field. With one eye closed, Odemog pinched thumb and fingers together, pretending to pluck the trees, like carrots, from a field and gobble them down. Skeeter was only slightly amused by what Odemog thought most entertaining. This was not new to either of them, of course.

Nassir began to turn away from the brook. Odemog looked in the direction of their changed course and saw what had also caught Nassir and Skeeter's attention: black smoke. It did not come from a clearing, but from a grove of trees. Nassir looked up for instruction and Odemog simply said "Yes, take us down."

Nassir touched down quietly, something a stranger would not think possible of a mordagha. Skeeter rested, still on Odemog's shoulder, on all fours as he considered the unplanned landing. Odemog slipped down from the saddle, touching the hilt of his sword as he took a first step. Skeeter took hold of Odemog's left ear and wrapped his tail around Odemog's braid for added security. Nassir sat down and began to tear at the grass and roots, quietly eating a luscious snack. In an attempt to conceal himself, Odemog crept toward the trees, leaning forward and with knees bent. Once amongst the gabelnut trees and firs, he could hear a small voice complain, then cry, complain again, then emit a loud, desperate sigh. He could see nothing.

"Oh bother," uttered the voice.

A few steps closer to the voice, he could smell the fire as it burned, and now could hear the fire, the voice, and still he saw no one. Even bent over, he should see someone belonging to the voice. Another quiet voice whispered to Odemog,

"Look left Moggie, down there." Skeeter gave his ear a tug as he flicked his tail quickly pointing down beside Odemog.

Startled, Odemog realized that, had his steps taken him a course any further left, he would have been right upon the little one. Well, there she was—the little voice. And a pretty little voice if there ever was one. He stepped away and went down on his knee.

In a kingdom where animals, beasts, and creatures are able to speak and understand one another, the wisdom of this moment was to have Skeeter, the smaller of the two, speak to the little one so as not to scare her. Skeeter knew his cue when Odemog touched knee to earth. With one spring, Skeeter was off the shoulder and on the knee.

"Good day little one, what brings your tears?" asked Skeeter.

They had crept forward so quietly that the words startled her in her place beside them. The little girl fell backwards where she sat. Looking up at what seemed like a monster, she looked frightened enough to scream. Undaunted, Skeeter continued.

"Little one, we are Odemog of Sweetbrooke and, myself, Skeeter—of Sweetbrooke also, you know, of course you know, I think…do you?" He was stammering now as his wording had confused him more than it had the little one. This caused Odemog to start to giggle. Now, Odemog had a funny way of giggling that one would not attribute to a giant of sorts. It was a small giggle, not tiny, but small; a tiny giggle might have made him look foolish. Combined with a charming twinkle in his eye, Odemog's laugh put smaller creatures at ease. And so it was, the little one began to giggle too. This, however, lasted only for a moment as she quickly recalled her plight and again her tears started to flow. Skeeter turned a circle twice, three times on Odemog's knee. Odemog stroked the squirrel's back to let him know all was well. It was the same gentle touch that came as an expression of gratitude, since the two were so greatly opposite in size they could never press hand to paw to clasp and shake.

"We saw your smoke and thought to come by to be sure all was well. But, seeing your tears and this unfriendly fire, I offer my aid in your distress."

Odemog bowed his head forward. Skeeter, pressing his right paw against his heart, did the same.

The little one stood quietly, looking at the pair of strangers who had come to her assistance. Collecting herself at once, she walked to the fire. She stopped, hands on hips and surveyed the area. Certainly, it was true, this was an unfriendly fire. The smoke was dark and black, showing that it was burning things one would normally not put to fire. As it was, she had not lit the fire, but a rough group of riders who, she thought, though they would have been well out of their way, were Khordrian raiders.

"The smoke," she said, "a signal that brought good fortune in your arrival, still could bring bad. We must make it white before it is too late." She spoke wisely for such a little one. The same thought was in the minds of the others as Odemog began to break dry branches to add to the fire. Changing the makeup of the fire with dry branches was just part of the solution. The first step was to remove that which caused the blackening of smoke. Boxes of products, foods and other sundries were knocked away with a large stick. Dirt was kicked on these items to smother the burn. No oxygen, no more fire; no more fire, no black smoke. And most importantly, no black smoke meant no unwelcome visitors. Skeeter raced around the pile kicking dirt in as he went, dousing hot spots. Odemog and the little one began to throw the dry wood on the remaining fire, causing the smoke to change to white, a fire for comfort. A traveller's fire. With this done, Odemog lifted and placed two logs as seats surrounding the fire. What was so easy for this giant would have taken at least two others to do, and twice the time.

Odemog gestured for the little one to be seated to rest. Joined by Skeeter, he sat on the log opposite, leaned both elbows on his knees to get closer to her and said, "Little one, if you please, who are you and how may we be of service? Darkness is soon here and we do not know from where you came or the direction you seek to travel. Pray, tell us your story."

"My name is Princess Lily," she introduced herself, "I am from Constantia Glen which lies at the foot of the Trezano Mountains and west of Mid Lake."

"Of course. Your father is King Magnus. I saw him on a visit to the Gathering only a few moons ago," said Odemog. "What brings you so far and away from home and how do you come to be all alone here?" he asked.

"It is my father's birthday this day and my brothers' birthday is coming," she began her story, "I wanted to get them something special. My father especially has been so full of sadness this past year. I asked to visit Trader's Peninsula. I have not been away for some time. Since my mother and my sister Annabella disappeared from the Gathering, father forbade our travels. So, when we were done, I begged my escort to take me up through The Meadow to see the mingling beasts. They are so happy and peaceful there. When we reached the lower of Twin Ponds, we were attacked by raiders who chased us north. They outnumbered us by far. You see, when I asked for the detour, my escort dispatched two riders—father says we must always travel in pairs for safety—to inform him that we would camp away into this next moon. I don't know if the riders found our messengers or simply found us, but they charged from the south. Kasell, the lead of our remaining team, thought they must have been hunting in The Meadow. Shame upon them for that." Princess Lily shook her head disapprovingly, referring to the pact of the Kingdom to leave beasts and creatures safe in the Meadow. As the pact amongst creatures and beasts forbids predatory acts amongst them, they ought not to be preyed upon by traders and travellers who pass through the Meadow.

Princess Lily continued her story. "After they chased us north for some time, perhaps a half of an hour, they seemed to break up. It seems that they had spread out with fast riders encircling us. Surrounded and cut off, we could hear their shouts to close in. Brave men were they, my escorts, they fell not far back," she gestured, pointing south, "to the swords and arrows of the raiders. My team of horses was frightened to a gallop and I was drawn here where raiders caught up with my coach. Kasell had told me to hide if we were separated. They did not find me, as I climbed that tree, yonder." She gestured to a beautiful willow tree, the skirt of which could hide even Odemog should he climb it for cover.

"And how did the fire begin?" asked Skeeter.

"While I was in the tree, I heard their leader, who wore a red tunic with, I think, a lion—some black beast—upon it. He told them to destroy all so that the one who escaped had nothing to return upon." She continued, "With that, they burned it all: foods, oils, clothing, gifts for my brothers—they won't like that—a fine gown for my twin sister, Tulip, and worst of all," bowing her head in her hands, she began to cry again, "my father's gift."

Skeeter crossed over gingerly, skipping the fire so that his tail was spared a singeing. He climbed her frock, it had a lattice of ribbon stitched across the front, brushed her cheek with his tail gently saying, "There, there, little one, your father's gift shall be your safe return."

"But first, we shall go to Sweetbrooke Wren," said Odemog.

2

Dusk would soon be upon Constantia Glen. The King's birthday had come and then gone with the setting of the sun. King Magnus stood at the northern window of his modest castle, looking west and east then west again where his gaze finally rested. 'Modest' really described the King more than the castle, if truth be told. For this wise king, whose heart was filled with kindness, was also one who loved his subjects. His wealth was shared amongst the citizens.

"As much as possible, we shall be equal in life," would say the King.

His council shook their heads and replied, "As King, you must be above your people or they will not respect you."

"On the contrary," King Magnus explained, "learn this: those who share in the goodness my family enjoys will value their homes, friends, and families all the more. For he who shares in our abundance appreciates and cares for others and enjoys continued abundance."

And so, the people of Constantia Glen loved their King, his family and all the goodness that his selfless, caring wisdom brought to their families, homes and lands. This was a place of peace and plenty as it had been for generations, due to the goodness of his father's father, and so it had continued, but for that one darkest of times of which one dare not speak.

In the Kingdom of Mazgamor, leaders take many shapes. Some, like King Magnus, rule by right of heredity and others are accepted as leaders for their skills and wisdom. Still others become rulers through fear and intimidation, as was the case in the province of Khordrya, east of Constantia Glen. Such an imagined kingdom was this, that Thane-Ra had taken it upon himself to name the compound within, Khordom Palace, to create the illusion of power and strength. And it was power and strength that he had, too, but only because of his malevolent and selfish ways.

It was the thought of Thane-Ra and his past actions that caused fear to grow in the heart of King Magnus on this day. His beloved Lily had not returned as scheduled from her sojourn southwest to Trader's Peninsula. The advance party informed the King's Court of her changed plans and intention to travel to The Meadow, a detour the King understood, but never would have approved had she asked prior to her departure.

Magnus knew the sadness and the restlessness of his children since their mother, Queen Madelina, and older sister, the Princess Annabella had disappeared while returning from the last Gathering. Disappeared perhaps is the wrong word; kidnapped was the true nature of the event. His heart was heavy.

3

As the moon began its slow rise to the top of the sky, on the ground the twigs broke and tall grasses parted as Nassir, filled with curiosity as to the whereabouts of his master, wandered to the three seated beside the fire. Odemog reached out as Nassir came to him. Taking hold of the base of Nassir's ears, he tightened his grip and gave Nassir's head a good rattle and shake, side to side. Nassir blew air from his nostrils and complained.

"Enough, enough, enough of that, you!"

"Nassir, my friend," man or beast, Odemog considered all to be his friend (except that little terror, the rabboo) "You are too serious, you know. Try a giggle once in a while."

He laughed as Nassir frowned and shook his ears back to the way they felt best, resting on his head. Odemog turned to Princess Lily and Skeeter. He held his arm out and down for Skeeter to climb up to his shoulder. Gesturing to Nassir, he said politely to the Princess, "Princess Lily, I invite you to ride with me home to Sweetbrooke Wren. I shall introduce you to our home and we shall take you safely back to your own home. I assure you."

The Princess tilted her head sideways, looking quizzically from Odemog to Nassir. She had never been on a mordagha before. In fact, her experience had been observation only. Worse still, what she had observed was her brother, Prince Fazzog, falling through the air from the back of a mordagha, landing on a branch, and then being sprung like an arrow into Mid Lake. Riding a mordagha had not looked promising then and it was less inviting now. Odemog sensed her hesitation and climbed aboard Nassir.

"I am a Master Rider, Princess. You needn't know your way about a mordagha. That would be my job. You may have Skeeter's sleep spot. I would call it the sweet spot for someone of your size." She was only four feet tall, just over half his size.

"Aye, it is the sweetest spot," Skeeter reassured her. "Between Nassir's shoulders and in front of the handle on the saddle where you can hold on is the perfect spot. Why, Odemog could loose his rope belt and tie you there if you are truly scared."

"Skeeter, it is not called a handle, but the horn of the saddle and—well yes, if you wish, Princess, I could secure you there. But Skeeter is right; between Nassir's shoulders you feel little movement of the wings or the down-up when he takes flight. Please, come forward."

"Odemog," Princess Lily spoke carefully, "I thank and trust you—and you, Nassir." She stepped forward and stroked Nassir's jaw line gently. "Let us take the next step in this adventure then, friend. Here I come, Skeeter!"

Odemog leaned down and held his hand out with fingers bent like a step. Lily grasped Nassir's wing, lifted her foot to Odemog's hand and pushed-pulled herself up to take her seat in the sweet spot between Nassir's shoulders. She half-sat, half-knelt, reaching back with her hand to take hold of the horn of the saddle. As she took hold, Nassir bounced back and forward then lifted his wings as he sprang to air. His belly went left, then right, then left again. Lily's eyes opened wide as if to pop. Her right hand came quickly around to grip with her left the horn of the saddle. They were away before she fully realized what had just happened. Skeeter, sitting up on Odemog's shoulder, smiled and said, "Hmmn, well, it's not as easy as it sounds. But we are away!"

Odemog set his hand on the young princess's shoulder to reassure her. Now airborne, she was more at ease. She turned to him and smiled.

"How far will we travel, Odemog, to reach Sweetbrooke Wren?" she asked.

"From here we go straight north. If you look ahead, Princess, below us Sweet Brook is running south. Wait till we arrive at the Wren and you can taste the brook. You will never have had water as sweet as this. No one knows why, but where the River Constantia crosses the brook the taste of brook water thereafter changes; it loses that favoured sweetness. Watch for the colour, it too will change. It is beautiful there, Princess. You will enjoy your stay—well, it is my wish that you do."

"Odemog, if the others in Sweetbrooke are as sweet as you, I am certain to enjoy myself."

"Mega will adore you," said Skeeter with great confidence.

"Mega?" The Princess looked puzzled.

"Mega, short for Odemega, is my dear mother. She always wanted a daughter but could have no more young ones after me as I was so big. Skeeter tells the truth; she will adore you." He went on, thinking of his mother's wisdom, "When I was young, other young ones in Sweetbrooke would run away because I was different. Or those who were truly scared would bully me. In truth, for a time they called me Eggmog because I tended eggs of our guinea hens. My dear Odemega always cautioned me, 'Odemog, my son' she would say, 'they speak truth that you are different, but only in stature. They are afraid of what they do not understand.'"

"At this age," he interjected into the story, "I was twice their height." Continuing, he recalled his mother's words, 'No one of Sweetbrooke Wren has ever been as tall as you at your age. You are unique. Your gift of added height was given to you to use to help others and so you must. Do not let other young ones disturb you with their bullying, rise above it and someday for your example, they will rise above their pettiness and respect you.' "And, you know, she was right. Some of the worst then are my best friends now. In truth, I cannot understand because I have never been afraid of anyone as they were of me. But I can tell you, I remain grateful for her wisdom to this day. She taught me patience and acceptance. And, you know, she, too, calls those who once hurt me friends also. Yes, as always, she was as right then as she will be with whatever she speaks when we arrive home."

He smiled. Odemog always smiled as he spoke of his mother, Odemega.

Her full name was Odemega Mary, but most called her Mega. As mothers go, Mega took no guff from her giant of a son but succeeded at spoiling him terribly. The way she spoiled Odemog just made him more grateful, rather than causing him to behave like a spoiled child. And this, of course, was why she so freely loved him. Giant in stature, he was gigantic of heart as well. Strong and able to defend others if called upon, but he would rather use his strength tending to the fields of vegetables at home. On behalf of his family, he would travel frequently to Trader's Peninsula to trade their vegetables for other staples and supplies that could not be found in Sweetbrooke Wren. Odemog was well known in many places within the Kingdom as a result of his trade and travels. His good nature and giant size made him all the more memorable. But it was home in Sweetbrooke that he was happiest. Adventures away always reminded him how much he loved to return home to Mega and his friends in Sweetbrooke Wren.

He had missed the landmark as he told his story. They had passed the cross point where the River Constantia divided and changed the waters of Sweet Brook. Had they turned and flown southeast, they could have followed the length of the River Constantia down through the mountains and over the falls to find their way to Constantia Glen, the home of Princess Lily. But they had always been closer to Sweetbrooke Wren. In light of the frightening situation the Princess had found herself in, Odemog thought it wise to give wide berth to those who had attacked her party and take her overnight to the safety of Sweetbrooke and the caring home of his mother.

Nassir tossed his head up and back, calling his rider's attention forward. Odemog pointed ahead to smoke rising through the trees, white smoke, welcoming smoke. As they approached, they flew over fields. Looking down they saw folks in fields who, in turn, were looking up at them and waving. Odemog waved back. Skeeter waved too but be assured not a soul saw his tiny wave. Still, he felt they were exchanging greetings with him as much as Odemog. And in truth, they were. For all who knew

Odemog also knew that his trusted small friend would be on his shoulder wherever he was. Crossing the fields, they flew towards a clearing, closer to several wisps of white smoke—a settlement. Nassir dipped and turned toward a thatched cottage at the western edge of the settlement. It was here that he landed, touching down gently. He stopped outside the cottage and settled down to a resting position before the riders touched foot to earth. This made it easier for Princess Lily and Skeeter. Princess Lily slid down and walked to face Nassir. She bowed her head touching Nassir's forehead below his horn with her forehead and said ever so graciously, "Nassir, my thanks to you for a lovely and safe ride; to have been escorted for the first time by a great mordagha was wonderful. That it was you, Nassir, makes it all the more grand." She smiled sweetly as she straightened up.

"It was my honour, Princess," Nassir replied, bowing his head in return. He, too, smiled and watched her as she followed the direction Odemog had taken.

Home at last, Odemog momentarily forgot his guest as he went to seek out Odemega. Perhaps it was his stomach that drew him away, for the smells that came from the cottage were truly irresistible. Recalling his charge, Odemog turned on his heel to see the Princess following.

Even Skeeter forgot her when he got wind of baking hazelnuts. "Mmm, pie," he muttered as he licked his tiny squirrel lips.

"Come along, Princess," called Odemog, whose face shone with a smile from ear to ear. He was happy to be home. Just then the door swung open and out came a smallish woman. Well, she was smaller than Odemog by far, but certainly taller than Lily. She was drying her hands in her apron, let go, and raised both arms high to her son. Odemog took two great steps forward and reached down to his mother. He wrapped his arms around her and lifted her off the ground as he gave her a gentle squeeze. Skeeter leaned over and kissed her cheek three times. She laughed and brightened still more as Odemog set her back to earth.

"Odemog, Skeeter! You are late, but that diminishes not my joy in seeing you. "Welcome home, son," she spoke quickly with pleasure in her voice. "Hello, Nassir, fresh greens and turnips at the side," she called to her favourite mordagha. She always loved his colour and thought him the most gentle of all the mordaghas in Sweetbrooke. Looking in Nassir's direction, she spotted Lily. She gazed back at Odemog as she turned, walking to greet the little one.

"Princess Lily,"

"You know me?" replied the princess.

"Princess Tulip? Have I mixed you up?" said Odemega, apologetically.

"No, you were correct," said the princess. "How is it that you know who I am?" She looked rather confused in that Odemog had not known her earlier.

"I would know you anywhere, Princess. Your mother is of our Clan. A beautiful woman she was, I should say, is. Your mother would visit here on her way to the Gathering before she had the triplet princes. Then with four little ones it was too much… with six…well, we have not seen her for some time." Odemega spoke cautiously now, knowing of the disappearance of Queen Madelina. "Pray tell, little one, why has my son brought you here?"

"Mother," interrupted Odemog, "the Princess must be tired. I will explain inside. Leave us enter and settle. I am sure, after her adventure today, Princess Lily would be grateful to rest and refresh herself with your aid."

"My manners, Princess Lily. Be welcome in our home. I had prepared a feast for my hungry son. There will be enough for all tonight and three hazelnut pies with fresh cream to 'stop you in flight' as Moggie would say." Odemega gestured for all to enter the house.

"Moggie. Is that you, Odemog? Do they call you Moggie?" asked Lily.

Odemog turned several shades of red as he answered the question with a slow, seemingly painful nod. Skeeter chortled. Moggie reached up to his shoulder and gave Skeeter a push with his finger. With this,

Skeeter clambered down Odemog's chainmail and jumped onto the back of a chair, leaped to the next and the next chair, then climbed up to the top of a cabinet so he was taller than Odemog and chanted, "Moggie, Moggie, Mog-gie!"

"Oh, Skeeter, that's enough," said Mega shaking her head at him. "It was a nickname from his father that has stuck." She looked at her son with a maternal smile and continued, "Our Moggie isn't too fond of his nickname nowadays. But he does tolerate those closest calling him so." She looked at Skeeter and frowned, "However, I do not believe this consent includes mockery now, does it, Skeeter?"

Skeeter ignored Odemega, trying to look busy up on his perch as he dusted the place with his tail.

"Skeeter?" she said again.

Still trying to ignore her, he inspected his tail, shook his head rapidly, stopped and sneezed, "Hhhaaachoo, achoo, choo, ahhhchoo!"

They all laughed at the squirrel fighting the dust that had drifted up his nose.

"Moggie it is then," smiled Princess Lily.

"Moggie it is," his mother agreed.

Outnumbered, Odemog went about busying himself by filling a pot with water and carrying it to the fire. He was heating it for the princess to refresh before they sat down together to eat. Odemega observed her son at his task and gestured for the young princess to take a seat by the great fire. In this cottage, so much larger than others in the settlement to accommodate this gentle giant and his family, there were three fireplaces: a cooking fire, a great fire for comfort while visiting, and a fireplace at the back for comfort at night. Residents of Sweetbrooke Wren loved to visit Odemega and Moggie because their home was spacious and warm. Others would never have these extra fireplaces; tending one fire was enough for most. In Odemog's case, he was large and strong enough to cut and keep enough wood at the ready for three or even more fires. In fact, he also took care of Morlog's woodpile.

Morlog lived only one cottage away, so this was not a burden to Odemog. In fact, it was a pleasure. Morlog was the closest thing Odemog had to a father. Zodemog, Odemog's father, had died when Moggie was young. Odemog remembered his father well and had been devastated when he died. Known as Zodem, a well-loved bard of Sweetbrooke Wren, he was said to have been victim of the Great Falls. He had gone in search of something and, on his journey, had slipped over the Great Falls. The falls, located on the northwest corner of Great Falls Lake, named so for the enormous falls from which it was filled, were not frequently travelled. His grief stricken mordagha, Vadim, returned to the settlement as fast as his wings could take him. Vadim told Morlog that Zodem was climbing about the edge of the falls, looking for something. Vadim was nearby, grazing on water greens when he heard a cry. He looked up to see Zodem falling. As quickly as Vadim took flight, Zodem was out of sight. Vadim flew over the edge of the falls, hoping to catch him mid-air only to see Zodem fall and disappear amongst the torrents of water crashing down the rock face. Vadim tried to fly through, but the forceful waters interfered with his wings. He shook it off and tried again, but it was futile. He waited at the bottom of the falls, watching for Zodem. While he wanted to stay there until he found him, Vadim knew he must return with the news that Zodem had perished. This was a wise decision as he would have waited and never found Zodem—never. In his grief, Vadim never flew again. He lives at the back of Morlog's cottage green. It is said that only Morlog knows what it was that Zodem searched for that day. Only Morlog knows what was so important that Zodem risked, and lost, his life.

There was a rap at the door of the cottage. Standing tall, as tall as a man who was not Odemog could be, was Morlog himself.

"Welcome, Uncle," called Moggie with a wave to enter, "I hoped you would come. We have a special guest joining us this night."

Morlog strode through the doorway with a confident air such that one would think this his cottage. Crossing the room, he went straight for the padded chair by the fire and sat. His actions were purposeful, but his shoes squeaked while he walked. For all his refinery and confidence, this surefooted man had a funny way about him. He gazed about the room with a serious face. His eyes stopped on Princess Lily, who by now knew not what to think, and he stared. She shrank, just a bit, for had she shrunk much further there would be no place to go at only four feet in height. Morlog's face changed, and a brilliant smile worked its way across his face. Odemog laughed. "Princess, I wish for you to meet Morlog." He looked back and forth between them. "You have frightened the little one, Uncle." Close as he was to this family, Morlog was friend, not uncle, but this was how dear he was to Odemog that 'Uncle' he was often called.

"I know you, little one," Morlog leaned forward on his staff to get a better look at the princess. "You are the fifth little one of Magnus of Constantia Glen and you are far from home this day." Without looking away from the princess or taking a breath, Morlog said to Odemog, "Explain how it is that you brought us a princess, Moggie."

With this, Odemega beckoned Lily to get up and go with her. She would take the princess to their sleeping chambers where she would assist her with washing and dressing for supper. Putting her arm around Lily's shoulder, Odemega spoke to her saying, "Little one, I have a frock that we can make fit you. It was a gift long ago from Zodem, I am sure a quick stitch will make it perfect. It is a lovely blue to complement your hair and eyes. This way." She guided Lily through a passage to chambers beyond. Odemog reserved comment, watching his mother escort Lily away. He had poured the hot water in a basin on a bench in chambers, anticipating his mother's care. He turned his attention back to Morlog, who was now watching Skeeter atop the cabinet. Skeeter, as usual, had fallen asleep but had shifted such that, with any further movement, he would fall. Following Morlog's gaze, Odemog strode over, reached up, and shifted his friend to safety.

"Raiders, Uncle," he turned and said, "Nassir was first to spot the distress from air. A plume of black smoke was drifting up from a place in the woods. So, we landed to determine if we could be of service. After we came upon the fire and located the princess, she told us of the attack on her party. By description, it seems certain they were Khordrian raiders. Although, I must say, it seems odd that they attack so far northwest."

"This does not bode well," Morlog muttered. "Northwest where, exactly?"

"They were attacked by the lower of Twin Ponds but chased further north for some time before she broke from her party. There was enough of a separation of her from the raiders that she was able to hide from those in pursuit, as instructed by Kasell."

"Ah, Kasell," said Morlog. "I know him to be a good and loyal arms man of the King. And what of Kasell, Moggie?"

"That's just it, Morlog, we found only the princess and the fire. There was evidence of no other souls. It seems as quickly as they attacked, they disappeared. By description, they were on horseback. I do not know how long she hid in the tree." He digressed, "A lovely willow it was, Morlog."

"Focus, Moggie. Tell me all."

"That is all there is to tell, Uncle." He shook his head saying, "All we could do was whiten the smoke of the fire to blend ourselves as any traveller in case they chose to return. After a respite, we embarked on our journey home. I felt it safer to travel here to put distance between the raider attack and the princess, rather than flying her home."

"A good decision, Moggie, that's true." Morlog nodded and sat quietly for a few minutes. Odemog knew these silences well and took his seat to wait for Morlog's next words. The fire dimmed, he set a log and fanned the flames. His stomach growled and Skeeter snored quietly from the top of the cabinet.

"Odemog, it seems Thane-Ra is making moves again," Morlog finally spoke. "We must not alarm the princess. In recent meetings, Magnus has learned details of the attack on the Queen. I do not know all as yet, but sounds are being made that Khordom Palace played a part. If these were Khordrian raiders—"

"Princess Lily described a red tunic with a beast, perhaps a lion," Odemog contributed.

"Well then, to be sure, these are Khordrian raiders. Something is afoot and all caution must be taken. Even bringing her here brings danger. What is your plan, Moggie?"

"We shall dine and remain here this moon rise. The morrow, then, we shall set out early and fly her by way of Siwa and Trezano Falls to Constantia Glen. I cannot imagine raiders travelling east and north of the mountains, can you?" said Odemog.

"True, it is a good plan. But Odemog," Morlog looked him straight in the eye and urged him, "do not travel alone."

"I will have Skeeter." Frozen by a look from Morlog that suggested he was a fool, he restated his plan. "Skeeter and I will take Samezog and perhaps Deronezog."

"They are master riders and strong in defensive skills," pondered Morlog. "But, I think, I shall accompany you also. It would be wise for me to confer over these matters with Magnus. No doubt he will have joy in the return of the princess, but there will be grave matters to discuss when he learns of this attack."

And so, it was agreed that Odemog would invite his two best companions; strong and able were Samezog and Deronezog. Odemog roused Skeeter to take the message to his friends. Without his usual fuss, Skeeter hopped down and sprang through the open upper half of the split door. A warm breeze drifted in and Odemog took in a long, slow breath, thinking ahead to their pending journey. At that moment, Mega returned with Lily, who shone. Her hair was brushed, cheeks rosy and the frock suited her perfectly. It was no royal gown by any means, but the stitching was of royal quality just the same. Both Morlog and Odemog admired her. Smiling, she curtsied and then offered to assist Mega with the table. Odemog quietly rejoiced at the thought that they would soon feast.

"Rabboo and Brussels sprouts, Mother?" he inquired hopefully.

"Eggplant, peppers, mashed turnips and yams, butter lettuce, sweet carrots, Brussels sprouts…" a long teasing pause…"And, yes, stuffed and roasted rabboo, my son."

If a stomach could smile, his did. Across his face the smile erased his tired expression from the day's excitement. More excitement followed as Princess Lily argued over rabboo with Odemog.

"Rabboo. You eat rabboo?" She shrank away from the platter that Mega held out for her to take. Mega stepped around the little one to set it on the table herself.

"Of course we eat rabboo," said Moggie.

"But we do not eat creatures," cried Lily.

"Well, this one we do," Moggie argued back as he would have once upon a time when he, too, was a young one.

"You talk with creatures and eat them too?" she argued, "How can you eat a peaceful beast?"

"Peaceful? There is not a thing peaceful about a rabboo." Odemog asserted. "You, young princess, are most confused. The rabboo is neither friend nor foe but a scourge on our fields and crops. To catch a rabboo is to save our livelihood. They are devious little beasts and spare nothing. Like a plague of locusts, just one rabboo can destroy an entire field in days if not caught." Now he puffed his chest and said, "And this fresh rabboo was caught by these very hands this morning before I left for trade." He held out his large hands, first palms up, then down, then up again, very proud of his accomplishment.

"In fact," he continued, "I have been waiting all day to feast on this beast." With that he sat down at the head of the table. Quickly, he stood again and gestured to Morlog to take the seat in his place as head of the table. Morlog and Odemega said nothing but listened to the argument.

Princess Lily looked utterly mortified by the end of the conversation. Still, being the daughter of Magnus and Madelina, she knew she must correct the situation. Rising to the occasion, Princess Lily cleared her throat and said most regally, "Odemog, you have your reasons and they seem honourable. But I cannot feast with you on rabboo." She looked to Odemega and said: "If it pleases you, I shall dine on vegetables; the Brussels sprouts sound lovely and I have heard they are the best in the land, Mega."

"Princess, you shall feast on that which satisfies you. Odemog is correct, the rabboo can devastate us and certainly has." She gave her son a sideways glance, "Moggie gets a bit excited about his favourite meal, it is true. We grow our vegetables as best we can and benefit from the nourishment of our Sweet Brook. Enjoy all that you wish; please, have some Brussels sprouts." With that, she lifted the bowl and served the princess two heaping scoops of the greenest Brussels sprouts the princess had ever seen.

Morlog nodded, cut himself a leg from the rabboo and lifted his carafe of Sweet Brook water saying, "Welcome, Princess, eat well and later sleep well, a great journey awaits tomorrow." In turn, each raised their carafes and drank with him.

4

Morzan stood back and watched. He said nothing and knew nothing should be said at this moment in time. They had just returned from Pierce Island and, while he found those trips satisfying, he did not gloat over his accomplishments there.

Although he was, by birth, of the Clan of Odem, Morzan had been gone from the north for too many moons to even try to count. He would certainly not wish to return. And, truth be told, were he to venture there he would not be welcome. In fact, Morzan was cruel and had worn out every welcome except the one he enjoyed at Khordom Palace.

Morzan walked in the shadow of Thane-Ra, companion, advisor, inflictor of cruelty. These were the roles he served to the leader who called himself king.

Thane-Ra glared at the lowly foot soldier cowering before him. The young soldier knew well that the mission he had been charged with could bring him only the reward of imprisonment or death. He hoped for death. To be sent to the prison meant death in no uncertain terms, but it would be a slow, painful process of torture, disease and starvation. Few who entered left alive and this young man knew of no one who had in fact ever left, except in a shroud. He had heard rumors of one light, one bright presence at the Pierce Island prison but it was just that, a rumor.

"And so, you bring news of the raid," Thane-Ra spoke carefully. "What say you then, messenger? That you are here at all, and not one of my generals, gives me pause. What say you?"

The young man looked around, hoping someone would have different, better news than the message with which he had been charged. Morzan stared through the young man and slowly began to sneer, waiting, waiting…

"My lord King," the soldier began to speak the inevitable, "I bring news from General Pervan. As charged, the raiding party followed the Princess's escort from Trader's Peninsula. We tracked them north to The Meadows and began our assault there. A chase ensued; raiders removed the escort." He hesitated, fearing the response to what would come next. "My Liege, the coach of the princess became separated from the party and raiders…"

"Well, get on with it, fool," shouted Morzan.

"Raiders lost sight ever so briefly, My Lord," he cleared his throat to continue and, at that moment noticed the figure he knew as Morzan nearby the King, smirking. "On locating the coach, there was no one to be found. The…"

"NO ONE?" shouted Thane-Ra in disgust. Now Morzan was amused. Thane-Ra continued, "This is a girl you are tracking—and you find no one?"

"My Liege, the scroll from the general reads," he looked down to the parchment he had already memorized, and read:

> *Lead raiders located the coach four lengths from where the escort was terminated. The coach was intact but there was no one inside or on foot. The party searched the immediate area. Following the search, they destroyed the coach and contents to leave any possible stragglers at a loss for transport or provisions. Without these and weapons or protection, one would not survive a day in the woods.*
>
> *The princess was not located. The raiding party concluded that she was not with them. Advance warning must have been received whereby she was hidden away by members of the escort. We return anon.*
>
> *Signed,*
> *Your Loyal General*
> *X. Pervan, III*

The young messenger now dropped on one knee, bowed his head and awaited instructions. All around him was silence. All eyes, but his and those of one other, were on Thane-Ra. He felt the piercing glare of his leader, the self-proclaimed king, and was sure he could hear the sound of Morzan, who was watching him tremble, rubbing his hands together with glee. All about him, it seemed, was evil.

5

A child pointed to the sky and tugged on her mother's sleeve. Her mother stopped washing their garments, shaded her eyes from the sun, and looked skyward.

"Oh no," she uttered softly. Looking around, she called out "Boy, you there, send word to the castle." And, as she uttered this last word, a raptor flew closer to ground. It was not the raptor that caused alarm. Great eagles were beautiful and peaceful hunters. It was that which the raptor carried in the strong grip of its talons: a man. And not just any man.

What the woman had seen was a tunic in the King's colors. The colors of Constantia Glen, the King, and his heraldry, were blue and gold. This man, clearly injured, wore the tunic of Constantia Glen—he was an arms man of the King.

As the raptor gently set him down, the great eagle lifted himself up and away from his charge and came to rest on earth beside him. He waited, guarding the man, until someone could tend to him. It would not be long as they were close to the castle. The raptor had flown far with a heavy weight and was tired. The woman brought water to the eagle and dropped to her knees to tend to the wounds of the arms man.

"Kasell!" The name burst from her as she realized this was the King's first arms man. She knew he was also the first arms man for Princess Lily on her recent trip away. She felt her stomach knot as her imagination went wild with thoughts of what might have happened to bring him here, injured, and unconscious. No sooner had she called out his name, than she heard the thundering sound of horses. Looking up, she saw King Magnus accompanied by the princes, a healer known as Forthrumal, and several arms men. Magnus leapt from his mount, recognizing Kasell before anyone. He waved to Forthrumal who followed him to Kasell's side.

"How did he come to be here?" asked Magnus who, standing aside to give way to Forthrumal, looked around to see who was before him. "Who shall be heard?"

"King Magnus, I am Leevon of Twin Ponds." The raptor spoke and bowed his head before the King. "I was hunting where Sweet Brook enters the lower of Twin Ponds when I heard the sounds of a chase: many horses, chaotic shouts, and clashing of weaponry. From the sky I recognized your colors on tunics and on the dressings of horses. I followed the melee from above though several times lost it in thick, wooded places. Once the sounds abated, I flew low and saw still tunics on arms men lying all about. As I lifted away, I saw one attempting to drag himself back up from a nearby ravine. I can only suggest that he feigned death and, since he was out of reach of his attackers, they did not bother to confirm."

All around Leevon of Twin Ponds, the faces slowly filled with a deeper fear. Magnus looked down at his first arms man lying still on the earth.

"Leevon of Twin Ponds, you have the gratitude of the King. My Kingdom is at your bidding, great eagle."

Leevon asked for nothing, only bowed his head to the King again and then began to spread his wings to fly home. Magnus raised his hand.

"Was there no one else? A coach, perhaps. My daughter the Princess Lily, did you not see or hear her as you flew over?" Magnus ached inside to hear the answer he longed for. Leevon closed his eyes, bowed his head, and slowly shook it from side to side: *no*. His spirit crushed, the King thanked Leevon of Twin Ponds again and directed the arms men to return Kasell by stretcher, in the care of Forthrumal, to the castle. The teenaged Princes looked to their father for direction—they too felt their hearts break—and saw that their father the King was so pained he could say no more.

By the time Forthrumal had Kasell cleaned up and reclining in a chamber bed, the arms man began to stir. At first, he did not know where he was. He drifted in and out of consciousness through the night. By morning, the tinctures and compresses brought him around. Sword wounds were treated and an arrow removed from his thigh. Poultices of yarrow root and white willow bark tea were administered for pain and swelling. Kasell's physical pain was easing but his heart was heavy. When the King finally entered the room to check on his loyal and trustworthy first arms man, they were both filled with sadness.

"Majesty," Kasell strained to speak as he was exhausted and still in some pain. "I do not know what became of the princess. I have failed you."

"Kasell, first you must know that you can never fail me. This I know in my heart. How else would I have entrusted you with Lily's care?" He sat down beside Kasell and placed his hand on Kasell's forearm. Looking him directly in the eyes, he could see Kasell shared his pain. "Tell me all you can. Start at the beginning."

Kasell closed his eyes and lay silent for a moment. Everything began to rush back and he shuddered at the thought of the surprise attack. For a moment, all he saw was a rush of red and black tunics.

"Raiders," he said. "Khordrian raiders, My King, from nowhere and everywhere they came upon us. I called to arms and raced our party northward. It seemed the least number of them came from that direction. Those in the rear went down first. Onward, I pushed the core escort and coach. In no time, the raiders spread further afield as if to advance and encircle us. I whipped the horses of the coach and called to Lily to get away and hide. No sooner had she broken away in the coach, than we were surrounded. As my mount fell, I was thrown and could not stop myself from falling into a ravine. I recall nothing from there. My King, I bring no news of Princess Lily to you. I have failed in the protection of your daughter. I cannot offer you anything. Forgive me, King Magnus. Forgive me."

Kasell had been in service to the King from the time he was very young. He was a stellar swordsman and rather a good singer as well. He had endeared himself to the King one summer's day and was promoted to first arms man for his skills, leadership, and his heart. The King and his new bride, Queen Madelina, had been out riding when two boys ran out from the trees. They ran in the path of the King and Queen's mounts. Both startled and the Queen's mount charged. Kasell broke formation, lunging ahead to take the reins of her horse. He was able to break the charge before the Queen could be thrown. Turning their horses back, he softly sang a tune that soothed the horse so the Queen herself remarked of this to the King. But it was not this alone that won the King's favour. Arms men were taking the boys to task for their raucous and dangerous race across a traveller's path. When Kasell heard them berating the boys, he stepped in. In the gentlest of words and gestures he soothed their panicked spirits and invited them to apologize, while expressing their concern for the Queen. This gentle yet firm leader impressed the King—he was naturally a first arms man—and so it was that they became friends and Kasell assumed his loyal and trustworthy place at the Kings side.

Seated beside his long-time friend and most loyal arms man, Magnus had no words to ease Kasell. Where he had gripped Kasell's arm, he gently squeezed and held tight for several moments. He understood Kasell's distress. And Kasell, in turn, understood his King's pain.

"King Magnus," Forthrumal interrupted. "If it please you, I would ask that Kasell try to sleep some more. Perhaps you could visit again later. I am not sure there is more to gain at this time." Magnus nodded and, rising from the chair, stepped aside so Forthrumal could offer Valerian root tea to Kasell to help him sleep.

6

Morning in Sweetbrooke is perhaps the sweetest time of day. Birds lyrically welcome the sun and villagers are busy preparing to work in the fields. But on this morning, as the sun is rising in the east, warming the earth, five villagers and their guest are hard at work preparing for a different task. A task that will take them away from the security of Sweetbrooke Wren and into the unknown.

Samezog greeted Deronezog with a smile and a slap on the back as they met on the path to Odemog's cottage.

"What say you this fine morning, Dero?" asked Samezog.

"Fine it is, Sam. Fine it is. All is well thus far," replied Deronezog.

The two old friends, who once called Odemog 'Eggmog' usually leaned toward the cheerful and optimistic. Knowing full well that this day would unravel in ways that not a one of them could predict, the safest way to start it would be on a good and happy footing. Sam and Dero, as they called one another with familiarity, were Odemog's two best friends, though they certainly hadn't started that way. Once fearful of their giant friend, they grew to appreciate his tolerance and genial nature. And sure enough, as their fear of someone so different from them diminished, they discovered how alike they truly were. Thus, they became fast and loyal friends. When Moggie called on them for support Sam and Dero never questioned, they simply came forth.

And so it was on this morning that the two converged on the road to Odemog and Odemega's cottage where they would meet up with their friend, Morlog and their charge, the Princess Lily of Constantia Glen.

"Good morning, Brothers! How are my best mates this sunny dawn?" called Odemog from his front garden. Mega had prepared a wonderful repast and served it outside to welcome the dawn.

"Happy to see you, Brother," they said in unison. The three called one another 'brother' from long ago when their roughhousing and games brought Odemega outside to put a stop to a particular fight saying, "Were one not aware, one would think this foolish sibling rivalry; you behave like bandit brothers. Cease this nonsense at once." Since that time, they call themselves brothers and since that time, they have felt just so.

"And what, Odemog, is the call to arms you so mysteriously bid us in service of?" asked Sam, "It surely is not in hunting rabboo." Dero laughed at the joke, for Odemog was known for his ongoing battle with rabboo. It was not his battle alone, of course, but he did seem to take it rather personally that these creatures would feast on his Brussels sprouts.

"Dero and Sam, this day you will join us in an adventure as yet unknown, even to me," said Moggie. "And frankly, I do not know exactly what lies ahead. For this reason, I will understand if you do not care to partake. Suffice it to say that the enjoyable part of our journey is to bring happiness to a princess as we safely see her home." He looked from one to the other and waited briefly before continuing. "My manners, Brothers; let me introduce you to…" he looked around for the princess. "Hmm." She emerged from the cottage almost on cue, startled to see visitors so early.

"Princess Lily, there you are. Let me introduce you to my best mates, my brothers. Samezog," he gestured to the taller of the two friends who placed his hand on his chest and bowed slightly. Samezog spoke with a deep, strong voice.

"My honour, Princess. Please call me Sam. I am at your service on this fine day."

"And this, Princess Lily, is Deronezog, whom we call Dero," Odemog continued as he stepped back allowing her to see Dero, the smallest of the brothers, who had been shadowed by Odemog's size.

"Princess Lily, it will be my pleasure to be of service to you," Deronezog spoke softly as he was quite taken by her appearance. He, too, put hand to chest and bowed, though he held his position much longer than Sam. Odemog patted his friend upon the back to signal that all was well, and Dero stood tall once again.

Morlog crossed the path from his cottage and stepped over a small fence, one post in height that was more decorative than barrier. Painted white, it served as a lovely background for the wildflowers that grew along the line of the fence.

"Good day to you, gentlemen. Ready to travel then, are we?" asked Morlog who, faced with such a journey, was all business. Odemega emerged from the cottage as if on cue with three bundles. One packed for each Samezog, Deronezog, and Odemog. Princess Lily carried two more, one for herself and one for Morlog.

"We have packed a feast and spare provisions for each traveller," explained Mega. She, too, was all business. It was not often that Odemog took trips such as this. She was accustomed to packing the occasional snacks or lunch for Moggie to journey to and from Trader's Peninsula, a full day at best but usually just more than half a day. By the looks of these bundles, she had taken the time to consider all possibilities. Sitting on the table as well were several flasks filled with the waters of Sweet Brook. Thirst quenching, sweet, and satisfying, these would carry them far. The bundles were set down and the six gathered at table for biscuits and tea, where Morlog would give clarification to what lay ahead. Sam and Dero were each served a plate of what remained of the substantial breakfast of leftover rabboo, hearty grain porridge with preserves, shaved and roasted vegetables, applesauce, biscuits, and a good slab of cheese with their tea. Once all were served, they turned to face Morlog. He sat silently sipping his hot green tea and when finally he spoke, all listened intently.

"There is much we do not know regarding what is taking place at this time within Mazgamor. There is some that we do. Sure or not of the accuracy, there is more that we may speculate. This I can tell you for sure: there is danger ahead and be confident that it will involve Thane-Ra and his raiders." Morlog turned in his seat to face Odemog squarely and carefully spoke, addressing him, and him alone.

"It is now—this time, these days ahead— that you will learn much of your life, your destiny. Know this, Odemog of Sweetbrooke Wren: your stature comes not from your size but from your destiny as it did for your father and those before him." Odemog looked to his mother, whose eyes, if he was not mistaken, tried to hide pain and hold back tears. He looked back at Morlog and waited.

"Odemog, one cannot know one's destiny, but only live one's best life in order to fulfill it. I cannot predict, foretell, or guide you in these matters. I can only share what I know of the past." Morlog then reached under his robe and produced a parchment. It was sealed with red wax and the stamp of "Z" – Zodem. He passed the parchment over to Odemog.

"Go on now, read it; the letter will not read itself," Morlog pressed him.

Odemog set down his tea and opened the parchment folded in three. It read:

My Son,

If it so that you are reading this letter, I am gone and you are a man.

I pray you have had a good life, made your mother proud and have benefited from the attentions and lessons taught to you by Morlog. He was, for me, a great teacher and the dearest of friends. As his counsel was entrusted to my father and me, so it is that he has guided you to this day.

Puzzled, Odemog stopped reading, looked up at Morlog, and asked one simple question.

"Morlog, just exactly how old are you?"

"Details such as these are not important now, Moggie. Suffice it to say, I knew your father, his father, and his father before him. There are many things for you to learn and, though I am here to guide you, most only you can learn on your own. Read on, Odemog, read on now." Morlog gestured to the letter with one hand and poured more tea for himself with the other.

> *I know not the means of my demise, my son, I only hope it in service of our Mazgamor. This is a Kingdom of many peoples, where we are joined with creatures and beasts in ways not known or understood in other lands. The saddest of all is that there exists one dark corner of this Kingdom where division, anger, jealousy, and deepest sadness flourish. It is a place of pain. It is the province of Khordrya, where lies Khordom Palace. For reasons unknown, our Clan, our family has been charged with a role known only to us and our Protectors, of which Morlog is one. He will guide you, but you will go the way your destiny guides you. Trust yourself, trust your heart, my dear Moggie. My son, that which lies ahead of you is adventure, true, but more so it is the hope of our Kingdom. You will be charged with great things, a great responsibility. If I have somehow failed in this mission and this is how you have come to read my letter, I know you will fulfill the destiny and responsibility of the Clan of Odem. Gods be with you, son. I will see you on the other side.*
> *Your devoted and loving father,*
> *Zodemog,*
> *Of the Clan of Odem*

Odemog read the letter twice, the second time quietly to himself. In his heart he felt pain reading a letter from a father he knew briefly and loved deeply. In his mind he felt confusion. He had lost his father to a mission. What mission? From where had this mystery, this mission, this responsibility, come? All he had done was pick up a little one yesterday, a princess to be sure, but it was only a good deed. Now, it seemed he was being prepared for something altogether different, a new road in his life, an extraordinary change in his path. His destiny seemed to be redirecting him from farmer and trader to—well, this was part of the mystery then, wasn't it. What was this new-found responsibility? What would be his ultimate destiny?

Odemog sensed that all eyes were upon him. He looked at his mother first, and then at Morlog. He closed his eyes, took a breath, and said, "My father perished on a 'mission' then, Morlog?"

"For generations, Odemog, the Clan of Odem, your family, has served as protectors of this Kingdom. Your father's father fulfilled his task. Your father perished as he sought to fulfill his destiny. It seems now, and we will learn more on this journey, that your destiny has been awakened. This is all I can say to you now, son. It seems, Moggie, that more answers lie ahead than within me." Morlog paused, took a long draw from his carafe of tea and set it down. He whistled three beckoning notes. From behind his cottage came Vadim.

Vadim stretched his wings and stretched them again. They spanned wider than Nassir's and were whiter still. It had been too long since he had taken flight, so deep was his sadness at the loss of Zodem. Many had said that Vadim was a lost mordagha, his spirit broken like the wing of a fallen bird. His wings were fine but there was truth to this if one were speaking of his heart.

"Vadim," Morlog gestured toward the mordagha, "will join us this day and provide flight for our Princess. He looked at Lily and continued, "Be assured, Princess Lily, that Vadim is a great and honourable creature who will attend to your care and safe return to Constantia. For all his strength, he is devoted and would give his life to protect yours."

"It should not come to that, Morlog," spoke the princess softly. "I am grateful for your service, Vadim." She rose and went to the low fence where she leaned forward to touch her forehead against that of Vadim. "You have my confidence for this journey."

To touch one's forehead to that of a creature small as a bird or as large as a mordagha and to have that creature return the touch is a gesture of great faith and trust between human and beast. When Lily touched her forehead to another there was exchanged an energy so beautiful that the peaceful bond between her and the creature was instant and would be enduring. Her gesture this morning gave ease and confidence to all.

From their seats at table, Samezog and Deronezog rose and bowed such that it was hardly noticeable to all but Odemog.

"Brother, we are at your service," said Sam.

"Brother, where you go, whatever this destiny, we are beside you," affirmed Dero.

"Besides," Sam joked to ease the tension, "a little adventure never hurt anyone now, did it?"

"Furthermore," added Dero, "it is not every day that one is invited to escort a princess, especially one so lovely, to her home." Having added the last words, Deronezog blushed slightly, causing Odemega to smile.

Out of nowhere came Skeeter who leapt onto the table and grabbed a biscuit. Before he could escape came the hand of Mega who, while scorning him, swatted Skeeter just hard enough that he dropped his precious biscuit.

"Drat!" he said turning and taking a running leap to land on Odemog's right shoulder. "At your service—yes, we are all in, Moggie, my friend, but I am hungry; you did not call me for breakfast."

"Now that is one way to refresh a table," laughed Odemog. "Skeeter, you really know how to break up a serious conversation." Everyone at table laughed, though it was clear that beneath the laughter was an anxious sense of the unknown.

7

Nassir stood close by the legendary mordagha, Vadim. Both, with saddle and satchels secured, waited patiently for the travellers to finish readying themselves. Morlog had called upon Lisan, a free travelling mordagha and friend to himself and Vadim, for his transportation on this day.

Samezog and Deronezog signaled their mordaghas, Bazat and Tovar, who came to them with saddles ready. Each secured their burlap parcels from Odemega; they would at least eat well this journey. With the fondest of farewells, the travellers mounted mordaghas. Odemog lifted Princess Lily to Vadim and instructed her in the manner of holding fast when Vadim lifted to air. Odemega stood close by to reassure the princess, who appeared very much at ease. Odemega stepped forward and took the princess's hand. She leaned in and kissed the little one on the cheek.

"Travel well and safely, Princess Lily," she said. Turning to her son, Odemega took hold of his belt and drew him closer. He lifted her and gave her a warm squeeze.

"I will return soon, Mother."

"Be safe and take counsel from Morlog, Odemog. Your father would be proud of you. Be strong and smart in all you do." She kissed his cheek, touched the other with her soft hand and smiled, a tear in her eye. Odemog set her gently down, walked to Nassir and climbed into his saddle. Skeeter climbed from Nassir's shoulder up Moggie's chainmail and took his place on Odemog's left shoulder. He gripped tight the braid and ear of his friend just as the command was given.

"Away all, our adventure begins," called Odemog to friends and mordaghas alike. At once, the mordaghas took flight, back legs down-up, lifting at front and bellies shaking left and right then left again. Wings lifting to air, they were off. Nassir, Vadim, Lisan, Bazat, and Tovar took to formation with Nassir leading them all. A flight (as a number of more than two mordaghas in the air is called) of five mordaghas lifted away from Sweetbrooke Wren and off on a journey, the likes of which they had never known before and would remember for moons yet to come.

Tovar and Bazat, brothers by birth, were known to be daring in flight. This, in part, was why Samezog and Deronezog, brothers by choice, enjoyed them so. As the day progressed, the brothers by choice, Sam and Dero, gave license for their mordagha brothers to fly free. In essence this meant that, destination in mind and course set, the two mordaghas could fly as they pleased. And so, the show began. Nassir, Vadim, and Lisan continued their journey remaining in pattern, Nassir in the lead flanked by the two. Tovar and Bazat flew ahead and behind conducting daring feats, with their riders laughing and hanging on for life.

Bazat's favourite move was to draw in his wings and, but for inertia, stop dead in the sky. A moment would pass—as would Tovar winging ahead—and Bazat would extend and draw his wings to lift him up and forward. The games in full heat, the two would perform this and many more stunts: circles, crossovers, loops, and such other flights of daring. Princess Lily flew mostly with eyes closed or covered by loosely held fingers, fearing for Sam and Dero, who seemed to thrive in the excitement, caring not for the risk. Odemog laughed at the stunts, ducked his head on seeing some crossovers too close for comfort and Morlog—dear Morlog—rode astride Lisan, feigning disinterest, though his heart leapt and dropped with every move the others made.

The miles slipped by as the minutes and hours passed. Several stops to ground were made for rest and refreshment. The group flew along the River Constantia and made the last stop there before reaching the Village of Siwa, where they were to rest for the night.

This was a journey that could, when travelled a certain path and pattern, could be completed in almost a day. But, bearing in mind the apparent growing unrest in the Kingdom, the wisest plan to get the princess home to her father and King was a carefully thought-out expedition. Travel away from the logical path of the raiders, follow nourishing waters on familiar routes, and rest overnight in a place that would be both friendly and familiar. And so, the Village of Siwa would be the safest and most protected location to ease tired bodies for the night.

8

"Ahead yonder," called Sam, as he pointed just north of the flight.

"It is Siwa, Princess," Odemog said matter-of-factly, turning briefly to face the princess beside him. He smiled as he looked at her.

Princess Lily leaned forward in her saddle as Vadim, sensing her movement, dipped down for her to catch a better glimpse of what lay ahead. Surrounded by trees on three sides, the village squarely faced the waters of Dragon Bay, a quiet inlet off the North Dragho Sea.

"Since you have chosen this as our resting place, am I to surmise that you have great faith in the people of Siwa then, Odemog? Morlog?" she asked.

"The people of Siwa are of the Clan Tsesiwa. They are known for their skills in archery. Mostly the women of Siwa, really," called Morlog from where he rested on Lisan. "They, the women that is, are known for their height. And somehow, though I know not how frankly, it is their height that is said to give them advantage in their accuracy. Regardless, my appreciation for these lovely women is in their wisdom. If you present an argument or puzzle of any kind that challenges the mores of man, a solution of sheer brilliance will always be proposed. The answer, seeming so simple, conjures the thought: of course, this is logic I should have come to myself." Morlog shook his head, smiling, "Their wisdom and logic give pause. One is inspired to consider the pattern of thought that draws these conclusions. Inspiring. These wise women are authentically inspiring."

"My mother spoke of an elder of Siwa once," said Lily. "Her name, I think, is… Kasr…"

"Kasreya," offered Morlog. "You speak of the elder Kasreya. She is also an elder of The Circle."

"Yes, Kasreya. They also call her Reya?"

"That is she."

"Mother spoke of Kasreya as if she leads Siwa. Could this be true?"

"Kasreya took the Clan leadership on the passing of her mother Artemeya. Her mother perished in the last Khordrian uprising ten years past. It was around the time of the twelfth Gathering. She was very young at the time. It was then that Khordom Palace sent raiders north through the Galdordon Forest. They took to water, avoiding the mountains, and attacked Siwa by night, coming quietly through the mists of Dragon Bay. It was most unexpected. There had been peace in Mazgamor for some time. Not since the arrow of gold stopped Thane the Strong Heart has there been any violence—until now."

"Teller, amuse us with legend of Thane the Strong Heart," called Sam from his perch atop Bazat. The flight had converged as one as they approached the edge of the village.

"Let us be settled first, impatient one!" Morlog rebuked Sam for his impertinent tone and gestured ahead with his hand. With that, Odemog directed Nassir to fly down to the center of the village. The rest followed closely.

9

A single archer watched attentively. She observed a series of spots in the sky growing larger as they came closer to her station. She stood on a square platform high above Siwa. From this platform set squarely in the center of the village, which could easily hold a dozen archers, she could see north and east to the waters of Dragon Bay, south and west to the woods surrounding her village. She waited for them to come within visual range, so she might make the correct call on her horn: one long blast–friends approaching; one short, one long–unknown travellers; three short blasts–danger is upon us.

Most who travel by way of mordagha are friends of Siwa. Those who travel the distance that would bring them from the direction these travellers have come would be master riders. Travellers of this skill most often come from Sweetbrooke Wren and thus, are always friends of Siwa. Still, as some enemies creep silently to shore out of darkness, so may others feign friendship, capturing free mordaghas to attempt a breach from the sky. This would take much skill, but enough time had passed to give Khordrians opportunity to at least attempt to master such skills.

And so, she watched with caution, having called a casual alert to friends passing below. Slowly other archers came and began to climb the ladders to the lookout deck, armed with bow and quiver, presenting themselves for what may or may not lie ahead.

As the shapes grew, one unmistakable shape answered her question, and she raised her horn. Drawing in a deep breath she blew one long note–friends approach. There in the sky the archers, now quite at ease, watched as the familiar form took shape.

"It's Odemog!" shouted the sentry archer.

"Odemog brings us travellers," someone called down to those gathering and passing below. A ripple went through the village and electricity began to build amongst the villagers.

Word travelled quickly to Kasreya, who sat with council at table. Happily, she adjourned her session. Kasreya was a very relaxed leader. Not all within Siwa were of this demeanour, so Kasreya was required to tolerate lengthy sessions with council each month. Walking across the council chamber, Kasreya beckoned to Amara, her cousin. As Amara came from behind the round table, Kasreya placed a hand on her shoulder.

"Cousin, it has been some time since we have seen Odemog. Please see to it that he has all he needs for comfort and rest."

"Assuredly, Reya, shall I take them to Holder Cottage?"

"We shall see first with whom he travels, but I think your suggestion is fine."

Holder Cottage stood at the edge of the waters and was a fine home to host travellers. There was room for three or five, perhaps even six, if arrangements were made and those who visit could share quarters with ease.

Kasreya, Mistress of Siwa, of the Clan Tsesiwa, stood tall amongst her own. She wore her long, thick, and full auburn hair in a twist and pinned up at the back. On any day, it was easy to identify her as their leader by the dignity and poise with which she carried herself. She wore a simple dress of cream colour with a blue overskirt. It draped her figure well and showed her athletic frame. Wrapped around twice, the overskirt was fabric enough to allow her to straddle her horse with ease. The one accessory distinguishing Kasreya from all others of Siwa was a flat pewter arrowhead trimmed with gold that she wore around her neck.

Reya and Amara emerged from the chambers to see the flight come into the village and make ground. A circle of villagers welcomed the travellers. Kasreya stood watching the reception given by her people. She smiled and quickened her step to join her fellow Tsesiwans in welcoming them.

Reya waved at Odemog with enthusiasm. She recognized Morlog at once and went to him directly. As she approached, she looked quizzically at Lily and back to Morlog. Odemog stepped down and away from Nassir to tend to Princess Lily's needs.

"Morlog, dear friend, welcome to Siwa," she stepped forward, taking him in her arms as she kissed him once on each cheek. He returned the kisses without hesitation.

"Reya, it has been too long."

"Not since the Gathering. You have been well, I trust?" Reya spoke with Morlog with great familiarity as they were old friends. He had been her greatest ally and supporter when she took leadership. Morlog was among the first who came to Siwa on hearing of the attack those years ago. He stood by her side as she sought his counsel, though all the while believing that she knew quite naturally what to do and how to revive her decimated village. The losses of those days still pained Siwa, the archer lookout was evidence of this. "Pray, Morlog, what brings you here where you are all most welcome?" asked Kasreya. leader of Siwa.

"All will be made clear soon enough. Now, Reya, it is a joy to see you. You seem very well and happy. For this I am grateful." Morlog observed her every move, expression, and word. Her happiness only served to expand his. He loved her like a daughter as he loved Odemog like a son.

Odemog came to Kasreya's side and put his arm around her. Although a giant to most, he still was required to bend down to hug her but did not have to go to his knee or lift her, like his own mother, to make contact. He loved to visit the women of Siwa for they were so much closer to his height. These were strong, intelligent women whom he could appreciate all the more as they shared a common trait. Tsesiwan women are taller by far than the men of Siwa. He valued their strength of character and spirit—the men that is—for what he knew was that men of other villages were rather intimidated by these creatures. The men of Siwa were smaller only in stature. Their spirits were grand and they adored the women who bore their children and contributed greatly to the security of Siwa by their definitive skills as archers.

"Kasreya, dear friend," Odemog squeezed her affectionately. "I want you to meet a new friend of ours. We are escorting her safely home by way of your peaceful village. It was the safest way for us to travel and surely the most hospitable place along our journey."

"You are always welcome Odemog, you know that unfailingly," Reya returned the hug and looked to the young one to whom he was referring. Kasreya stepped away from Odemog and held out her hand.

"Welcome, little one, to the Village of Siwa. We are honored that Odemog brings his friends to us for nourishment and rest."

"Kasreya, leader of Siwa, please accept the introduction of Princess Lily of Constantia Glen." Odemog stepped forward to bring the leader and princess together.

"I am most pleased to make your acquaintance." Lily bowed to the leader of Siwa, as she had been taught by her mother to defer to all elders and leaders with reverence. "You have a beautiful village; it is so lovely here by the sea."

"Princess Lily? Daughter of Magnus and Madelina! I am so pleased to welcome you. Something about you struck me as familiar. I know your mother well, the Queen. Have you any more word?"

"More word?" Lily turned to Morlog, questioning. Morlog stepped forward.

"There has been word, Princess. It has been learned that she is alive as is your sister the Princess Annabella."

"You have known this before now, Morlog, and not told me?"

"I could not utter a word until I knew we were safely under way, Princess."

"For how long have you known of this?"

"Word came by raptor before you rose this morning, Princess. The King sent word as his arms men uncovered the news. I sent return word with the raptor that you also were alive and would return after a couple of days. In this message I told him of your escape from raiders. He will be relieved to know you are on your way home."

"But why must you keep it a secret and not share all that you know?" Princess Lily was intent on finding out why such cloak and dagger methods were applied at this time and on this journey. Kasreya set her hand upon Lily's shoulder saying, "Princess Lily of Constantia Glen, let us pause here now. We should move our conversation away from this open place. Join me at my home for tea and I have no doubt that Morlog will answer your questions." Kasreya beckoned with her arm for the travellers to follow her. Amara took up step behind her cousin, who walked with Morlog, Lily, and Odemog at her sides. Sam and Dero tended the mordaghas, intending to follow thereafter.

The home of Kasreya, leader of Siwa, loomed large on the Bay, though set back from the waters. To the south of this home lay Holder Cottage. To the north were two much smaller cottages. They appeared as cottages but, in fact, were actually stations of defense. These were occupied from moon to moon with sentries on duty all hours of the clock. Their appearance as such was to both calm villagers and deceive intruders. Kasreya had well prepared a defense of her village in the years after the attack on her family and people. What happened then, she had vowed, would never occur again.

The travellers were soon united as Sam and Dero entered the large and ornate cottage, escorted by two archers. They handed off the five satchels brought on their journey, lighter now for having feasted along the river, and took each a cloth to refresh themselves before joining the others. Amara directed them to basins in an antechamber.

It is true that these were loyal friends and worthy warriors if called upon, yet nothing would stop them from playing about like fools with the water basins and cloths. One would shake one's head at the mess they made.

As Sam and Dero left their mess to rejoin Odemog, Morlog, and Princess Lily, they heard but a hush in the room. On entering, they found Princess Lily weeping softly with her head in Kasreya's lap. The brothers shot a questioning look to Odemog, who, catching it, shook his head telling them to take a seat and be quiet.

Watching the two stride across the room to a bench by the window, Morlog drew a deep breath and spoke gently to the little one.

"Princess, please understand, with so many rumors making their way about the Kingdom, it was imperative that the King not alarm you, Princess Tulip, and your brothers."

"He should have told us," came a muffled cry from the head resting in Reya's lap.

"Understand, King Magnus would have risked the lives of your mother and sister had he shared this knowledge and had it been released. Thane-Ra cannot, must not, know that spies have released such prized and sought after secrets. You cannot know the pain and fear your father has been through since you, too, disappeared from your escort. So many lives have been lost through this all. It seems a sign of much more to come."

"Pray, Morlog, what does Magnus seek to do?" asked Reya.

"This he did not reveal to me. Truth be told, I believe he does not yet know himself. We shall join in council on arrival at Constantia Glen. There, a plan shall be revealed. It seems, as I thought on seeing the Princess in Sweetbrooke, that the destinies of many are to show themselves soon. I can only hope—pray—that uprisings of the past do not repeat themselves in this age.

Kasreya set her hand upon Lily's back and gently stroked to soothe her. The princess lay still as her tears began to dry. She knew that Morlog's words were true; to have known would have been certain death for some, if not many. She also knew he was right in his supposition that many more lives could yet be lost. This pained her heart greatly. Deep inside she felt a new hope kindled in her heart, knowing that her beloved mother and sister were not yet lost to that most evil of men, Thane-Ra.

10

When Leevon of Twin Ponds had aided King Magnus by bringing safely home his first arms man Kasell, he had, to himself, vowed continued service to the King. So, it was no surprise to him when a messenger bade him return to Constantia Glen at the behest of King Magnus.

"Welcome Leevon of Twin Ponds. I continue to be grateful to you for saving the life of my man, Kasell." King Magnus gestured to his right. Leevon looked over to see a smiling Kasell standing by his side. He did not yet appear at full strength, but his eyes greeted Leevon's warmly and with gratitude.

"Sire, if I may address your man," Leevon lifted the shoulder of his wing in a gesture of sort towards Kasell. King Magnus smiled and nodded.

"It is most satisfying to know, sir, that you are well and healing. May your health return fully that you may continue to serve your gracious king."

"I cannot express my full gratitude to you, raptor," Kasell addressed him.

"I am Leevon of Twin Ponds."

"Beg your pardon, Leevon," Kasell was not at his full strength. He knew the name of this great eagle but it had not come to him.

"All is well, friend. You are a good man in the woods and meadows; I have watched you moons over. It was my honour to come to your aid."

"Again, my gratitude. I am always at your service, Leevon, for I am indebted to you for my life." Kasell finished speaking and nodded, deferring back to the King.

The King rose and stepped down from his dais and approached Leevon. He held out his hand and a page rushed forward with a cylinder containing a parchment.

"Leevon of Twin Ponds, I must ask of you a great favour. I have an urgent dispatch that is not safe to travel by ground. I feel I can trust only one to safely bring this by air to the one for whom it is destined. Will you do me this honour?" It was clear that the King had no other option or desire. By ground was a risk with raiders about. A man by air on mordagha could be shot down. A great eagle, a strong raptor, may not draw as much attention. And so it was that Leevon agreed with the King and consented to fulfill his wish. Leevon knew only his destination and not the contents of the cylinder. If attacked, the King explained, he could drop the cylinder to a source of water and when it struck rocks, a vial within would break. The contents of the vial would cause the parchment to disintegrate entirely, thus protecting the message.

Leevon left Constantia Glen at once with the cylinder, which had been wrapped in fur to conceal any shine. With the cylinder clenched in his talons, he flew directly on his northwest journey and by pre-dawn, with only one stop in a small meadow to briefly rest and refresh, he had arrived at Sweetbrooke Wren at the cottage of Teller Morlog.

Leevon landed silently at Morlog's door. He set the cylinder down and stepped forward to tap his sharp bill to the door. A moment passed and he heard the door latch click. Morlog opened the door and welcomed him. Leevon deliberately raised his wings to lift himself away and back in order to present the cylinder to Morlog. He was conscious of the vial within and did not want to break it.

"Leevon of Twin Ponds, welcome." Morlog spoke quietly, not wishing to wake his neighbours.

"A good morning to you, Teller Morlog of Sweetbrooke," he replied. "I bring you this urgent dispatch from King Magnus of Constantia Glen. He requires an answer. I shall away to hunt a meal. If you would kindly prepare your reply, I shall return anon to take your parchment to the King. Be aware of the vial within, Morlog, it can destroy a parchment."

"I thank you Leevon, I know these vials well. I will be cautious. Give me some few minutes and I will offer my reply. Can I not prepare you something to eat?"

"I shall be more satisfied to find something fresh, friend. Still, you have my gratitude." And on these words, Leevon spread his wings and lifted himself away.

Morlog closed the door and returned to his table. He had, himself, only just risen before Leevon arrived. The pot he had set was now boiling so he added loose green tea and let it steep. Mug at the ready, he sat down to open the cylinder. First, he slipped out the vial and set it carefully in a bowl to his side. He would want to place the vial back in the cylinder when he inserted his own returning parchment. Morlog set the cylinder down only long enough to fix his tea. Comfortable now, he removed the parchment, unrolled it, and set four river stones on the corners to lay it out before him. Looking it over, he observed the seal of the King. The parchment read:

Morlog, I beseech you:

Your counsel is required in matters most urgent.

Word has come from Khordom Palace and area.

Our agents tell us they have succeeded in locating my beloved Queen Madelina and daughter, Princess Annabella. While I am overjoyed at this, it falls short.

I have learned that they are being held in the prison tower of Pierce Island. This does not bode well.

Since learning this, my darling Princess Lily has disappeared also. Kasell, recovering from injury, has recalled details of an attack that is surely of Khordrian origin. The raiders wore tunics that suggest this.

Should this be the case and, having confirmed the whereabouts of my Queen and eldest daughter, I dreadfully fear that Thane-Ra is planning a new uprising. We must take seriously the acts

of one who has all a man can require yet desires still more. The Kingdom of Mazgamor is in grave danger, Morlog. There is not time to call a Leadership Circle, so I am seeking your counsel as an elder of the Circle. You must inform Kasreya. I welcome her, too, to my Castle. Wiser and calmer minds must prevail and this is best done if we are united as one.
I await your reply,
Magnus II
Of Constantia Glen

Deeply disturbed, Morlog set down his tea and reached for a clean sheet of parchment.

11

In the house of Kasreya, the travellers gathered at table with Morlog at one end and Kasreya at the other. Amara directed young servers from the kitchen around the table. Each of the guests was served a portion of delicious fish and vegetables. Dero and Sam pushed the fish around on their plates until Odemog unceremoniously kicked both under the table. Most everyone loved fish, save these two. It was easier to have them eat the fish of Sweetbrooke coming from waters so sweet. But other fish, they would say, tasted like fish. To them, there was nothing palatable about that. So, they picked at the morsels with Odemog throwing them periodic glares.

At any feast worthy of a Clan, it would be expected that a storyteller would entertain those gathered. Tonight, a guest would assume this role. This was unusual as one of the Clan elders would typically do so. However, at table this night was Morlog, a Teller of stories of great renown. Moreover, Morlog is the elder of the Gathering who represents tellers across the Kingdom. It would be rude for another to entertain on this evening.

But entertaining was not at the fore of Morlog's mind. Tonight, his story would be to elucidate. And so it was…

"I know that you have heard tell of Pierce Island," Morlog began his story with a firm and conclusive statement.

"Some say it takes the shape of an arrowhead. Others say, because the prison of Khordom is located there, where many innocents have perished, that it pierces the hearts of mothers to think of it. In truth, the story of the naming of Pierce Island is based on the story of the great ancestor of Khordrya, the province in which Khordom Palace and Pierce Island exist, who met defeat at the hands of an unknown assailant. It has been said that his death came when his heart was pierced by a golden arrow that was said to have been made by an ancient somewhere in the northwest of the Kingdom. So sharp was the arrow in the way that it pierced his body, it simply slipped through him quietly. Not knowing he was injured, Thane of Khordrya commanded a boat back from the Island, marched miles to the Palace and feasted with others for the last time before collapsing at the table." Morlog paused in his story and looked around the table, assured he had the full attention of his audience. His eyes rested at length on Odemog.

"The healer who tended Thane of Khordrya later found the precise cut where the arrow had entered. A soldier of Thane recalled seeing him brush something aside as he fell, which must have been the shaft of the arrow. He had risen so quickly, the soldier thought he had simply lost his footing. So finely honed was this golden arrow tip that, when the healer opened the wound, he found it resting inside the upper right chamber of the heart. It should have felled him almost immediately, but Thane was so strong-hearted and had such great will that even his heart could not be stopped and so he became known as Thane the Strong Heart… or so the story goes."

As any good teller would do on completion of a story, Morlog bowed his head, closed his eyes, and stayed this way for moments as he allowed the story to be absorbed by the guests at table. Morlog waited, knowing the rest of the story must be told. It was time for it to be brought from legend to truth.

Those about the table began to applaud his magnificent story. No one could tell a story with such effects as he. Princess Lily, agog, looked to Morlog as if to ask a question. He raised his hand to silence one and all. On regaining their attention, he continued.

"The people of Thane the Strong Heart grieved angrily and vowed revenge on the rest of Mazgamor. In the generations since, his descendants have plotted to take control of Mazgamor. As a province of our beloved Kingdom, Khordrya has the right to send membership to the Gathering each summer. And, for the most part, they have observed this right. This has never been questioned or revoked. Some time ago, their inconsistent presence or absence was observed to align itself with various raids on peaceful villagers around the Kingdom. They have secreted themselves in and out of places in ways to cause ripples of fear throughout Mazgamor. There is no pattern or apparent intention, except to incite fear in the hearts of many. The raid on Aureopiscis two summers ago was timed with attendance at the Twentieth Gathering. This, of course, makes sense when one considers geography. It was a bold attack in daylight during the parade of healers and tellers in the hills between the Point and the border of Aureopiscis." Morlog paused to ask a question of his listening audience.

"And do you know how this village came to such a name, friends?" He stared from Sam to Dero and fixed on Amara. She shook her head 'no.'

"It is so named for the golden fish. A delicious species of fish known only to their northern waters, it is similar in size to your favourite brook trout," he gestured to Odemog, who nodded in agreement. "The difference lies in the golden flesh of this water creature. It is rich in oils that are used in healing, and it is soothing to the diet unquestionably." He paused.

"These fools came to a notion that traces back for decades and is part of the source of their hatred and anger. Thinking that such a golden fish must come from a golden place, therein must be a magic source of gold itself. Fools, degenerate fools," he inserted his rarely offered opinion. "And so, they did great damage to village and resources in search of their precious gold. Innocent fishermen and women lost their lives defending nothing but a peaceful life and fish of golden flesh. A great tragedy was this. What made matters worse at the time was the smug denial of those who stood for Khordrya at the Gathering. They professed innocence. They professed ignorance of any such plot and, while others slept fitfully that night, grieving for the distress of the villagers of Aureopiscis, these villains slipped away quietly in the dark, leaving not a trace of their ever having been at table."

He paused in the story now for a question or two, seeing the disturbance his words had generated. Samezog, always ready to debate or raise questions, was first to speak to this part of the story.

"Morlog, there is no logic in allowing them to continue to attend the Gathering. Tell us why we would be so foolish to welcome such evil to a meeting intended for education and celebration. It simply makes no sense." He shook his head in frustration.

"Who would be the fool to banish them from sight?" replied Morlog. "It is good to keep one's friends close, Sam…but still better to keep enemies closer." He smiled at Sam and, looking to Kasreya, he continued. "It is true that when they attend, they cannot be trusted and when they are away, we should be wary. And so, the Gathering Circle—leaders of provinces and practice—set guard on high upon leaving their homes for our gatherings. Yes, we are a Kingdom on guard. We keep them in sight as much as they permit, that we may observe and note patterns and changes. They believe we do this from fear, but it is our wisdom that shall prevail." He smiled and nodded looking at Reya who said, "I could not agree more with Teller Morlog. We, too, have been witness to the raids of Khordrya. Our losses painful, our learning great, we should never fall victim again. Never."

"Now," Morlog continued his story. "You must be questioning this vile search for gold. And so should you. And you especially, Odemog, must heed these words: the quest for gold by the Khordrians is one born of rage. That arrow, the golden arrow that pierced the heart of Thane, gave them much to think about. It is said that, in a glass case in Khordom Palace on a swatch of blue velvet, lays the arrow that felled Thane the Strong Heart. It is this which serves as a reminder of a battle lost and a leader destroyed. It is this which fuels their hatred.

It is also believed that it was not so much the arrow but the purity and purpose of this gold that felled their leader. So much so that the generations of leaders to follow believe that to possess this gold would give them power that cannot be fathomed. They believe that only an arrow of gold, or other weaponry composed with this very metallurgy and only the source of this specific gold could cause the demise of their leader. Thus, the violent and vengeful quest, foolish or otherwise, to find the source of this gold for both power and protection. It is said of the gold of this specific arrow that its composition is strangely different from other gold found within our Kingdom. But now, I know," he tapped his hand to his chest. "In your hearts, you pain over the questions this gold brings to you. Give some thought to this: you have no hatred or anger and the gold gives you angst. Those of Khordom Palace fuel their hatred further just by thinking of this gold. Imagine the power it generates."

As if on cue by Morlog's earlier cautionary note, Odemog leaned forward. He reached to his side as if to handle the hilt of his sword, which he had removed from his belt earlier. Morlog observed this movement, noting a modicum of discomfort in his charge.

"Teller Morlog," he addressed the storyteller as one would at such a time when the Teller held the attention of a group. "You singled me out as you have often this journey. I must ask why. What is my place in all of this, Morlog?"

"You ask of your destiny, Odemog, and this I cannot tell you. You have been told you must live it to fulfill it. Your destiny will present itself to you. There is one thing, and one thing only, that I can tell you. You, and only you, will know the location of this purest of gold. On your guard you must be, for there are others who know your place in this revelation."

"I know of no such thing, Morlog. I have never seen a place where gold is sourced. Neither have I mined gold, nor have I sought gold for any cause or reason. Morlog, you know as any, I am a farmer as was my father and his father before him. I travel to trade and take pleasure in the beasts and creatures of our Kingdom. What causes have I to be searching for gold?"

The room took on such a quiet state that it would be difficult to know that there was anyone other than Morlog and Odemog present. Hushed, all beings followed the conversation with their eyes only. Kasreya, unlike the others, closed her eyes and bowed her head for she knew that this was the beginning of a new age in the Kingdom of Mazgamor.

12

Mother and daughter huddled close together in their cell, high above the cliffs and surrounding waters, in the prison tower of Pierce Island. Outside their window and over the sound of crashing waves below they could hear gulls calling to one another.

Tired and losing strength, Queen Madelina held Princess Annabella close. They had shared their close quarters for over a season and, because of the proximity to the ocean, the weather had not been kind. Annabella gave her mother strength, as she was known to see the bright side of everything. She was a source of great frustration to Morzan when he made his visits upon them.

Each morning on waking, Annabella, struggling to track time except for the changing of seasons and temperatures, would spend her first moments calculating the day. This morning, she was half certain it was a special day for her mother. Today would be the birthday of the prince brothers, Fazzog, Mezzog, and Borzog. In any other time and on any other day she would consider them a nuisance but now she longed for her brothers. Such was her sadness that Queen Madelina sensed a difference in her daughter.

"What grieves you this day, Annabella?" the Queen asked.

"Mother, I think today is my brothers' birthday."

"So then, we should feel joy," her mother responded in a manner fit to cheer anyone. She felt a deep pain for her daughter, who rarely showed such sadness. The Queen shifted and drew Annabella closer, tightening her hold. If love could infuse another by the strength of an embrace she was, this moment, filling her daughter full. Annabella wrapped her arms around her mother and held her tight in return.

"We should celebrate my brothers."

"And how do you propose we do that?" Madelina asked as she stroked Annabella's hair.

"I think a story would do, don't you? If we celebrate them, our hearts will grow lighter. Then, when that wicked Morzan appears again, our strength will outdo his."

"A wonderful idea, my love," responded the Queen, marveling yet again, at the creative ways in which Annabella could muster strength. She thought for a moment and said, "Aha, Annabella, I have the perfect story for you. I am most certain I have never told you about the birth of my triplet sons, have I?"

"I have heard you speak of Lily and Tulip only, Mother. I can't imagine much pleasure in birthing three—boys especially!" She laughed.

"Alright then, prepare yourself. There were three, as you know, so this is a long story."

Annabella stood up and extended her hand to her mother. Queen Madelina took her hand and rose from the floor where they slept on a bed of straw. She pushed the hinged hook, on which a pot of water hung, forward until it hung over a small fire. Once boiled, she made two cups of weak tea. Such a luxury they were afforded infrequently so they used the leaves again and again until they coloured the water no longer. A fractured excuse for a table and two rickety chairs beckoned to them where they sat and took their tea. With her free hand, Madelina reached across the table and took Annabella's as she began her story.

"The healers came regularly after my belly continued to grow and grow with each passing day. They measured, they weighed me and served me strange concoctions and strange, to be true, they were. King Magnus, your father, distressed at my size, for I was so very much smaller as I carried you." She squeezed Annabella's hand as she smiled at her daughter.

"When the day finally came that your brothers would enter this world, I felt such pain as I had never known giving birth to you. A Tsesiwan healer who practiced midwifery was by my side. She was tall and strong and commanded the chamber as none before her. She was called Kayrana. I have seen her only once since, with the birth of your sisters Tulip and Lily. A lovely and kind woman is she. But I digress…" The Queen paused as she recalled the memories of those days.

"Kay, as she bade me call her, spoke of miracles that day but, to be honest, there was nothing miraculous in the pain. I know that hours passed, and day turned to night, and I felt no relief. Your father came and went in and out of the chamber. As the day went on Kay approved less and less of these visits. I would scream in pain with a contraction and your father," she laughed, "your father would turn white as a cloud. With this, Kay would shoo him from the room. Eventually, she banished him altogether."

Annabella pictured the story in her mind. Her father, such a loving and gentle man, she knew could not bear anyone suffering. He would, could he do so, trade places with anyone that they not suffer. She smiled and listened.

"Finally, your brother Borzog began to make his way into the world. He was a struggle. Kay gently prompted my pushing and breathing. For all the struggle and pain, she made me feel less fear and more ease. And so, he arrived but I was still with child. We had thought twins and twins it would be. In but a moment Mezzog burst into the world with a howling performance like none other of you. At this moment—imagine the scene, dear one—your father had entered the chamber against the wishes of Kay but on hearing Mezzog, he turned on his heel and was gone before his body knew he had even been in the room. I am told it was a sight. Now, fearful was I, Annabella, for I did not feel quite right. I knew from your birth that after childbirth things were not quickly righted. But this was a different feeling and I complained bitterly to Kay. Now it was Kay's turn to be amused with my ignorance. She had seen this before and I was to see it now—a third child. It was but a few moments when Kay stroked my belly to ease my pain and before I knew it, she held in arms a tiny boy. Triplets they were, to my great surprise…triplets! And so, your brother, Fazzog, arrived with neither pomp nor circumstance. He simply arrived."

"Were there no triplets before, Mother?" asked Annabella. "How did this come to be? I have not seen three alike brothers before."

"This, too, is part of the miracle, daughter, for you speak truth. There are but few known triplets to survive in our Kingdom. And, with your brothers, except for their difference in size, they are completely identical. Poor Fazzog is a shadow of his brothers and this was part of his struggle from birth. We did not know if he would survive his first night. Your father always said that Borzog, the leader of three, commanded him. Mezzog, the most vocal of three, demanded him. And Fazzog, the gentlest of three, obliged them. They are my beautiful sons and I do love them dearly, for all their mischief, mix-ups, and foolishness. They are bright and delightful."

"And their names, Mother, how did they come by their names?"

"The naming of a child is a noble and thoughtful process. A name honours the one who receives it and the one from whom it may be taken. In our family, your name and your sisters' come from your father's lineage. Your brothers' names come from my ancestors. This has been the way of our Kingdom from the beginning. Borzog is named for my father from the Clan of Odem. My uncle, Mezzog, was a storyteller and teacher of students of the Gathering. And Fazzog, dear Fazzog, was blessed with his name from one who was not a blood relation but an honoured member of my Clan. Fazzog was the father of Zodemog, who was the father of Odemog of Sweetbrooke Wren. Fazzog, like Odemog, was a gentle farmer. He was destined to be a Protector of the Kingdom. It was he who felled the one who built this prison. We owe much to Fazzog and for this reason I chose, with the King, the great name for your brother. A small boy needed a great name to inspire his confidence and bravery with brothers such as his. And this, Annabella, is the story of your brothers. What do you say, child?"

"There is one certain thing I take from this story, Mother," her expression gave away her intention as she beheld a rather sheepish grin. "I cannot complain of nuisance or pain from them, as you suffered the greatest in childbirth, no doubt."

The Queen laughed at her daughter's understanding of the story. And Annabella concluded with a comment that would serve to inspire their continued time on Pierce Island.

"As we endure our time here then, I shall take faith and inspiration in the name and namesake of my smallest of brothers. Fazzog's legacy is one of courage and strength and so I shall reach deep inside to enlist the courage to withstand all that may lie ahead. Knowing that a power associated with this dreadful tower was destroyed gives me strength. Thank you, Mother, for inspiring me with such a story. And happy birthday, Brothers." She raised her mug as if to toast them and took the last drink.

As Annabella swallowed, she heard the sound she dreaded most of all: a key in the lock of the arched wooden door that kept them from leaving the tower. As if on cue, Queen Madelina rose from her seat. She stepped in front her daughter who rose beside her, reaching back she placed her arms protectively holding Annabella.

A guard pulled the door open slowly and Morzan took a step forward. His unwelcome visits had been stepped up of late.

"Happy birthday? I am sure I heard you say happy birthday. Well, well, well. So, which of you could it be then?" His voice was caustic and sounded not the least bit interested or sincere. Still, there was a commanding tone that required response.

"There is no birthday here," the Queen responded. "We were simply reminiscing. You will find nothing interesting in our conversation, Morzan."

"I will find what I wish. And you, Queen, will come with me."

"No!" cried Annabella as she sprang from behind her mother. A second guard stepped forward and pushed her aside. She fell to the bed of straw and quickly tried to rise to defend her mother. The guard stepped forward, pointing a spear down at her. She fell back on her elbows. The first guard took the Queen by her arm and forcibly removed her from the cell. Backing out of the room, the other guard reached for the door, waiting for Morzan. A guttural laugh emerged from this heinous creature as he spoke acridly to the princess.

"Patience, Princess, your turn will come." With that, he turned on his heel and left the dank chamber, the door slamming shut behind him, lock turning, leaving nothing but a hollow silence with the princess.

13

The limestone steps sounded hollow as Morzan and the guard marched the Queen down the curving stairwell from the tower. The tower had long been reserved for the important 'guests' of Khordom Palace. These current guests had long been planned for the tower cell and Morzan was enjoying playing with them. He delighted in stretching out the angst of the Queen and Princess with new and different torturous experiences with each visit. But rarely did he or his minions actually touch them. Like Magnus, the Queen and Princess were gentle and kind, as was their nature and that of Constantia Glen. Logic had proven correct for Morzan, who believed that they would feel more pain in observing the pain and torture of others. And so, he delighted in creating merciless means by which to make others suffer and cause suffering in turn to the Queen and Princess.

On this day, a spy would be punished. A loyal servant of Thane-Ra had turned coward in the eyes of Khordom Palace and sent information to Magnus on the whereabouts of the Queen and Princess. This was unforgivable. Though such a revelation had been planned from the beginning, it was much ahead of Thane-Ra's plans. This, of course, angered him greatly and, after much searching and punishment of many, the spy was ferreted out to meet with certain death, a slow, painful, certain death. Perhaps what was worse was the process by which he would accomplish this. The soldier of Thane-Ra who would conduct Morzan's bidding would, himself, be the next victim. Morzan's cruel methods were consistent and informative.

A soldier messenger who had returned from a recent raid with news not pleasing to Thane-Ra was dispatched to the Island to suffer a horrible end as reward for bringing unwelcome news. And so, to extend his suffering, Morzan would introduce this soldier, named Nordhal, to his own end by making him conduct the series of torturous tasks upon another.

"Learn of your unspeakable death by doing so to another," Morzan laughed gleefully as he watched the sickened look cross Nordhal's face in a slow and painful manner. Morzan seemed to gain strength from the suffering of those at his mercy.

Guards at her side, the Queen was brought to a dark chamber far below the tower cell. There, about the chamber, were chains and remnants of past victims of Morzan. She cringed at the horrid smells of sweat and blood mixed with fear that enveloped the entire space. Her stomach turned as she looked upon a small and filthy man chained and hanging in the center of the room. He raised his head and moaned.

"No, it cannot be—Constantia's Queen!"

"Silence, traitorous fool," Morzan sniped, raising a whip, and cracking it across the man's chest. His head dropped and he fell into a state of unconsciousness, a saving grace in this agonizing place.

"You," Morzan turned and pointed at the Queen, "are witness to the rewards of treachery. Though you would not think him a treacherous man for he has revealed your whereabouts to the King—the fool."

The Queen felt a weight lift from her soul as she thought of what and how the King would come to their aid. She feared for her beloved Magnus at the same time and she was right to do so. But she would not betray her feelings to Morzan. Still, he seemed to read her thoughts.

"Were I you, Queen, I would not breathe too easy. This cretin has only served to advance a plan that was already in the making. It was the intention of Thane-Ra from the planning of your capture to draw that simp, Magnus, to us in order to rid Mazgamor of his influence and expand the bounds of Khordrya even further, as it should be. Our timeline has changed but our plans have not. And for the inconvenience, we shall send a message to those who betray and those who fail Thane-Ra. Stupidity shall neither be tolerated nor forgiven." He turned abruptly and snapped the whip in the direction of Nordhal. A guard reached out with his spear and prodded Nordhal forward toward Morzan.

"You will take this whip and give this pathetic beast 100 lashes. Make him bleed!" Morzan uttered a guttural command that dripped with gratification.

Shaking in anticipation of what would come, Nordhal raised the whip and began. Watching, Queen Madelina stood her ground. The chained prisoner raised his head, gritting his teeth and, on making eye contact with the Queen, found peace in her gaze. For the duration of those torturous moments, she held his gaze as she prayed inside for strength for all, especially for this man who had risked himself for her possible rescue as well as Annabella's.

14

Leevon of Twin Ponds had taken to air from Sweetbrooke Wren not an hour from his arrival. Again, in his talons he held an urgent dispatch. This time, he returned to the King a message that would put him at ease.

As the sentry sent word that Leevon had been observed in the sky drawing nearer to King Magnus' castle, the King hurriedly made his way to an upper court upon which Leevon would be directed to land.

The Great Eagle Leevon landed gracefully and, releasing talons, stepped back from the cylinder. He picked it up gingerly in his bill and gave it to King Magnus. He would not let the King bend to pick it up from the ground out of respect for the monarch.

"My thanks to you, Leevon. You have fulfilled your mission and I extend my gratitude." He beckoned to a page near his side who brought forth rewards for Leevon. There on the tray were rare delicacies that would please his palate. A healer offered relaxation in the form of a soothing elixir that would ease his tired wings and give him comfort and rest. After all, this had been a long and tiring journey. Independent and strong, Leevon would typically decline such offers graciously. But on this day, after a long day's quick speed of flight he was, in truth, exhausted. And so, Leevon imbibed the potion and was shown a quiet place to rest where he indulged in the delicacies before nodding off to sleep. As he fell into a deep slumber, Leevon considered the last time he had enjoyed the rarities of stip flungi, a nutritious and filling fungus that was known to grow only along the shaded banks of upper Sweet Brook. It was rare, for few places along upper Sweet Brook were sufficiently shaded. And, like all other things of the brook before being crossed by the River Constantia, stip flungi enjoyed a hearty flavour, savory and sweet with earthy aroma. He was grateful for the care of the King.

Retreating to the Royal Halls, King Magnus met there with Kasell and other advisors. He had passed off the cylinder to Kasell as they made their way to the chamber.

Kasell approached a great table that could seat twenty. It was round and sturdy with the crest of the King inlaid in the center with shells and stones. Crushed abalone was used to represent the teal within the crest. This table had been host to many meetings and plans. As Kasell opened the cylinder and carefully removed the contents, King Magnus took his seat at table.

"Read on then, Kasell," the King gestured with an open palm to Kasell, drawing listening ears and attentive eyes to the man. Kasell nodded and presented the room with the contents of Morlog's parchment.

My King,

Warmest wishes for safety and health to you, your family, and people.

I received your word by the grace of Leevon of Twin Ponds and send return findings with urgency. I send you good news! Odemog has stumbled upon your beloved Princess Lily in the woods north of the Meadow.

With this news, the room erupted in cheers and Magnus touched his right hand over his heart as he took a deep breath and sighed with relief. Tears filled his eyes and somehow even the room seemed brighter.

"Praise to Odemog, he has found my sweet Lily," the King rejoiced.

Smiling, Kasell continued:

Odemog wisely brought her to safety in the arms of Sweetbrooke Wren, believing it best to travel away from the possible path of the raiders. Mega cared for her this past night and all is well. This morning, we prepare to leave to bring her safely home. Our journey begins shortly. I have cautioned Odemog of the dangers. He has been told of your news and readies to join you, as service requires, to gain the freedom of your Queen and daughter, Annabella. We bring other worthy warriors to protect and serve the Royal family of Constantia Glen in service of the Kingdom of Mazgamor.

Magnus, Odemog has been introduced; the letter has been passed. We travel by Siwa to pick up the others and join you in correcting the evil. I offer my allegiance to you and will join Constantia Glen in battle anon.

In Loyal Friendship,

Morlog,

Clan of Odem

Kasell set down the parchment and gazed over at his King. The silence was brief. With strength renewed, Magnus rose from his throne looking larger than life and uttered three determined words. "To battle plans."

The room cleared of all those listening. They would gather again, in preparation, at the next sunrise. Kasell remained at the King's side to hear and relay expectations.

To plan for battle in Constantia Glen was not a common practice. But games held regularly had honed the skills of arms men, should such occasion be upon them. It was only four Gatherings past that a lack of preparation and training had caught them off guard and they fell as victims of Khordom Palace to the greed and evil of Thane-Ra. Never wishing to repeat such pain in his province, King Magnus prepared his arms men for all that could come their way through organized tests of skill. They also applied their skills by patrolling the restless foreign traders at Trader's Peninsula in support of Thorandal. Though the Princess Lily's escort had been caught off guard and the Queen and eldest daughter kidnapped, his men were strong and determined. In his heart he believed the only reason his men had been overtaken was because of the strength of the evil they opposed. And so, with the greatest resolve and truest of heart, he would lead his arms men against them. A true heart filled with love can outlast and overcome the most horrid of evils. This, Magnus knew in his head, heart, and soul. He would see the return of his family and the Kingdom he loved would be safe again.

Mezzog entered the Royal Hall, followed by his brother Borzog. Approaching their father, they came to stop at the other side of the table and together bowed.

"My sons, where is your third?" King Magnus inquired of their brother, Fazzog.

"Fazzog is in the library, Father," Mezzog spoke confidently, still addressing his father with reverence.

"Word has come we prepare for battle, Father," Borzog pressed. "What roles have you for us in this? We prepare to rescue our mother and sister, then?"

"My sons, Fazzog has chosen the wisest path at this time. I sense your determination to join in battle but we are much against the unknown. Our own spies bring little word of the resolve of Thane-Ra. Thankfully, news received has been the good news of the Queen and your sister, so I shall not minimize our spies. What we do not know tells us much of the secrecy of the plans of Thane-Ra."

"But Father, my King," Mezzog knew to win argument with his father would only be accomplished if he presented himself with the strength and maturity of a loyal arms man. "Borzog and I can, at least, offer our honed skills at battle. Fazzog offers his strengths in his way. You must consider us not as princes but as trained arms men with the advantage of both skill and strategy."

Borzog was a victor in all categories of arms. On successive skill games days in Constantia, though he was not yet of age for the Gatherings, he won all events in which he competed. Those who came up against him were sure to meet defeat. Mezzog was a good strategist who had consistently outsmarted their teachers. Of the three, Fazzog enjoyed the lessons and absorbed everything he read or was taught. On the other hand, Borzog could always count on his brother, Mezzog, to determine a way to finish lessons early or distract a teacher to another task. What they did not know was that this, too, was a strategy of the Teachers. The Teachers were a select membership of educators, healers, and tellers led by Gimrial who, together, planned lessons that would guide the princely brothers on the path to the throne in moons to come. As triplets, they confounded the tradition that the first-born son would ascend the throne to succeed the King. And so, succession was argued in many ways. Some said they should share. Others saw this as a foolish division of power. Still others saw Mezzog as their future king— after all, he showed strength as a leader. Logic suggested it should be Borzog, as he was the first born of the three. Fazzog was gentle and kind, others said and would continue traditions. There was an opinion for every one of the princes. But what mattered to the identical triplet princes was that they knew who would succeed the throne and this was all that counted.

The King listened to Mezzog as he argued his points, all the while smiling inwardly. He considered all points of the argument which he thought a valid one. King Magnus knew that, should he say yes, he would never hear the end of it from the Queen. However, as King, he had a responsibility to the future of Constantia—a duty—to prepare the future monarch, whichever of the princes it would be. To be a part of the battle at arms, or in strategizing, would give them experience the games and Gatherings could never provide.

"My son, your argument is solid, but you have not identified the role that Fazzog would play here. I cannot permit you without a complete argument. I encourage you to consider this and return to plead your case again. You, Mezzog, are one of three; each strengthens the others. One does not stand out or contribute more than another. Thus, when you can present a complete argument, you will once again have my ear."

"But Father," Mezzog knew he would not win but elected to press the King. "There is no time for debate. You must let us serve."

"Serve you may, should you convince me. But only fools rush in, my son. We take the time to prepare. At this moment it is you who wastes time. Be off to prepare a thorough debate."

Mezzog bowed without further argument and took leave of the Royal Hall. Borzog loitered to hear the discussion of armaments. The King continued his council with senior arms men who had studied the secret raids and warfare of Khordrya.

"Marsdell, you led the defense of our land in the Khordrian raid, during the Nineteenth Gathering. What say you of our strengths and challenges?"

"My King, those embattled arms men gained much experience of the fighting ways of Khordrian raiders. Suffice it to say, raiders have no real strength, just determination, anger, and fear. Those who fail Thane-Ra face death if they do not die in the heat of battle. They have nothing to lose. Perhaps this is their strength: return a victor or die. Thane-Ra cares not who he extinguishes, for he has loyalty to no one but himself. He thrives in a place of greed and hatred. He only fears the arrow. Thus, his obsessed quest for the gold."

"And you, Kasell? What have our spies given us in ways of attack on the Palace and prison? Are there weaknesses we may exploit?"

Borzog could hear Kasell imparting details to his father but had become distracted, thinking of Mezzog and the debate he was preparing. Excusing himself with a step backward and a silent bow in the direction of his father, Borzog withdrew from the hall.

In anticipation of the Gathering of arms men at sunrise, the meetings to develop a plan to free Queen Madelina and Princess Annabella continued through the night.

15

Mezzog sat across a long, heavy dark mahogany table with his fists clenched and resting one atop the other. On top of his fists, he had set his chin and he stared straight ahead. His gaze fell upon Fazzog across the table from him. For a long time, he watched Fazzog page rapidly through books and piles of parchments: letters, decrees, and ancient cartography. After some time, Mezzog's eyes had glazed over and he appeared a solid statue compared to busy Fazzog. Occasionally, Fazzog would speak with words and phrases such as "aha", "I see," "good gracious," and the like. It was not until he spoke these words that Mezzog was brought back from his trancelike gazing state.

"This cannot be. How did this letter come to be here, I wonder. Should this be authentic…hmmm…if this is true…" Fazzog enjoyed a deep conversation by himself but peaked his brother's curiosity.

"What could be true, Brother?" Mezzog demanded in his assertive manner. "You are making no sense, though this would not be unusual," he joked.

"What would not be unusual, Brother?" Borzog asked of Mezzog as he strode into the Royal Library. After leaving the Royal Hall, Borzog had gone straight to the library hoping to find his brothers together. He knew his first stop would find Fazzog and found fortune with both present there.

"Fazzog seems to have a story to tell, Borzog," Mezzog said, gesturing towards their studious smaller brother.

The two stared at Fazzog who sat shuffling documents from one side to another. It appeared he was attempting to place them in some sort of order.

"A moment to think, my brothers, and I will share what I believe I have found," replied Fazzog without raising his head.

It suddenly dawned on Mezzog that this was the last piece to the puzzle that formed his debate. The answer lay in the strength of the three, not one over another. Borzog brought strength and skill at arms, Mezzog brought wisdom of strategy, and Fazzog brought knowledge of history. Each brother's strength empowered the others. It was simple and obvious: they were brothers together, identical and connected in more ways than a birthday or in like appearance. Now he could convince their father to allow them to assume their rightful places to bring their strengths to battle. In this revelation, and unbeknownst to him, the moment of truth had come, and the Teachers had succeeded.

Fazzog now looked up, observing Mezzog's excitement. But rather than asking for enlightenment on his state, he now looked over at Borzog and began to speak slowly.

"We are at the fore of a changing tide in this Kingdom. I have found here, amongst these parchments, information that must not leave this room. I am certain that Father holds this knowledge as well. But to share it ourselves could mean certain death for many. My brothers, pledge now your silence."

"Our silence is yours for the protection of the Kingdom," the brothers said in unison. Fazzog acknowledged this with a firm nod.

"Here, I have found a record, dating back to the attack on Khordom Palace. In fact, it expounds greatly on the strategy and plans to attack and stop construction of the prison tower on Pierce Island. Then ruler, Thane, the father of Thane-Ra, also known as Thane the Strong Heart only because he knew not how to die properly," Fazzog rarely made snide remarks, but his brothers enjoyed a guffaw over this one before he continued. "He commissioned the tower to imprison all who disagreed, failed, or disobeyed him. In that period, the people of Khordom Palace travelled freely and visitors went to the province to trade openly in the street markets. But Thane had developed a lust for power like none other. He was advised to build armaments and facilities to protect his reign, which then could not be challenged or dissolved. He would be the undisputed ruler of Khordom Palace. Until that time, it was simply the province of Khordrya. Thane so named his castle to distinguish himself as ruler and king over the people and this was when circumstances began to change. Thane's lust for power grew and, with that, his paranoia. This began the culling of his people he believed to be plotting to betray and destroy him. Visitors never returned to their homes outside of Khordrya as they were captured as spies. Spies, in turn, were taken to Pierce Island, where they were enslaved to finish work on the prison. Few escaped and rarely survived, others perished from exhaustion, torture, or lost hope. The stories I have read are ugly and dreadful. Things settled somewhat over time. Then the raid took place. An amalgam of arms men from around the Kingdom came together in the effort to stop Thane. Unfortunately, due to his enslavement of so many, the prison was completed before it could be stopped. When arms men arrived by boat to Pierce Island, they did so under cover of darkness, surprising Thane's men. And, in fact, they surprised Thane himself, who had arrived to inspect the prison before sundown. A battle commenced, where many slaves joined the brave warriors, freeing themselves from captivity. It was this battle where Thane was pierced by an arrow—the very golden arrow that ended his life. The evil of Khordrya, the threat to Mazgamor, was eradicated. The one who strikes down such evil can only be a Kingdom Keeper." Fazzog paused for his brothers, who were taking this all in. A shadow appeared in the archway entrance of the library and hovered.

Fazzog continued now more deliberately, "Brothers, this is what you must know: the one who brought and let loose the arrow that struck down Thane was none other than the grandfather of one we know today—Odemog."

"Odemog's grandfather was Fazzog, was he not?" asked Mezzog after brief thought.

"Yes. It was he who fashioned the arrow and he who shot it from his bow. You must know what this means." He looked to his puzzled brothers and answered his own question. "This makes Odemog one of the Kingdom Keepers about which we have been schooled."

On hearing this information from their brother, they pondered what was now taking place in the Kingdom: kidnappings, attacks, and Odemog on his way to Constantia with their sister in his protection. As this revelation began to sink in, the shadow moved closer to the table at which the princes were gathered. They did not notice the presence of another until a voice interrupted their dialogue.

"That will be enough now."

"What did I say?" asked Fazzog looking to the voice.

"More than is wise," replied King Magnus, who had heard much of this conversation.

Fazzog, Mezzog and Borzog had risen from their seats on hearing their father's voice.

"I do not understand, Father." As he pulled a chair out for the King to join them, Fazzog challenged his father for chastising him. "What I have read and shared with my brothers, who have pledged secrecy, must be a matter of some public record, for I found it here in the Royal Library."

"Fazzog, this is the Royal Library and not public record. Further, I do not know how you found access to secret archival documents."

At this comment, Fazzog turned a shade of red, realising he had exposed himself. Because of his insatiable appetite for knowledge, the Teacher, Gimrial, had shown him the way in to the Royal Archives. Perhaps it was a deliberate way of preparing Fazzog for his future, but it was not the King's intention for these facts to be revealed in such an uncontrolled way. Sure enough, his father was right and Fazzog had made a grave error. He had gone to the library to learn more of historical battles and skirmishes to prepare for this impending battle. Unsatisfied with general documents, he snuck into the archives and dug where he was not welcome.

"Father, I ask your forgiveness."

"Your initiative is commendable, my son, but as I said, what you have revealed is neither wise nor is it the way it was to be. This is a dangerous time as you are each now aware. What has been revealed here has yet even to be revealed to the Kingdom Keeper, Odemog. This is a life mission and potentially perilous destiny that has been passed down his Clan from generation to generation. While he is not alone, a Kingdom Keeper is only informed of this charge when the time calls. The identity of a Kingdom Keeper is known at their birth, but only by the Protectors. When they are called, a letter is passed from their predecessor who, having been called before them, has prepared to inform them of their destiny early in their mission. This way, no evil can come to a Keeper before their time, thus protecting them and the Kingdom. Your logic prevailed and you have discerned what has never been revealed and no one has deduced. Now you three Princes, my sons, must withhold your knowledge until the reveal or to your deaths. Will you affirm your pledge with me?"

"Ours is a pledge to you and the Kingdom, Father," said Mezzog.

"From the heart, Father," agreed Fazzog.

"To the death, my King," swore Borzog.

"Then, my sons, I invite you to join us at table in the planning of the rescue of your Queen and your sister, Annabella. You have shown me today that you have learned your teachings well and are united in your knowledge, skills, and loyalties. Come with me."

Together, the princes and the King rose from the table and returned to the Royal Hall to join those who had continued devising strategies. All they waited upon now was the arrival of Odemog, his fellow travellers, and the others who would join them.

16

Skeeter was the first to rise as his stomach behaved much like an alarm on this morning. It growled and grumbled so disruptively he could sleep no more. He stole his way down from his perch high atop a cabinet. He always chose a cabinet top to sleep upon when indoors or the branches of a tree when outdoors. The elevation gave this small creature a sense of safety. It had paid off for both him and Odemog many times in the past when creatures and beasts attempted to come upon them in secrecy. Skeeter slept lightly, as most small creatures would, to protect themselves from predators.

On this beautiful, crisp morning with the sky filled with ribbons of pink and orange on the horizon, Skeeter was happy to be alive. Perhaps less for the beauty of the sunrise and more for the fact that he had just spotted a bowl of plump nuts sitting in the center of the dining table. On the floor now, he selected his path to the tabletop and hopped to the seat of a chair, then climbed the back, and jumped to the table. There he began to feast on walnuts, hazelnuts, peanuts, and gabelnuts. He ate till his belly was full to bursting. Skeeter was surveying the room when the sleepiness from eating a rich meal overtook him. Yawning, he leaned back against the bowl, rubbed his bloated belly, and fell asleep exposed to the world.

Moments passed and another emerged from a chamber. Odemog gingerly crept across the room to a bucket of water. He took the ladle in his hand and scooped enough water to fill a mug. Odemog turned around to see his little friend perched and snoring on the table. He could not hold back the giggle that erupted. Taking his mug of water, he sat at table and withdrew a parchment from his waist pouch. He stared at Skeeter for a moment then reached for a half shell of a walnut and placed it atop Skeeter's head. The look of this tiny helmet amused him immensely. Odemog turned his attention back to the parchment, sipped his water and read, once more, the letter from his father. He puzzled over this destiny of which his father spoke and gave further consideration to all that had occurred to date. Then he thought back to the day he remembered less clearly with each passing year: the day his father left for the Great Falls. He recalled cautionary words exchanged between his parents, loving embraces, and his father climbing into his saddle atop Vadim. The last image of his father was of him in the sky, flying away from their home. He felt the pain of his loss for just a moment, then returned to his present situation.

Today they would travel together—himself, Morlog, Princess Lily, Sam, Dero, and those who would come along from Siwa—Kasreya, Amara, Juliet, Stronleya, and her band of archers. The Tsesiwans would travel on horseback and raft. Experienced in travelling the Trezano Falls, they had rigged a system of rafts with finely woven hemp ropes anchored along the rock face. A number of lives had been lost in the construction of this carefully engineered system, which enabled passage in relative safety through the three falls down the canyon passage. There were four options to reach Constantia Glen: by boat along the coastline, but this required a lengthy portage to reach Mid Lake before crossing to reach Constantia, through Trezano Falls by rafts, across land, and through the mountains by way of Volcanic Valley, which was a treacherous journey, or the longest route, and the way most commonly taken during times of peace, and when one could travel a leisurely pace, was across land to The Meadows and back again. Now was not the time for long journeys, rather expedient ones, even if there was some risk. So, Odemog and his travellers would fly above them to make sure the Tsesiwan party made it safely through the mountains by way of the Falls. He and his party would then continue ahead to return the Princess to her father and ease his angst. After a brief respite, Odemog and any other master riders available would travel back to ensure the safe arrival of the

Tsesiwans. It would be a long day of travel but, unless some misfortune should come upon them, all would be well.

Sam and Dero were next to join him at table. Kasreya followed and announced that the princess would follow with Amara anon. They began to discuss their travel plans when Juliet arrived on the heels of Kasreya. Morlog still had not joined them when Amara and Lily arrived, carrying platters of food.

"Kasreya, have you seen Morlog this morning?" Odemog asked as he turned to face Kasreya who was pouring hot tea near the fire. She turned, bringing a tray of mugs to the table and shook her head 'no.'

"I cannot say that I have seen him since rising to observe sunrise," she said. It was a morning ritual of many Tsesiwans to rise and consider the beauty brought each day by a new dawn. During her morning meditation she had not observed Morlog strolling the beach.

Morlog had, in fact, risen just ahead of Skeeter. Perhaps he had been wakened by the grumblings of the squirrel's stomach. On waking, he had elected to take a long stroll to give his body a chance to catch up with his already racing mind. This morning had brought, with the rich colors of sunrise, an uneasy feeling in his heart and mind. He had great concern for Odemog, who was just coming to the knowledge of being a Kingdom Keeper. Since one does not choose this mantle oneself, it could take some time to accept such an ominous duty. Morlog pondered how he could best guide his young friend and the one whom he had spent his life in protection of, just as he had Odemog's father and his father before him. On Zodem's passing, Morlog had sworn he would do better by Odemog, in spite of the fact that he could not have foreseen or changed what had happened to Zodem. It had not been his fault.

Morlog was making his way back to Holder House when he heard the archer in the tower sound an alarm–three short blasts. He watched as, in just a matter of moments, the pathways filled with villagers armed with bows and arrows. Still more came with swords and Kasreya emerged alert and ready to lead.

The archer who had sounded the alarm had done so as a precaution. Archers awaited Kasreya's command. Morlog strode toward the tower observing Reya climbing to the deck to determine her next course of action.

"Report please, Stronleya."

"I beg your pardon, Kasreya. I sounded the alarm as I saw approaching strangers by sky. I thought them to be mordaghas and riders at great distance then realized they were smaller than those who come by mordagha. I looked away but a moment and they were gone from the air. I then observed them to be amongst the woods, at a distance. I have lost sight of the strangers at this time; please forgive my error." Stronleya was a young archer and new to this post. A post at night was reserved for an experienced watcher. The sentry archers had just changed over. Newer sentries learned their role in daylight hours, a quieter, safer time.

Frustrated but forgiving, Kasreya allowed the archer's apology. Still, she beckoned to others to join the watch. Fearing the worst, Kasreya returned to the ground to discuss this development with Morlog and the rest of the travel party. They convened back at the table with reports every fifteen minutes whether the strangers were spotted or not. A ground crew was sent out to expand their perimeter guard just to be sure of ample warning of attack, should this be the order of the day.

"Sounds like horgles to me," Juliet offered, looking to Kasreya.

"Mmm" Kasreya looked only at Morlog, who had returned with all involved to Holder House. "It seems, Morlog, there are others than Tsesiwans aware of your presence here."

"Odemog, our journey must be advanced. The sooner we depart, the safer it will be for Siwa and the Princess," Morlog pressed Odemog to finish preparations for departure.

"Little horgles are no match for us," spouted Sam with unflinching confidence.

"What is a horgle and where did it come from?" asked Princess Lily.

"I shall say this: a horgle is not the worst of our concerns; it is that which may be upon their backs we should be concerned about." Morlog set his hand on her shoulder in an effort to reassure her but he only added to her anxiety.

A horgle, while rather attractive to view, is a winged creature smaller than a mordagha, but faster. They are able to travel and flit about the skies in tighter circles and dives, by far, than a mordagha. The origin of a horgle is questioned by many. Tellers say they are the result of an experiment by a healer scientist of long ago who crossbred a species of small woods horses with a colorful winged raptor. Enchanted by the results of his experiments, he continued to breed them, calling them horgles. They were intended solely for his amusement until he realized their swift and fleet form of flight. He thought they would be excellent messengers and prepared to introduce them to King Magnus I at the thirteenth Gathering. This scientist, known as Storsumal, lived the life of a hermit on the east coastline at the north edge of Galdordon Forest. A kindly old healer, he was neither enemy nor friend to anyone for he largely kept to himself. However, on returning from the raids on Siwa, Khordrian Raiders saw the horgles dashing about in the air above Storsumal's cottage. A party was sent to shore to investigate. To protect his home and livelihood, Storsumal fearfully gave a pair of horgles to them which the raiders presented to Thane-Ra upon their return to Khordom Palace. Delighted, Thane-Ra began to breed them himself but for reasons other than Storsumal had intended. Thus, the sad truth became that, when a horgle was spotted, there was likely a raider on its back.

"What then shall be the new plan?" asked Dero of the others.

"Juliet, Kasreya, if the away party can be ready at once, we shall leave immediately." Odemog looked to the two women as he strapped on his sword and hoisted his bow and quiver. On cue, Sam and Dero did the same as Princess Lily rose.

"Princess, you are well intentioned," Odemog observed. "Skeeter, buck up now and give her a hand will you. Hop to it."

Skeeter, well roused from his sleep and feeling, ever so slightly, a building indigestion, hopped into the bowl of nuts and started pitching them out to roll to the end of the table. From there, he leapt to a chair where a satchel hung and loosened the drawstring. With one paw he grabbed an edge and jumped back to the table. Holding the bag open, he kicked the nuts into the bag, one after another, until the weight of the bag pulled him off balance and yanked him off the edge of the table with a great *thump* as he hit the ground. Odemog shook his head and carried on.

"I think, Morlog, if we can steal away before these visitors arrive, we may gain advantage."

"Perhaps, but by what route? Stronleya gestured in the direction of the Falls. They come from our route already." Morlog was willing but he needed to know that Odemog's plan was well formed, before taking the Princess directly into the face of danger.

"To leave now would surprise them. One would think we would stay to defend Siwa. Kasreya, will your archers be safe if we leave them the fight?"

"By now, Odemog, the route will matter little. They are too close to surprise or deceive. Still, we have long prepared for an attack and I have every confidence in my archers. Our away party will be fine to depart but Morlog poses the wise question. Just how do you propose we get around an enemy virtually upon us?" Kasreya's reply generated a quickly formulated plan that could work if they timed it just right. Juliet was quick to call for a revised report of observations from the tower.

Relieved from her post by a senior archer, Stronleya arrived breathless with her hand in the air pointing to the woods. Juliet placed a hand on her shoulder to calm her.

"Take a breath, child, and speak."

"The sentry has identified six, possibly nine, horgles and mounts. The pattern by which they fly is vertical peaks. And so, it has been hard to distinguish the precise number. As they get closer, some colour and patterns of movement become more clear and sentries are able to mark more features, thus distinguishing the number of attackers."

"It is nine, the word is nine," a second young sentry came flying through the door shouting a new message. "Further news of another casting that may have been spotted at far greater distances and approaching but not yet confirmed."

Kasreya calmly suggested that a panic amongst younger sentries could have generated this unconfirmed sighting.

"Thank you, sentries," she said. "Step outside and await instructions, please," Kasreya remained calm as she spoke every word carefully.

"It is quite simple," Odemog spoke up. "My plan, that is. We begin to walk south along the coast, so they do not see a flight embark directly from here. That is our first move. At the same time, a pledge of sentries begins a very noisy advance in the direction of the incoming party. The horgles will advance both above the trees and below so it is safe to suggest that the pledge advance both on horseback and on foot." Odemog considered the numbers to be sent to the woods. A group of twelve constitutes a pledge. He considered the number of attackers and added, "There will be two more pledges. These will flank the first on either side, advancing quietly until practically upon them. Once within striking distance, they will erupt with as much noise as possible to confuse and disorient the cast of attackers."

"I suggest we send drummers with each pledge to add to the confusion, then," offered Juliet.

"The more the merrier," added Sam.

"It will not reflect merriment, friend, but pure distraction." Dagger in hand, Odemog fiddled with his braid. Skeeter watched as radish-colored strands of hair fell away. He jumped over and climbed Moggie's chainmail and gingerly reached around until he could touch Moggie's hand at the hilt of the dagger. This gesture quietly signaled Odemog to lower the blade. Odemog squinted and finished his plan as he stuck the dagger in a round of cheese sitting on the table. With his other hand gently stroking Skeeter's tail, he continued. "The beauty of the plan is in the distraction. With much noise, we build the frenzy, dismantling their attack. In the confusion, our party slips quietly into the woods until it is out of range where then it may meet up with the mordagha group. What say you of this plan, Kasreya?"

"We shall put it to the test, Odemog. Juliet, send word for the away party at once and map the route with your pledge leads. They should prepare to advance with the departure of the away party."

With the plan in place and Juliet off to organize the Tsesiwans, Dero and Sam emerged from Holder House to prepare the mordaghas for their journey. It would take a bit of convincing, however, because mordaghas despised walking. They were not built to travel by land. However, this was why Odemog had suggested they travel the coastline. Because of their awkward shape and girth, a mordagha could walk easier when buoyed, at least somewhat, by water. This plan would be a safe one, as long as no airborne horgle and mount strayed to the coastline in the manner of a scout.

The Tsesiwan away party, a pledge of twelve eager young archers, gathered at Holder House, ready to depart. The young archer Stronleya sat atop her horse and held the reins of three others without mounts. There, the group awaited further instructions.

Behind them, the excitement grew as three other double pledges prepared to advance into the unknown.

17

Dero spoke softly to Bazat and Tovar, offering reassurances of comfort and safety. Lisan stood nearby, listening to his words. As a free mordagha, Lisan had enjoyed not being at the beck and call of any creature. Neither did he have to listen to such piffle. Mordaghas roamed freely and lived with masters. Those known as masters were not master of the beast but of the privilege of ridership. They had mastered the skill of staying safely atop their escort in spite of the unusual manner of flight. These mordaghas enjoyed living with creatures most familiar to them as well as enjoying the spoils of such a lifestyle. Free mordaghas never adjusted to any creature as their masters. They lived a life of leisure and adventure, befriending only those to whom they chose to warm. Although friendly and kind, Lisan always found that such closeness with other creatures complicated life and so he remained a free spirit. Listening now to Dero did nothing to endear other creatures any closer to his heart.

Vadim and Nassir were restless. They had heard many stories of air challenges with horgles. Vadim himself had been in a brief tussle with a smart aleck horgle once when he was very young. At the time it was one smart aleck horgle against a quick-witted mordagha as they challenged and out challenged one another until they were exhausted. It ended in a draw and each went away with respect for the skill of the other. Vadim was neither in the mood, nor was he young enough to look forward to such a tiresome prospect. He would be happy to walk for a while. Nassir would accompany Vadim wherever he went for he respected this mordagha above all creatures.

Grounded temporarily, the flight of mordaghas went to the water and began their solemn march south along the shore of the North Dragho Ocean. Walking at their sides were Sam, Dero, and Morlog. Odemog remained with the Princess and the Tsesiwan pledge. The journey had begun.

Odemog lifted Princess Lily to her mount and stood at her side. He would not leave her on this leg of the trip. He entrusted the care and guidance of the mordaghas to his brothers and Morlog. They would soon meet again. Odemog, far too large for a horse, would walk and run beside the Princess until they would reconvene as a group again, once safely away from danger. Thinking he would help to make the Princess feel safe, Skeeter sat in the saddle with her and held tight to the saddle horn with his tail. She held fast the reins and held her elbows tight to offer more protection to Skeeter, thinking she would help make him feel safe. Joining them, Kasreya and Juliet took to their mounts as a horn was sounded atop the tower.

Kasreya turned in her saddle, looking over at Stronleya. "Thank you, Stronleya, for tending to our guests' horses. Ride out now and join Morlog's group. Should they need assistance or require conveyance of a message, you will act as messenger."

"Thank you, Mistress, I am away."

"Safe journey to you," Juliet called to Stronleya as the young archer manipulated the reins, directing her horse as she rode away from them.

Two long blasts of the horn was the signal to advance. And so, each pledge moved forward and entered the shade of the woods. The sun became hidden by the dense foliage of the gabelnut trees and broad boughs of evergreens. The center pledge stepped forward in unison, drummers beating their every step. Each of the two flanking pledges moved in time with the same drummer as their own drummers marched alongside in silence. The sound of the drummers began to fade as they marched deeper into the woods.

Atop the tower, the lead sentry called down, "There comes the second grouping of horgles, in view now, a dozen more, at least."

"What say you of the advance horgles, then?" Juliet called up to the tower as the travellers moved away toward the edge of the woods.

"They shall be upon our archers less than a quarter of an hour."

"We have less than fifteen minutes to make ourselves scarce," Juliet looked to Kasreya with concern.

"Best we move quickly, then," Kasreya raised her arm and gestured forward. This motion signaled the group to pick up the pace. From a slow walk, they broke into a canter. Odemog braced his sword and began to run. Protected by a tightly formed pledge, the Princess, with Odemog keeping pace at her side, was led into the woods with Kasreya, Amara, and Juliet behind her.

Just as the group disappeared into the woods, the first horgles made contact with archers. A horgle screamed as it was struck with an arrow and came down to crash in a gabelnut tree above the archers. The rider fell from his mount and crashed, unconscious, to the ground. And so, the battle continued with drums beating and arrows flying through the air. The horgles flew in and out of the trees, as Khordrian raiders fired arrows back or came in fast and low and swung long arm swords to cut down archers unaware. Overly aggressive horgles took swipes with their sharp bill to grab an archer or two by their garments and swung them into the air, disarming and incapacitating these unfortunate ones. The flanking pledges began beating their drums as they came around to form a circle around the skirmish started by the first pledge. More horgles came down from above the trees and a battle ensued. As riders, pierced by arrow or sword, fell from their mounts, fleeing horgles could be heard screeching as they returned on a riderless journey south to Khordom Palace. The Tsesiwan archers fought long and hard, taking casualties as they valiantly struggled to keep the raiders from entering Siwa. With wave by wave of attack, one or the other, archer or enemy, rose and fell to victory or defeat. The fight continued for half the day as horgles flew away and Khordrian raiders regrouped to attack again and again. But, in the end, the Tsesiwan mission was accomplished, the distraction a success. The travellers and their escort secreted themselves away to safety, continuing their journey southward, where they would again meet to challenge Trezano Falls.

18

"We stay beneath the cover of trees at all times," Odemog instructed the travellers, who had stopped to rest for a moment. He pointed to the sky where a screeching horgle flew overhead. This horgle flew riderless. As they watched the skies, two more flew over, both with riders who looked very much worse for wear.

"By appearance, the first cast must have followed the same path as we, coming from Sweetbrooke Wren, searching for us. But they will take the shortest route back to Khordom Palace. The same path we travel, through Trezano Falls," Odemog explained as he looked around.

"We should see the others soon enough," Kasreya responded confidently. "But take nothing for granted. Odemog is right, keep clear of any openings in the canopy above us. Stay as close to the gabelnut trees and evergreens as possible."

They began to make a rough camp, where they would wait for mordaghas, Morlog, Sam, and Dero to join them before they continued to the top of the falls. The pledge dispersed to encircle those they protected. A quiet came upon the travellers. Before long, Stronleya rode in with news of the others.

"Mistress Kasreya, Odemog, I have been sent forward to tell you the mordaghas and their companions are en route but very tired from walking." Stronleya gave details of the state of the travellers and finished saying, "We are due west of your camp, a mile, perhaps two I would say by my time."

"I suggest we break this camp and make our way to them," Odemog proposed.

"You are right, Odemog," Kasreya responded, directing Stronleya back to the others. "Tell Morlog and the others to please rest. As we are not far, we shall come to them."

"I shall bear the message forthwith," Stronleya bowed from her saddle, pulled her reins left as she nudged then kicked her horse to move quickly.

As Stronleya made haste back to Sam, Dero, Morlog, and the mordaghas, the pledge was called back in to assemble and make tracks to meet up with their weary friends. They travelled light; it took only moments to gather and redirect the group.

* * *

There was a sense of relief in Morlog's travellers when Stronleya returned to tell them to continue their rest. Vadim smiled and closed his eyes on hearing the news they would soon be joined by Odemog and his group. It had proven to be a good idea when Stronleya arrived to join them shortly after their departure from Siwa. Kasreya had considered communications between the two bands of covert travellers and felt an archer on horseback to be an asset to Morlog, Sam, and Dero as they escorted the mordaghas by the water route. Kasreya never surprised anyone. Any strategy she presented, regardless of timing, was always received with a tone of gratitude and acknowledgement of the wisdom of her foresight.

"I see them," Dero beckoned to Morlog, who sat rubbing Vadim behind his ears. Vadim, the eldest of the mordaghas, was the most exhausted of the group. He lay in a bed of evergreen boughs Sam had cut and laid out with care for the venerable creature. Lisan had found a sweet spot of grass and had torn away some clusters, bringing them to Vadim. Nassir had pouched extra water and passed it to Vadim as well. While all felt the fatigue of the long walk in the sand and water, they respected the journey made by Vadim. He was fine for distances in the air and could find relief in chest deep water, thanks to his buoyancy, but wore out quickly on the ground. The ground simply was not a travelling friend to a mordagha; it never had been. Lisan was heard to say, "If a mordagha was meant to walk, he would not have wings." And there was nothing more truthful in this moment than those words.

Right then, the two groups were united. Seeing Vadim on the ground, Lily quickly dismounted her horse, named Armus, and ran to him.

"Vadim, dear Vadim, you are injured!" she called anxiously.

"No, my Princess," he spoke softly. "Do not be alarmed, I am just an old, tired beast, not created to walk on all fours. I shall rest a while and we shall away. My wings have not been tested today and they are ready to carry you and your lovely spirit." Vadim smiled as he spoke with the Princess. They touched foreheads and held there for a moment. This, alone, lifted Vadim's spirit. Soon, very soon, he would be ready to fly.

19

Travelling south, the united group soon happened upon a clearing. Two scouts entered the clearing, breaking away from the pledge and those they escorted. Odemog signaled for everyone to wait quietly as he stepped to the edge of the clearing, watching the scouts. The two rode tentatively around the perimeter of the clearing; one looked skyward in all directions while the other scanned the trees. After some time had passed, they signaled back with a raised sword in Odemog's direction.

"That's it, then," he said as he turned to the others. "The sky is clear, and all appears well. We can only make haste from here. Nassir, are you ready?" Odemog looked to his mordagha who, hearing these words, had taken steps toward him.

Dero was standing next to Princess Lily who waited atop her mount, Armus. "The waters are not far from here, Princess," he said.

"Yes, I think I can even hear the waters moving, Dero. But I admit I am rather afraid for those taking the rafts."

"It should be fine, Princess Lily." Amara attempted to put her at ease but her movement in the saddle betrayed her own anxiety.

"Our people constructed the rafts upon which we will travel the waters, Princess. They have been tested again and again. Already this season they have been checked and repaired, is that right, Juliet?" Kasreya now added to the conversation.

"Yes, Mistress, all was well, with repairs only to the third of Trezano Falls." Juliet referred to a number of rope replacements that had been made to stabilize and secure the rope and raft system.

"Mount up! We are away," called Odemog.

And, with those words, the travellers settled on their mounts—mordaghas and horses—readying themselves for the next phase of their journey to Constantia Glen.

"Odemog, we shall see you at the top of the Falls?"

"We will be waiting for you," Odemog gave Kasreya an informal salute, something he had never done before.

"Take caution, Kasreya," Morlog smiled at his longtime friend as he bade her good journey. With these words, Lisan lifted to air followed by Bazat, Tovar, Vadim, and lastly, Nassir, with Odemog on his back and Skeeter hanging on for life.

The riders advanced into the sunshine that warmed the circle of green. Princess Lily looked down from her place on Vadim at the pledge that encircled Kasreya, Amara, and Juliet, watching them as they advanced through the pasture.

In short order, those who flew by mordagha bore witness from air to the beauty and rage of Trezano Falls. Leading the group now, Odemog and Nassir circled the top of the falls, looking down at the first and most hazardous of the three. Skeeter leaned out from the security of Odemog's shoulder with claws clenched tightly in the weave of the chainmail tunic his friend wore when travelling. Overwhelmed by the sights and sounds below, Skeeter wrapped his tail around and across his eyes, shielding him from the view of the watery danger as if to eliminate it altogether.

"Moggie, if you ever set me on one of those rafts, I shall have to disown your friendship." Skeeter shouted to Odemog's ear above the din of the roaring water. While he tried to veil his words in a harsh tone, Skeeter only conveyed his fear of water in general for he knew not how to swim and the thought of being thrown about on giant, sharp rocks terrified the little grey squirrel.

Odemog laughed quietly to himself, knowing both of Skeeter's fear and that he would never allow such things to happen to his dear little friend—never. At this moment, Odemog leaned forward to Nassir's right ear saying, "Let us go to ground, my friend." And Nassir led the mordaghas down to the side of the river where the greenery looked most appetizing.

For a mordagha, the best place to land would be where the best greens beckoned. It was there that the group settled to wait for the riders from Siwa to join them. As a precaution, Morlog encouraged the travellers to move away from the River Constantia, which fed Trezano Falls, to the shade and protection of nearby gabelnut trees. While they waited, Morlog set about gathering gabelnuts, herbs, and other healing plants and berries he observed around and about their rest stop.

Odemog watched as Sam followed Morlog about, asking him questions about the different plants and their uses. For every gabelnut that Morlog gathered, Sam snacked on two as he knocked them from the trees with his sword. Skeeter had climbed a most unique gabelnut tree, shaped like the palm of a hand with finger-like branches extending skyward. There he sat in the 'palm' of the tree, resting against the thickest branch where he cracked and gnawed on nut after favourite nut, filling himself to near bursting. The shells piled up around him until they overflowed, falling to the ground below.

Below Skeeter's perch sat Dero, who had rolled out a blanket upon which Princess Lily rested. Dero was explaining the rope and raft system to Lily when he was hit in the head again and again and again by gabelnut shells as they fell from Skeeter's perch. Lily couldn't help but burst out laughing at the sight of Dero as he jumped up, startled by the attack. Dero spun around in a circle as he drew his sword and took a defensive stance. Odemog, too, watching from afar where he sat leaning against a tree, could not help but erupt with his famous giggle on seeing his friend in a squirrel-generated panic.

"False alarm my brother," he called to Dero, who took a swipe at the tree as he realized what gravity had brought down upon him.

"Skeeter, you pipsqueak! I ought to—" Dero stood shaking his sword in the air at Skeeter who, looking simultaneously guilty and rather pleased with himself, peered over the side of his perch at his unsuspecting and unplanned victim.

"I would say I am sorry, Dero, but you have made this so amusing, I should say thank you instead," Skeeter held back a laugh himself as he now scurried up the branches to find a few more gabelnuts. A drooping branch heavily laden with nuts sparked an idea. He grabbed at the nuts, quickly picking and tossing them down one after another at Dero, who fended them off with the broad side of his sword, lest they hit the Princess.

The battle continued until one gabelnut caught the blade of the sword such that it flew back up into the tree and hit Skeeter square on the head, knocking him from his perch. Skeeter tumbled down through the air and landed squarely in Princess Lily's lap. Odemog leapt up, fearing for the squirrel; Dero let go his sword and dropped to his knees, terrified he had killed Skeeter. Startled by the deposit of a sharp-witted squirrel in her lap, the Princess cried out his name and gently picked him up to be sure he was breathing.

As Odemog approached, Dero looked up at his brother, terrified he would be hit by the broadside of a blade. But, in truth, never would such a thing occur to Odemog. He came to Dero's side and, placing his giant hand on the shoulder of his brother, he watched, as Lily tended to Skeeter.

With both hands, she cradled him gently. She raised Skeeter up close to her face and stroked his head with her finger. She blew a small breath over his face and head and spoke his name softly. She repeated this several times until his eyes fluttered open. Odemog gently squeezed Dero's shoulder and dropped to one knee across from Lily.

"Now that is a special touch you have, Princess," he observed as he held out his hand to her.

"Nothing a little love can't heal, Odemog." Princess Lily leaned forward and passed Skeeter over to the care and attention of the one all knew to be Skeeter's best friend and protector, Moggie. Skeeter fit perfectly in the palm of Odemog's hand.

"He's a bit of a silly fool, my Skeeter but a loyal fool, I admit." Odemog smiled as he gently prodded Skeeter's belly with his large finger.

"W-what's going on?" Skeeter lifted his head and looked around, seemingly unaware of his fall from grace or, at least, from the gabelnut tree.

"It seems, my little friend, that you should have kept your walnut shell helmet from this morning's feast!" Odemog joked, recalling Skeeter with the half walnut shell perched on his head earlier that day. "You might need wings too."

With all at ease for his recovery, they did not notice the pledge coming quietly through the surrounding trees. Their arrival largely being drowned out by the din of the nearby Falls.

"From one adventure to the next, I see," Kasreya greeted the travellers with a smile, observing the scene before her. She dismounted and approached. Lily rose from the ground and went to offer a hug to Kasreya.

"You made it! Welcome." Lily was becoming fond of Kasreya, who emitted calm and warmth that was readily reassuring to the young Princess.

"I'm so happy to see you again, Princess. The worst of the journey is over for you. Now where is Morlog?" Kasreya hugged Lily back and turned, looking for the Teller.

"I am here Mistress Kasreya." Morlog emerged, following Sam from behind a large stone near the river. "Your journey went well, then?"

"Yes, efficient and uneventful. Are you ready to move on?"

"As ready as can be," Odemog interjected. "This silly creature," he lifted his palm in a gesture showing Skeeter who was still reorienting himself, "thinks he can slow us down with stupidity but we shall away quickly to preserve the light of day for safer travels."

"Well then, with Skeeter's permission, perhaps we can get moving," Juliet returned, having ridden forward to do a quick visual check of the rafts and ropes. "Everything is in order. Will you see us off before taking flight, Odemog? Morlog?"

"Amara, why don't you take the princess to see the rafts?" suggested Kasreya.

"Certainly. Join me, Princess?" Amara climbed down from her horse and held her hand out to the princess. The two young women walked to the edge of the river, past the stone from which Morlog and Sam had emerged. There, on the other side of the enormous granite stone, were wooden pulleys secured to the granite with large, wound wraps of thick, braided ropes draped on a horizontal post above the largest pulley. These would unfurl as the raft made its way down the Falls. Securely tied to reinforced pilings in the water was a large raft with posts and slats forming an enclosure on both sides, and a ramp that hinged up to complete the enclosure on the side that meets the riverbank. The raft was clearly large enough to hold more than a pledge of horses and riders. The rafts took on a shape similar to a regular boat, narrow in front, wider at back for ease and management through the rocky white waters. They were constructed of wood with a double deck; the lower met the water and the upper deck, on hinges and ropes, absorbed the shock from the raging water and bumps to stabilize and absorb the tumult of the ride as much as possible. It was not perfect, but it made the ride one even a horse could withstand. As Amara gestured to the different parts of the raft, she explained how the overhead ropes anchored to the raft with hooks and pulleys in strategic points allowed them to control the direction of the raft along the river and over the falls. They only had partial control of the speed because of the currents of the white water. Still, it was probably the safest and most well-tested way one could keep one's life and travel the River Constantia over the Trezano Falls to reach Princess Lily's home. If it were not for this efficient system, the falls could not be passed.

While Amara and Princess Lily looked over the pulleys and raft, Juliet gave Morlog and Odemog details as to how long it would take them to navigate Trezano Falls. They pulled together the plan for the next phase of their journey.

"We shall fly Princess Lily to the waiting arms of King Magnus," Odemog repeated the original plan to those listening.

"It will take us approximately four hours, Odemog, to navigate the Falls." Juliet explained that, while the equipment had recently been inspected, there is always the chance that a rope would become snarled on a rock or branch, in spite of their protective riggings.

"And then, two more hours on horseback to reach the castle at Constantia Glen," Odemog added. "Our flight to Constantia should take less than three hours from here, I should think."

"Closer to two hours, Odemog," Sam clarified.

"Alright then," Morlog took over. "We shall see the Princess home, rest briefly and then return to meet you safely at the base of the Falls. From there, we will escort you into Constantia Glen."

"I think, Morlog, if you don't mind," Odemog set his hand on Morlog's shoulder as he continued to cradle Skeeter, still groggy, in the other hand. "It should be Sam, Dero, and me only who return to meet Kasreya and the pledge."

Morlog looked around the group and over to the mordaghas grazing nearby.

"I should not disagree with you. Someone ought to look over your vain little furry friend, too." Reaching into the satchel at his side as he spoke, he removed a sprig of mint leaves and, tearing off several leaves, he rolled and crushed them in his fingers. Morlog held the crushed leaves in front of Skeeter's nose where the sharp fragrance perked him up.

"Morlog, I thank you." Skeeter took the leaves and began to chew, enjoying the dual sensory experience.

"Pleasure, little friend. Juliet, shall we depart?" he said, turning his focus away from Skeeter who was much happier now for Morlog's efforts.

"Let us take leave," she confirmed, gesturing the pledge forward. They moved out past the stone and began to walk the horses onto the raft, where they would carefully secure them for the trip down the river. No horse enjoyed this ride, but their faith in the Tsesiwans was strong so they boarded the craft with ease. Riderless, now that Lily would again fly with Vadim, Armus was last to board the raft. Seeing Lily, he raised and lowered his head in a gesture of acknowledgement and good wishes. She called to him in gratitude and waved back.

As the travellers watched the pledge and their leaders prepare, they, too, prepared and mounted mordaghas. Lily came back around the rock to Vadim, who waited patiently for her. Small though she was, Lily was becoming increasingly familiar with the ways of the mordagha. She now climbed to her saddle with relative ease. It helped, however, that Vadim would kneel to enable her to use his foreleg as a step to climb aboard. Odemog watched his young charge with pride for her growing skill, trust, and comfort.

In no time, the travellers took to air, circling long enough to wave good wishes to their Tsesiwan friends as they embarked upon their journey down the River Constantia and over the first of the three waterfalls. All were safely on their way.

20

King Magnus watched the grains of sand streaming through a funneled hourglass to form a peak below. He had watched the turn of perhaps six or eight glasses this day. In moments, the glass would be turned, yet again and he had received no further word as to any sightings of the travellers, who would come from the north.

Magnus wondered what could be keeping them but knew in his heart that he worried prematurely as they were still not expected for several hours. The journey by way of Trezano Falls would take a full day, barring any dangers or challenges that could arise.

Sitting at his side along the table of the dining hall were his daughter, Tulip, on his left, son, Borzog, to his right, and Mezzog and Fazzog sat at either of the group. Few words were spoken aloud, but much churned about in the minds of those who shared in a midday meal at table.

"Father, you are miles away," Princess Tulip, Lily's twin sister, spoke to the King in a soft voice. "I can feel already that Lily is safely on her way home."

"I will trust the feelings of a mirror-child," the King placed his hand on top of Tulip's as he made reference to the undeniable telepathy shared between the identical princesses, which was also true of the identical princes.

"Father, you trust Odemog. He would not let you down." Fazzog spoke confidently, which was not always his way.

"My son, you cannot know what it is that I am thinking," the King scolded his youngest son. "You do not understand the gravity of danger the Khordrian raiders present. They lack compassion, fearing their own demise at the whim of Thane-Ra should they fail in their missions. Odemog's journey to bring your sister safely back to Constantia Glen is only just the beginning. I worry for our Lily but my greater concern is for that which is yet to come."

Tulip, sitting beside Fazzog, reached out to her brother, took his hand where it lay on the table, and gently cupped it to reassure him.

"My brother, have faith. We shall all be united soon—Mother, Annabella, Lily, and we who sit here at table." She turned to her father and continued, "What can we do Father? How may we help you?"

"Tulip, my sweet girl, just be your refreshing self. Your patience and optimism warm the room and all who are in it. We shall be together soon; patience and good fortune be upon us." The King glanced around the table, casting a long gaze at each of the four of his six children who sat with him. "I welcome what is to come; that we will be together again. I welcome what is to come; that we should eradicate evil in the Kingdom of Mazgamor. My children, I welcome your trust and your unique contributions." So that he may raise their spirits, he lifted his goblet as if to toast, "To the future of our home, Constantia Glen and the Kingdom of Mazgamor."

Each of his offspring in turn raised their own goblets and replied, "To Constantia and to Mazgamor!"

"Sire, a messenger arrives!" A boisterous call erupted from the entry to the dining hall.

"Speak now, you are in the presence of the King," Borzog rose from his seat and gestured with his arm from the messenger to the King.

"My Liege," the messenger took a deep bow as he approached the table at which the King sat. "Mordaghas approach from the north; there appears to be five on first sighting. It is clear that one rider—by his obvious size—is definitely Odemog of Sweetbrooke Wren. A greeting party is preparing for their arrival in the Queen's Meadow."

On hearing Odemog's name, King Magnus rose quickly, pushing his chair from the table, and strode in the direction from which the messenger had come. He beckoned to his children, who had also risen, to follow him.

So overcome was he on the news that Odemog was arriving, he was speechless. For where Odemog may be, so would be his cherished daughter, the Princess Lily. The family hastened past the confused messenger who had not been discharged from his report. He stood facing an empty table, not quite sure what to do next.

The Queen's Meadow was located just outside the gates to the castle. It was a lovely green pasture where deer, rabbits, birds, and even bears were found resting and grazing often. It would be a perfect spot for a mordagha to land and find rest after a long journey. And this, with ample greens and a quiet place to rest, this spot would surely do.

As King Magnus, Princess Tulip and the three princes arrived in the Meadow, they could clearly see who approached by air in the distance. As Tulip's eyes met her sister's, she began to jump and wave with great excitement. The anticipation of seeing Lily again overcame the King and he stood motionless, watching her shape grow in the sky as she flew closer on Vadim. King Magnus recognized Vadim at once and felt all the more at ease, knowing that Odemog and Morlog had trusted her care to such an honourable mordagha as Zodem's truly was.

Memories of times past rushed over him as he pieced together what had happened long ago with this moment and those yet to come. Here came a Kingdom Keeper whose journey as such had begun before he even knew the full impact of what was about to take place. King Magnus marvelled at the accomplishment of generations of Kingdom Keepers and this newly presented soul to a destiny unknown.

As his mind cleared, Magnus heard the cheering voices of Borzog, Mezzog, and Fazzog.

"Welcome! Welcome!" they shouted in unison.

He refocused on the Meadow in time to observe a perfect landing of the perfect flight of mordaghas. At once he saw Lily and his heart rejoiced. He scanned the group, recognizing first Odemog, then Morlog, and did not know the other two faces accompanying them. Sam and Dero dismounted from Bazat and Tovar. Dero promptly rushed to Vadim where he reached up to assist Princess Lily safely to ground.

"Dero, you are truly gentle in nature," Lily looked him directly in the eye as she spoke causing him to blush. She pretended not to notice. Odemog, always watching over her, noticed his friend and brother's blush for he missed nothing when it came to his friends. Lily squeezed Dero's hand in gratitude and immediately turned to rush to her father.

"Father! Father!" She ran towards him with open arms. "I am so happy to see you." She threw her arms around him and held him tight, that they may never again be separated. As they held one another they were overcome by her brothers and sister, who joined in wrapping arms around to form a tight bundle filled with love.

"Oh Lily, how I have missed you," cried Tulip as tears wet her face and soaked into Lily's dress. She let go of her embrace and cupped her hand to her sister's face, who did the very same with the opposite hand at the very same time. Mirror sisters they truly were. The King stepped back for only a moment, long enough to watch his daughters reunite. Stepping between them, he placed a hand on each of their backs and pulled them into his sides once more. Magnus leaned down and kissed each of them on the head and a second kiss for Lily. His heart was filled with joy.

Borzog approached Odemog with arms outstretched. Odemog stood beside Nassir, scratching the mordagha behind his ears. As Borzog approached, Odemog glanced at Morlog, who nodded his head for Odemog to step forward. As he did, Borzog raised his arms and wrapped them around in the warmest of hugs.

"Friend Odemog, welcome. You have the deepest gratitude of the people of Constantia Glen."

"My honour, truly my honour. The princess has been a joy to escort. Still, business has not yet been completed, Highness." Odemog remained concerned about the party from Siwa.

"I am Prince Borzog, please call me by name."

"Thank you, then, Borzog. I welcome your friendship."

"In what way may we serve, that you will be at ease?" asked Mezzog as he, too, approached.

"Find us water for these mordaghas, Prince Mezzog," Morlog directed the group now. "Sam, Dero, see to it that these creatures receive all that they need."

"I like the look of these greens," Lisan, bold as ever, spoke out of turn, causing Morlog to nudge him with his hip.

"King Magnus of Constantia Glen, old friend, you are a welcome sight," Morlog now approached the King with open arms.

"A sight for sore eyes are you, good man," replied the King. "I am weary for the wait yet rejoice in your safe arrival! Pray tell, how went your journey?"

"Odemog leads well, Magnus. His vision for planning is strong."

"So say you, Morlog, but it is all new to me," Odemog interjected. Morlog waved off the comment.

"Ignore him for now, Magnus. We have one more thing to do now that Lily is safe with you. We shall return…"

"We, not you, Morlog, shall return to the base of the Falls to greet Kasreya and escort her party back here to the castle." Odemog interrupted Morlog to bring clarity to the task at hand.

"A brief rest, Odemog, and you shall be on your way." Morlog smiled at Odemog's kind assertion showing concern for his well-being. He knew well the next step but prompted Odemog's voice to test his resolve and attention.

"Dero, Sam, once our winged friends are ready, let us away to meet up with our travel mates at the Falls, as promised. Lily, I am pleased to see you safely home." Odemog spoke to each quickly and without hesitation. He would fill his role as Kingdom Keeper well.

"If you have a moment," Kasell interrupted the group to offer refreshments to all. He gestured to several court pages who brought forth trays of fresh fruit, nuts, fish, and cheeses, along with large carafes of tea, juice, wines, and Sweetbrooke Water. On hearing his voice, Lily jumped and ran straight into his arms, a most informal gesture from a happy young girl whose heart had just overflowed.

"Kasell! Oh, Kasell! I am so relieved, so happy. I am overjoyed to see you!" Lily showed no restraint as she danced around him, holding his hands, then wrapped him in the tightest of hugs. This alarming breech in protocol stumped Kasell and only made the King laugh out loud.

"Child, give this man some air," he called to his daughter. "Surely, such excitement will wear out a man recovering from injury."

"Injury? Oh, Kasell, what has happened to you? I am so sorry." She stopped in her tracks and stepped back looking him up and down. "Father's healers have attended to you, I expect?" She looked to her father, then saw Forthrumal standing not far off. "Kasell, are you truly well?"

"Princess, my heart is stronger now for seeing you. I have agonised over your disappearance. You have my apologies, as I have offered them to my King, for letting the raiders take down your escort." Kasell gestured to Forthrumal and continued, saying, "and as for my health, I have been in none but the finest of hands with Lord Forthrumal."

"I am both relieved and pleased for you. And, no, I hold no grudge for what happened with those raiders. I know that you and the arms men did all that you could. After all, it was you who gave me direction to save myself. Were it not for those words, who knows what would have become of me. You, sir, saved me when I could otherwise have been lost." As Lily spoke, she squeezed, then let go of Kasell's hands with a thought now occurring to her.

"Lord Forthrumal," she called over to the healer. "I have a small task for you now." She bade him come closer to the group that had been talking. As she gestured him forward, she walked toward Odemog. Odemog knew exactly what she was thinking and reached up to his shoulder. Taking Skeeter gently down, he held him in both hands. Lily approached and waited for Forthrumal to come.

"This, Forthrumal, is Skeeter," Lily gently scratched the innocent-looking squirrel under the chin. He loved this and feigned a dizzy spell hoping for more. Odemog recognized the signs of mischief immediately and jerked his hands slightly, signaling to Skeeter that he knew what was going on. Skeeter glanced up and sideways at Moggie, then rested a paw on Odemog's thumb as if to catch himself from falling. Lily, not knowing Skeeter's mischievous side, looked upon him with concern.

"Skeeter was hit square on the head with a gabelnut that was travelling with great force through the air." She omitted the details of the foolishness that brought about the flying gabelnuts. Very seriously, she continued outlining the outcome of this thump on the head.

"Will you be able to tend to his injury, Forthrumal?" She asked the healer with sincere concern. Forthrumal stepped forward, bent down, and stared directly into Skeeter's blinking brown eyes. He looked up at Odemog.

"May I?" Forthrumal held out his two cupped hands to take Skeeter for further inspection and treatment.

"By all means you may take this little nut off my hands," Odemog laughed as he dropped Skeeter in the healer's hands. "Get well Skeeter, my friend. We shall see you anon!"

With a smile on his face, Odemog turned to see how his friends were faring with refreshments and how attending to the needs of the mordaghas was progressing.

"What do you need, Odemog?" asked Kasell.

"All appears well, thank you, Kasell. I think we will be ready to depart shortly."

"May I join your return to meet the Tsesiwans? I am no Master Rider but fare quite well with the winged beasts."

"You give yourself away as unsure with such a phrase, 'winged beast'. There is not one beast amongst them. Vadim will remain here to rest but I am sure Lisan will be pleased to take you, with Morlog remaining behind. What say you, Lisan? Will a new rider please you?"

"Anything to keep flying, Odemog. I am enjoying this adventure. And, I should add, if there is a beast amongst us mordaghas, it would certainly have to be me!"

Lisan joked, making reference to his life as a free mordagha, unhitched to any master, free to fly and dare as he pleased. This statement, however, clearly unnerved Kasell, who was far from being close to a master rider. In fact, Lily had outridden Kasell's skill in just the last two days of flight. Of course, she had the gentlest mordagha of all tend to her travelling and learning needs. Vadim had provided comfort for both the master and non-masters amongst them. His patient and caring ways relaxed all riders, thus helping them to find their centre and ride comfortably. Lisan could prove a challenge to Kasell but in truth, his talk was worse than his lift and ride. Lisan would look out for Kasell.

"We should make a good pairing then, Lisan," Kasell addressed the mordagha directly. "We are both adventurers. If you will be patient with a somewhat weary arms man, I will attend to your every movement to make your flying easy."

"My flying is always easy; I hardly notice my rider. But we shall pair just fine, rest at ease, no flying tricks for you. I see you are still recovering from other adventures."

"I thank you, Lisan."

In short order, on Odemog's signal, the group of Sam, Dero, Kasell, and he mounted their respective mordaghas and took flight. Kasell's face turned the color of his favourite white cheese as Lisan lifted from ground to air with an up-down thrust and his belly swaying from left to right, then left again. And they were away.

21

"Well, Magnus, it begins again."

"So it does, my friend, so it does. And is he ready for what lies ahead?"

"Who can ever truly know?" Morlog posed a fair question and answered it himself. "I should think our safe arrival here an indication of his readiness. I guided him little and he took well to Kasreya's direction. It seems to flow naturally for this young farmer."

"You have faith in his leadership, come what may?"

"What will come, will come and he will stand the test of time. You ask for answers I cannot give, my friend. But what I have observed is a selfless young man, taking the task set before him in stride. Either he sees no danger, and thus is a danger to himself and others, or he is innately aware of what lies ahead and accepts a destiny beyond his imagining with strength and courage. The Odemog I have watched grow leads me to think it the latter. He will meet the challenges presented to a Kingdom Keeper, Magnus, have faith. He executed this first test of will flawlessly. Yes, have faith, friend."

King Magnus led Morlog from the Queen's Meadow through the halls of the castle and into his private chamber. It had been many moons since Morlog had visited the castle, though he had spent time with Magnus deliberating over various topics each year at the Gathering. The private chamber in which they consulted required passage through two corridors whereupon each arched doorway was secured after passing through. There were three long arched windows that peaked in the center letting in much light but were so narrow no man could fit through. It was a virtually impenetrable room in which to consult privately. A great fire warmed the room. On the wall opposite the fireplace hung a magnificent tapestry featuring the royal crest. To the right of the doorway hung a portrait of the King, to the left of the doorway a portrait of the Queen. The light from two of the three windows cast brilliantly upon the portraits, illuminating them in such a way as to give them life. Though absent from the room, portraits of the three princes and three princesses hung along the wall of the staircase they had travelled on their way to the chamber. Finally, a statue of a great eagle with wings spread poised on a stand before the center window, which was filled with the most brilliant stained glass. The statue shimmered with coloured light, giving it a sense of movement.

As they entered the room, Magnus directed Morlog to sit in a high back chair with a curved seat to give comfort. They sat angled toward each other before the fire.

"Your words give great ease, Morlog. Still, you can imagine my fears."

"I would be fool not to anticipate your emotion in a matter that affects you personally. I, too, share your concern for Queen Madelina and Princess Annabella. I grieve what happened at the Gathering."

"I am long past the deceit brought upon us and look to the future now. What concerns me is the unknown that has joined with Thane-Ra."

"I understand."

"I am sorry to raise this with you, Morlog, but there is no one else with whom I may confer in this matter."

"Again, I understand. You speak of Morzan and I do not know what to tell you." Morlog looked away from Magnus and stared into the fire. "It pains me to say this, but he is as evil as that fire is hot. I could never have foreseen this; never in countless moons could I have believed…"

"Morlog, we can never know the path our children might take."

"I vowed never to speak of this son of mine, ever again." There was silence for a while until Morlog could find words other than those that caused him so much pain. Anger and betrayal dwelt in his heart.

"When his mother perished at the Gathering upon which Thane-Ra brought down his evil, I could never have anticipated that he would have chosen to align with the one who brought such a horrible end to her life. Morzanega, his mother, was a treasure of a woman. She asked nothing of others and shielded many during the attack before she died so bravely."

"Your wife— and my friend—remains a hero in our Kingdom to this day. No mother should die as she did, with a poison spear to her back."

"Healers could do nothing," Morlog felt his heart ache as he recalled a scene so painful he had vowed never to speak of it again. Yet here he was faced with the same pain and so much more. "Such an evil deed should have strengthened his resolve against Thane-Ra. I have never understood what changed Morzan so and drew him away from me."

"Do not try to understand something beyond our own nature. As parents, we learn from the errors of our ways when we are young. We try to impart our strengths and knowledge to save our children from pain. But they must feel the angst and learn on their own, regardless of what good or evil comes upon them as they grow. It is their innate nature that will lead them closer to us, or away from us. We can only hope for the best outcome for each child. There is something in Morzan that takes him away from you, Morlog—from all of us. He bears a burden, a sickness, it is true, and a malevolence lives within him. You could not see it then and you cannot see it now because you do not possess it. All I ask of you is to recall, simply for the benefit of our advance on Khordom Palace and the prison, what you sense yourself, innately about him."

"What you ask of me is understandable yet still painful. It has been a long time since I have either seen or heard from him and the letting go has given me peace. I am not so certain what I may recall could be of any service to us in our mission. But give me time and I will find what I can in my mind's eye to move us safely into his lair."

"Morlog, dearest friend," the King leaned forward and placed a hand over Morlog's on the armrest of his chair. "I know full well the painful thing I ask. I want you to know my heartfelt gratitude. I love you like a brother and would take the pain for you if I could, but this is one thing I cannot do. My castle, my lands, are yours—whatever your needs may be—all you must do is ask and it shall be yours. I wish you peace dear friend, only peace."

Morlog nodded and closed his eyes. They had filled with pain and a single tear hardly noticeable in the light formed in the corner of his left eye. Sitting so still, gravity left the tear where it was and it only dried where it sat from the heat of the fire. This was a pain so great to Morlog, the living loss of his only son to the greatest evil in the entire Kingdom, that even Magnus's generous and thoughtful words could not soothe his inner being.

22

What lay before the guests at table was a feast not seen before. Servants bustled about, bringing wines and delicacies to all who dined with Thane-Ra. To his right, as was always the routine, sat none other than Morzan, who sat picking food from between his teeth.

"Really Morzan, could you not wait to clean your teeth. Behold the women at table find you disgusting," laughed Thane-Ra, nodding in the direction of the women whose expressions conveyed their horror.

"By now you must know their disgust gives me pleasure, Sire."

"Well, then, you disgust me. Enough now, what is your latest plan?" Thane-Ra waved his hand in the air and the table cleared of women and those of his court whom he did not hold in such esteem or trust that they should be a part of such a conversation. Morzan waited for the room to clear before answering Thane-Ra's query.

With such a change in the mood of the room and purpose of conversation, servants grabbed what they could in an effort to clear the table and cleared themselves from the presence of Thane-Ra and his preferred guests, Morzan and the senior militia.

"Thane-Ra," Morzan began, "our spies outnumber and out-power those of Magnus and his fools. He gathers others from abroad—Siwa and Sweetbrooke Wren. It is unknown as yet how many from Siwa, three clusters of horgles were sent to Siwa to determine activity. We have been alerted to only a small contingent of four from Sweetbrooke Wren and I don't expect them to be of any threat. They were seen to be escorting the young princess. The trailing party elected to break off, to alert the horgle clusters rather than attempt to recover her. I suppose this was wise for it would have been a waste to alert them, causing them to change up their plans."

"Well, Morzan, so you say, but we have lost that princess again. Such cowardice will weaken, not strengthen our position. I am not impressed by this news."

"Sire, I assure you there is better news. The horgle clusters attacked Siwa and drove the travellers out. They were seen on horseback heading into the woods. After that, I regret, they were lost for some time as the raiders battled those wretched archers of Siwa. But a dispatch located them as they rafted Trezano Falls. Earlier efforts to sabotage the Falls were obstructed by the Tsesiwan engineering party, and repairs made."

"You know, if you wish to lose favour with me, you should keep going. If not, then shut up. Just shut up, Morzan. What is it that you don't understand about this? It is not simply an exercise, Morzan. We are —I am—conquering Mazgamor. I do not want to hear any more failure. If you and your miserable spies cannot fulfill missions… why-y-y are you even here?" Thane-Ra bellowed with rage. Spit bubbled at the side of his mouth and the veins of his neck bulged with each roar. His hands shook as the rage overtook him.

"Thane-Ra, Sire, I can most assuredly tell you that we remain in control of the situation. We have a spy within the walls of his castle."

"Hmm. You begin to redeem yourself. Go on then."

"Magnus has called for the leaders of the Gathering. We stopped Piralius and his party on their way from Aureopiscis. It seems they had not heeded Magnus's warning of danger and they travelled light in armor and weaponry. Our raiders encircled them by day and took them easily. Piralius is dead, Sire; one has been eliminated. There are three remaining."

"Who are the three and what of the other two in the count?"

"Magnus called upon Kasreya, who travels to Constantia presently. The old fool, Morlog," Morzan hesitated as he referred to the one he knew most intimately, and quietly feared, for reasons obvious to himself and Thane-Ra only. "He is part of the Sweetbrooke Wren travellers. Somehow, he and the mordaghas have disappeared. I have no word on them. A party is underway to stop Thorandal of Trader's Peninsula. He arrived only yesterday on his ship, *Venusia*. Word will have only now reached him. He will take time to assemble after returning from a long journey. I have no concern of him. The only one who has yet to move bears great mystery to me. This is MaginTor, the keeper of Dragho Point. We camp nearby and spies watch over The Point. Word will come when he moves, be assured."

"And what of Kasreya—she travels south now? What do you propose we do to stop her and those archers of hers?" Thane-Ra's temper began to ease as he listened to the details Morzan now presented.

"She is of no concern." Morzan considered the time of day, and the party of raiders camped at the base of the Falls, then finished his thought. "Yes, by now she is no more a concern of ours." Morzan smiled as he said this, causing Thane-Ra to erupt in laughter.

"You are a malevolent beast, Morzan. Sweetbrooke Wren was too charming for your wicked ways. Your betrayal those years ago amused me then, for the pain it caused Morlog. Still today you amuse me and for this I thank you." Thane-Ra considered the room occupants for a moment and then called for more wine.

"Tomorrow, Morzan, begin the actions at dawn. Send word to the sleeping raiders to wake and begin their assault. You will take Constantia Glen and, by all that will keep your breath alive, you will find the rare gold and bring it to me. I warn you only this once, do not fail me in this or death will be upon you."

"With pleasure, Thane-Ra, with pleasure," Morzan gulped back his wine and rose clumsily from his seat. "I depart to affect the outcome you desire; your new Kingdom is upon you. Goodnight, Sire." Morzan bowed as he removed himself from the cold and barren dining hall. In spite of the oversized fireplaces and pits strategically constructed around the room, no amount of burning wood or peat could warm the room and remove the icy cold that hung in the air. The evil of frozen hearts and wicked intentions was upon this place.

23

Slightly inebriated, Morzan stumbled every few steps as he went to his bedchamber. From there, he would send directions by messenger to the six strike points: Trader's Peninsula, Constantia Glen, Siwa, Sweetbrooke Wren, Aureopiscis, and Dragho Point. It would be a sweet victory. By the end of the next day, he should be appointed leader of the North. He would prove himself to a leader. Morzan worshipped Thane-Ra, who represented power, strength, and supremacy over others. All would fall to Thane-Ra. All would bow to Thane-Ra. Enough of these petty little villages and their proud villagers. They would soon bow to the enforcers, who would show them how to pay homage to their new King and his united kingdom. The terror to be brought upon them would encourage them to comply. And Morzan himself would delight, as usual, in setting those straight who would think they could fight against the power of Thane-Ra. This new darkness brightened Morzan's heart. He was the only one for whom darkness represented light. His core so immoral, he no longer saw goodness, only pain and it was pain that brought him pleasure. Morzan's wickedness was experienced by many and understood by no one. This would now be exponentially true as his cruel touch would reach farther and wider across Thane-Ra's new reign. For a moment he felt sheer delight and then went about assembling his plan for the sunrise.

"Bring me hot tea, the hotter the better," Morzan said to his chamber page. "Send for Walcod—quickly now. Move." He shoved the young page and dropped himself into a large chair swinging his legs over the side. Morzan's build and looks did not match his ways. Fair hair and colouring, deceptively handsome except for a scar that travelled from his left ear to the corner of his mouth, he all but looked princely in many ways. His behavior suggested he was a spoiled child but in truth this was false. He had been well raised by a cautious, yet loving, mother and father. He was well taught in every way and had been brought up to be a Teller like his father. But he was always attracted to the darker stories. There was no explanation for this. He had not been beaten but loved. He had not been deprived but educated and cared for. There was no reason for the behaviours that should have betrayed him. Yet, when a creature was injured, he did nothing but watch it suffer and die.

At the Tenth Gathering attack by raiders, His mother stood to protect Morzan from a raider's dagger. She pushed him away, so the dagger merely grazed the side of his face. Recovering from his fall, he saw a raider move in behind Morzanega with spear raised. Rather than call out a warning, Morzan stood and watched the raider drive the spear into her back. He was fascinated by her agony as she writhed with the rapid effects of the poison on the tip of the spear. But no one noticed these moments of happiness, as seen in the eyes of Morzan. He travelled his journey into darkness alone.

Morzan and his father were delayed at Dragho Point for several moons after Morzanega's death. The Circle Leaders elected to confer longer to attempt to resolve the trauma and conflicts born of the raid. Morzan had removed himself from everyone. They spoke of him grieving, but inside he played the death scenes he had observed over and over, delighting in the carnage. He would pull back his bandages to observe and pick at the scar on his face as it attempted to heal. He relished how it made his left side look ugly and angry while the right side of his face looked content.

On returning to Sweetbrooke Wren with his father, he stood in the doorway of their family cottage but never crossed the threshold. Instead, wordlessly, he turned and walked away, never to be seen again by the villagers of Sweetbrooke Wren. It was some time before spies brought word to The Circle of Morzan's new-found home. There were no words to describe the pain that rippled through the members and, that day, tore out the heart of his grieving father, Morlog.

"Master Morzan, you have sent for me?" Walcod stood in the arched entry to Morzan's chamber, waiting to be invited in.

"Walcod, we take action this night. Tomorrow, Khordom Palace becomes the seat of Mazgamor and all who dwell will bow to Thane-Ra. Rejoice in this and let us get to work."

"At your ready, Master. This is a great night for us all." Walcod spoke with fervour.

"To the six parties of raiders send two messengers, one north and the other south. Send the same parchment with each messenger.

All raids to commence as the sun reaches the peak of day. Villagers shall perish in the light of day. They must fall knowing who, and from where, their enemy attacks. Thane-Ra fears no one. Thane-Ra directs them to take no prisoners but destroy all those who bear arms of any kind. Surrender is acceptable only to allow a village to remain productive. These will now be the subjects of Thane-Ra's kingdom of Khordrya, north, south, east, and west. Long live Thane-Ra."

"The messengers will depart first thing, Master Morzan," Walcod said after repeating the dictation back to Morzan.

"Fool, it will go now. Send them by horgle to ensure they reach the raiders in time to organize their assaults. There is no time for error or delay in this matter. Off with you and attend to this at once."

"At once, Master Morzan, I shall dispatch the parchments at once." Walcod bowed his head and backed out of the chamber in three long steps. Relieved to have left the room, he took a dark round column of tightly placed stone steps down to chambers well below Morzan's own chamber and set about his business there.

Satisfied things were progressing as planned, Morzan kicked off his sturdy black leather boots, removed his over shirt and fell onto his bed. He pulled two sheep fleeces his legs and torso and fell immediately into a deep sleep.

24

The small flight of mordaghas had left the castle of Constantia Glen and was met by five additional Master Riders who had been sent word from the castle on the arrival of the travellers. 'All available Master Riders are bid welcome to join a security detail to bring safely visitors from Siwa.' It was a simple instruction that drew no questions, only commitment to a cause. The two flights converged over the north corner of Constantia Glen. They continued northeast to greet the Tsesiwan riders at the foot of the falls.

As they flew in, Odemog was disturbed to see something he had not anticipated. There, below, was a skirmish between the Tsesiwan pledge and what appeared to be mounted Khordrian raiders. Odemog drew his sword and cried out in a voice none had heard before. "Swords! To ground!" Master Riders alongside of him drew their own weaponry and echoed his cry. "Arah! Swords! To ground!"

Mordaghas adopted a more aggressive manner of flight and dove from the sky to bring their riders to bear upon the raiders.

Most Khordrian raiders are masters of broadswords and few adept at the bow and arrow. In the party of raiders, several archers turned and sent fiery arrows skyward. Skillful as ever, the mordaghas pitched and dodged the arrows. Bazat took an arrow in his wing and tumbled from the sky. Sam clung to his saddle and waited. The flame did not have time to catch his wing on fire. It pierced and travelled through the wing, hampering flight more than causing pain. It was, however, a temporary state. Dero witnessed the arrow and directed Tovar to the aid of their friends. Tovar dove below Bazat and came up suddenly. He tucked in his right wing and, angled, flew at Bazat to carefully nudge him correcting his erratic flight. The maneuver worked perfectly.

"Brilliant, Tovar—thank you!" Bazat called to his old friend.

"Smashing move, Tovar! I would not have thought of that," Dero slapped the mordagha on the shoulder in congratulations.

"Onward!" Sam raised his sword, then pointed it directly at the archer, prompting Bazat to dive deliberately at the archer. At the very same time, having sheathed his sword, Odemog raised his bow and fired an arrow in return at the archer below, sending him crashing to the ground. The archer's horse reared up in a panic and came down on the raider. Confused and distressed, the horse spun around and galloped south toward Galdordon Forest.

The mordaghas swooped low and all method of assault was imposed upon the raiders in support of the pledge that gallantly encircled and defended their leader. Lisan, with Kasell astride him, attacked with powerful wings knocking raiders from behind. Odemog again drew his sword and lunged at the various attackers as Nassir popped and weaved as best he could, for he was no horgle. Odemog then beckoned him to land at the edge of the battle. He leapt from Nassir and sent him airborne to be safe. He turned and raced to the scene on foot. Such a giant took great steps and came upon the fight with unbridled passion. It was only in play and at games held at the Gathering that Odemog, a farmer, not a warrior, honed his fighting skills. Today was proof that he had learned well; he showed himself a natural warrior.

Juliet positioned herself back-to-back with Kasreya and Amara, forming a wheel of three within the circle of the pledge. Odemog observed both Juliet and Kasreya to bear arms of a most unusual design. He had not seen this most effective horizontal bow before. Odemog had observed unusually shaped saddle bags straddling Juliet's horse and realized these were the contents. They each held not a long bow, but a short bow with a stock and trigger. A spring mechanism helped fire three arrows at a time. It appeared there was a mechanism to fire one to three arrows and directionally aim each one, thanks to a small adjustable arrow slot. These were deadly weapons that increased their defense exponentially. A brilliant design, he observed.

Dero directed the additional riders to ground where they could attack the perimeter raiders. Again, mordaghas were sent to air to protect them from attack. Sam circled above and called down to Dero, who continued directing his riders in their attack. Suddenly Sam and Bazat turned and darted southward. Dero whistled to Tovar who came down to pick him up.

"Kasell, I'm after Sam. Take charge of your riders." With that, Dero was away after Sam.

"Attack!" Kasell raised his sword high in the air and charged with the other Master Riders of Constantia into the fighting battalion of raiders.

Immediately a rider was struck down by sword. Kasell turned and took vengeance on the raider who had struck down his man. The raiders' numbers were dwindling but they would not give in easily. It was true what was said of these Khordrian fighters: die in the field if victory is not upon you or die at the will of Thane-Ra. And knowing the ways of Morzan, who took pleasure in enacting the will of Thane-Ra, no one wished to return if victory was not their own.

Away from the battle, Sam flew in chase of a rider who headed to Galdordon Forest. No one must return to Khordom Palace. No word must get back to Thane-Ra. It was imperative that they prevent communication. Sam took this seriously and, though Bazat was not fully himself, he, too, recognized the importance of this detour from battle. But Bazat was unaware of how seriously his wing had been injured.

"I cannot go in chase, my Sam," Bazat spoke in a tone of shame and disappointment.

"Go to ground my friend, all will be well, Bazat," Sam rubbed the mordagha's shoulder. "All will be well. We shall land and I will take a look at your wing."

"Samezog! Sam, behind you!" It was Dero upon Tovar who called to his friend.

"By all that is welcome, Dero, you are a sight for sore eyes!"

"I shall follow. Go to ground, Bazat; we shall return."

Tovar and Dero flew past Sam and Bazat and the chase continued. Bazat went to ground and rested. Sam stepped away to cut him some greens and find water. Tovar and Dero flew on and continued the chase to catch the escaped raider.

From his place in the air, Dero could see the raider in the distance. A small grove of trees concealed him moments later and Tovar slowed his flight. He circled the grove and came in lower. Dero saw the horse collapsed on the ground. It had been injured in the battle. A broken arrow protruded from his neck.

"He ran himself to death, this poor creature," Dero observed as he shook his head over the sadness and waste of it.

"I am certain he had no choice. Look at the whipping marks on his back." Tovar commented rarely but was clearly disturbed at the violence brought upon his fellow creature. "This creature's service ended in wrong. Dero, we must find the raider."

"Hush Tovar, conceal yourself," Dero whispered.

Almost before Tovar could lower himself in the long grass, Dero drew and was swinging his sword over Tovar's head. He ran at the trees and knocked a second airborne arrow to the ground as the first flew past his head. "Arah!" he shouted as he leapt at the raider who dropped his bow and fell to the ground. Dero kicked him over on to his back and held his blade against the raider's throat.

"You will not live another day if you move." The raider took a breath and stared up at Dero.

"Kill me now. Death by your hands is more desirable," the raider spoke through gritted teeth.

"I'll not kill you but take you back with me, fool. Where did you think you were going?"

"I failed in battle and would have died a worse death by Thane-Ra. I was taking refuge in Galdordon Forest with others who camp out there living in fear also."

"Then rise and come with me, but a false move will see your end quickly."

Although it was not ideal to take a second rider, Tovar was young and strong; he could manage this for a short distance. They took to air and returned to check on Sam.

In the meantime, the battle at the base of Trezano Falls was coming to an obvious conclusion as the pledge broke ranks to chase down remaining raiders and end their tenure within the Kingdom. Not one of them would return to Thane-Ra. Not one of them would tell of victory or defeat. Odemog and the Tsesiwans would, exhausted, make haste to Constantia Glen to prepare for what was still to come.

"Kasreya, your good health is a relief to my eyes." Odemog strode quickly toward Kasreya, who now stood by her horse with Amara and Juliet at her side. Juliet held out her hand to take back the weapon Kasreya had brandished with great skill.

"I don't know how you managed to come into possession of such a magnificent weapon, but I must say I am most amazed and impressed." Odemog looked to Juliet.

"She is not just your average engineer or archer, my Juliet." Kasreya reached over and set a hand upon Juliet's shoulder. She gave it a squeeze as she said, "Well done, most effective. These will do more than nicely. Thank you."

"You handled it like a master, Reya," said Juliet, "I must say I was impressed for only your second go at it!"

"I've never seen this short bow before," added Amara whose eyes remained wide and in awe of all she had just witnessed.

Smiling, Odemog added, "Well, to each of you, my admiration of Tsesiwan Archers —warriors—is ever growing. I am not sure you would have required our assistance in the end, but we perhaps helped to end this skirmish early enough to get back for dinner. Magnus awaits you, Kasreya."

"I cannot agree with you, Odemog, we were tiring quickly. They came at us with a vengeance." Kasreya, looking unflappable as always, betrayed a fatigue as she now spoke.

"I marvel at their knowledge of our arrival here."

"I would be inclined to think this was planned all along, Mistress," Juliet interjected. "It seems their strategy was to separate us and wait until we came to the bottom of the falls. They were ready for us here. I expect they did not anticipate Odemog's return with these brave riders." Juliet looked around at the Master Riders who had joined the flight as added security for the Tsesiwans.

"There is wisdom in keeping some plans between us," Kasreya said, "Gentlemen, Master Riders, and mordaghas, you have our gratitude for your willingness to come to our aid."

The mordaghas, now on ground, stood by, enjoying the grasses growing at the water's edge. Nassir, watching and listening to Kasreya, now looked skyward to see Sam and Bazat flying unsteadily toward them. Dero and Tovar followed closely. All who followed Nassir's upward gaze noted that Dero was not alone on Tovar.

As the two mordaghas landed, another Master Rider approached Bazat and encouraged him to go to the river's edge. There, he inspected Bazat's wing with Sam and it was treated with a poultice of healing herbs.

Dero, on the other hand, received a different sort of welcome as Tovar landed. Swords and arrows pointed to the rider tied up behind Dero.

Sliding from his saddle, Dero turned quickly and pulled his companion down from Tovar's back.

"This wretched beast rode his horse to death in a cowardly race. He attempted to hide away from his own death, by battle or Thane-Ra, in Galdordon Forest. Sam chased him, fearing he was taking word back to Thane-Ra. His cowardice leaves him a burden in our hands now."

"Find him a horse then; he shall ride back by ground. Sam will need to ride with you, Dero, to give Bazat an easy trip home." Odemog gave instructions to those around him. "Let us not waste any more time here. We don't know who may emerge from these woods while we stand here. Are you and your horses ready to travel this moment?" Odemog looked to Kasreya and Juliet for their readiness to move.

"We should not stay a moment longer than necessary at this point, Odemog. What is our path, then?" asked Kasreya.

"Stay alert, all," Odemog spoke to the pledge and master riders with their mordaghas. "I think the most direct route to Constantia is in order, so we make a hasty arrival. Riders, mordaghas, spread out in pairs to fly over the path of the pledge. All eyes to air and ground; we may be looking for horgles as well as horse mounts. It is safer to expect another attack than to be foolish and think they prepared only one assault. Riders, both air and ground, we will go easy to protect our mounts. This has been an arduous trip for all. We shall rest on reaching Constantia Glen. We are away, then."

As Odemog took his place on Nassir's back, other riders mounted their horses and mordaghas. Odemog took to air first, having observed that Sam and Bazat were as ready as they would ever be. He took the front of the flight ahead of the lead pledge rider. Looking back and down at those for whom he now acted as guardian, Odemog suddenly felt the mantle of his task and began to realize all that had occurred and all that lay ahead of him meant, most assuredly, that his new destiny would be that of a Kingdom Keeper. He quickly dismissed this thought, realising there was still much more to learn. His mind raced with thoughts of his mother, his father, Morlog, the princess, his friends, and his little companion, Skeeter. Where was this mayhem taking him and what was to become of him? Odemog puzzled over it all as he watchfully guided the group forward to the safety of Magnus's castle within the boundaries of Constantia Glen.

25

Skeeter paced back and forth on the mahogany table in the Royal Hall. Magnus drummed his fingers on the table, where Fazzog pored over maps and documents.

"Tell me again what you know of their attack," Mezzog drilled the messenger who had arrived in the dark of night. "You must not fear for yourself, you are safe within these walls." Mezzog looked to the King, who nodded in agreement.

"No one in the Kingdom of Mazgamor is safe. Should they discover that I bound the other messenger and locked him in a root cellar at the edge of Khordom Palace, I will be a marked man."

"You took great risk, and you will be rewarded for this," the King spoke unequivocally.

"Sire, expect the worst." The messenger withdrew the parchment from his sleeve and presented it to Mezzog, who broke the seal and read it aloud to the King. As Mezzog read, a grave look crossed the face of the King, who gestured to Marsdell.

"Take this man and determine the path of the other messenger, should he be found and released. Man, tell me, did he know it was you who bound him?"

"I think not, Sire, as I surprised him from behind. But I cannot be entirely sure."

"We plan for both possibilities then, Marsdell. If he did not see this messenger, then fortune is in our favour and they assume he got through with his dispatch. If he did witness his attacker, then they will hunt him to the death and a new plan will be sworn."

"If the expectation is that they attack our villages at noon, we must be ready to depart long before dawn," Mezzog proposed.

"We have yet to hear from our Northern friends and this concerns me greatly," Morlog interjected. He then observed the messenger shake his head. "Speak man, what do you know?"

"I know only that they were being watched and one of them was killed."

"Killed? Of whom do you speak?" thundered Magnus.

"Sire, his name was unknown to me...Parel..."

"Piralius of Aureopiscis—rest his soul." Morlog shook his head.

"Then there will be hope for MaginTor and Thorandal?" Borzog posed the question directly to Morlog.

"I should think if there was a successful attack on Piralius that MaginTor may also have perished. We can only hope otherwise."

"Of Thorandal, what have we heard?" Morlog looked to Magnus for his input.

"Word returned from his second that the *Venusia* made haste in its return to Trader's Peninsula. They readied an army to join us on Thorandal's arrival. He was expected any day."

"Our plans must adapt to what we have." Magnus spoke with confidence and determination, yet his heart pained for Piralius and all that was now unknown to them.

"And Odemog? We have yet to see your man, Morlog," Borzog spoke curtly to Morlog, forgetting, for a moment, the place held by the Teller in governance of the Gatherings and therefore, within the Kingdom.

"You shall rephrase your address of Morlog, Prince Borzog," the King rebuked his son.

"Humble regret for my tone, Teller Morlog. I await the leadership Odemog brings us." Borzog had begun to feel the urgency of the moment as his confidence had now been rocked by the appearance of the Khordrian messenger and their new awareness of what was intended to be.

"Who speaks my name in my absence?" Odemog spoke from the archway at the entrance to the Royal Hall. Skeeter bounded across the table, leapt to the floor, and raced toward Odemog who, as he approached the table, bent forward with arm outstretched so that Skeeter could race up his sleeve.

"Moggie, what a relief to see you!" Skeeter had complained and cursed from the moment he had learned his friend had departed without him. In spite of being told he was safer in the castle for the time being, Skeeter was miserable to all, including Morlog, whom he felt betrayed him by allowing Odemog to leave him behind.

Morlog strode to greet Odemog with a generous hug and a slap on the back.

"The riders will be here presently. I stopped the guard from disturbing you and asked them to attend to the others. I wanted to greet you first."

"Welcome back, Odemog," Magnus approached with outstretched hand. They shook hands and embraced.

"Ours was a journey with incident, I am afraid," Odemog related news of the attack he and the other master riders happened upon as they flew to meet Kasreya. "Fortune was with us, injuries to the pledge were minor. Bazat, too, was injured by a flaming arrow. Perhaps your Lord Forthrumal could see to him and the others?"

"At once," the King spoke the words and, on command, a page was dispatched to Forthrumal to attend to the injured.

As the page ran from the hall, the archway filled with arriving guests; there came Kasreya, Juliet, and Amara, who appeared surprisingly alert in spite of their fatigue. They were still buoyed by the rush of adrenalin from the day's adventure.

"Morlog, so good to see you again. And Magnus, dear friend, you are a sight for sore eyes." Kasreya, ever gracious, appeared to float forward as she came toward the two men. Arms in the air, Magnus grinned from ear to ear seeing his fellow Circle Member and beloved friend of the Queen.

"Reya, great blessings! It is a relief to have you in my home. The hour is upon us, however, and there is no time to rest now. We must immediately review tomorrow's mission." He called for food and liquids for the travellers. Magnus then directed the group to take seats at table where Fazzog had spread maps of Khordom Palace and Pierce Island in the center.

Kasell came forward with Dero and Sam. He introduced them to the princes, whereupon they shook hands and took their seats at the table. Morlog directed Juliet to the table and he took a seat beside Kasreya. Amara elected to stand behind Kasreya's seat, where she felt most comfortable. Tea was served to the travellers with side plates of a rich pudding for sustenance and energy.

"Kasreya, I regret that the first news I must share is not good at all. Our friend and Circle Member, Piralius, is dead. We know not the fate of MaginTor of Dragho Point. But these circumstances, we do know, are part of the plot of Thane-Ra and Morzan."

With mention of Morzan's name, she looked briefly with sadness to Morlog who, looking back, showed no emotion. Odemog observed the exchange, puzzled. He found more mystery everywhere he turned.

"A messenger has come this night, one of our spies in Khordom Palace, with the gravest of news. He broke word of Piralius, not knowing the significance of such news. But more heinous than this was the revelation of Thane-Ra's plan of attack and conquer. He has planted sleeper raiding parties around the Kingdom. They await word from Morzan to commence their merciless attack. Our fortune is in the unknowing trust that was placed in one of our spies. Still, the risk is great for there were, in fact, two. The second was temporarily silenced by our spy. Marsdell is determining the path the spy was to take to deliver his dispatch so we may intercept if a second messenger is sent."

"If there are hidden raiders, we must send our own messengers to alert the others immediately," Kasreya pleaded to Magnus. King Magnus looked to Kasell, who was absorbing this information at the same time as Kasreya spoke.

"Kasell, we need every arms man we have for the morrow. Can you suggest alternative messengers?"

"My recommendation would be three of the master riders, Sire," Kasell had been most impressed by the riders who had joined the detail to meet the Tsesiwans. "They will have to fly at greater elevations to avoid detection if the raiders are watching the skies. And, they will have to depart in the night. Are mordaghas comfortable with night flight, Odemog?"

"It would not be their first choice for flight time but it would be the least visible. If seen, however, it would be the most suspicious. A master rider knows his mount and would be best asked individually for his preference." Odemog looked to Sam and Dero, "Brothers, I entrust this arrangement to you. We need you here but if you would engage the other riders to determine who should attend to this urgent mission, I would be grateful."

"At once, Odemog," Sam spoke for both of them as they rose and turned to leave.

"We shall return but require specifics of the message to be delivered." Dero stopped long enough to pose this question then continued out with Sam.

Magnus turned. "Morlog, perhaps you would draft the message?"

Morlog stepped away from the table and tapped a nearby scribe on the shoulder. Gesturing to the woman, he moved with her to a side table where she provided clean parchment and ink. He set to his task immediately.

"I require clarification, King Magnus," Odemog rose and bowed slightly to the King, who sat to his right. "We move forward tomorrow with one pledge from Siwa, your arms men of numbers I am not aware. We have no known support from the north of the Kingdom and wait, without word, for armies that may or may not come from the west in Trader's Peninsula."

"Sent before your arrival at Siwa, Odemog, were six double pledges at Magnus's request," Kasreya interjected. Finally, Odemog was puzzled beyond his ability to remain quiet.

"When did this all begin? I cannot understand who knows what and when forces began their movement to bring this all about. Someone, Morlog, your Majesty, Kasreya, please—someone impart to me your knowledge of this process."

Magnus looked between his fellow Circle Members and spoke very deliberately to Odemog. "This entire battle began at the Gathering when Queen Madelina and Princess Annabella were misled and seized from our midst. The actions taken by Thane-Ra were, in themselves, an act of war. He took them to provoke me and the others. At first, we were not sure of the well-being of the Queen and Princess. Without certainty of their survival there was little we could do. We began to plan to move on Khordom Palace but delayed our actions until more information could be revealed. That you came to be a part of this in the way in which you did was unintentional. Your rescue of my daughter, Lily, was entirely unexpected, heroic, and an action for which I am grateful. But you were to be called to action by much different means, Odemog."

"Called to action?" Odemog shook his head and stared from Magnus to Morlog who, having completed his task and sent the parchments by way of the scribe to Dero and Sam, now returned to the table. He placed a hand on Odemog's arm and bade him return to his seat. Morlog now sat beside him, hand still on his arm.

"Moggie, you were presented a letter from your father, Zodem. He, like his father and, in truth, some members of your Clan for generations back, are what we call Kingdom Keepers. It is an honour and a gift to be chosen. When one is called to action to serve as a Kingdom Keeper, it is held in the greatest of secrecy. In your lifetime, you have served your family and community as a gifted farmer and respected trader of goods. As you have grown and while you travelled, you have been watched over by Protectors, of which I am one. The Circle Members are the only ones who know the identity of a Kingdom Keeper as they grow. Until one is called, it is even kept from the Keeper him or herself. Thus, we present the letter of the previous Keeper to commence the revelation."

"But it was a simple letter. It doesn't say 'Moggie, welcome, you are a Kingdom Keeper'. In truth, it was rather cryptic. Tellers speak of Keepers of the Kingdom, and I admit that the past days of adventure caused me to consider the possibility."

Morlog nodded, "Thus, the letter. Such a great responsibility is the calling and service of a Kingdom Keeper, that it is revealed gradually. That this is revealed to you now, so publicly, is

only because of the changing times. We are in an urgent and desperate time, with the lives and the safety of the entire Kingdom of Mazgamor at dire risk. Moggie, you were born to this. All that has come your way—your mother's teachings, and lessons with me, training at the Gatherings—all of this has served to hone skills of which you are both aware and unaware. These past days, you have begun to prove all this as true. You were born to this, and you are a Kingdom Keeper of Mazgamor."

As Morlog finished speaking, Odemog looked about the room to see Sam and Dero, having returned from their task, now standing away from the table with looks of awe. In that moment, those around the table stepped forward and those seated at table rose, whereupon Magnus now spoke. "To each of you present at this moment, I present to you the Keeper of the Kingdom of Mazgamor, Odemog, Clan of Odem of Sweetbrooke Wren." The room erupted in a cheer.

For many present, including Odemog, a Kingdom Keeper was more legend than reality, resulting from their youthfulness. Odemog had not even known his father to be a Kingdom Keeper. The revelation of a Keeper in their midst sent a wave of hope and confidence through the room.

Borzog, Mezzog, and Fazzog were the first to move in to congratulate him further. They had been waiting with hope and eager anticipation for this moment, after their own discovery of the truth in the Royal Library. The feelings shared were of pride and jubilation. In spite of these feelings, there were three at table for whom such feelings were stored, knowing the greater urgency of the task at hand. These were the Protectors, the members of the Circle: Magnus, Kasreya, and Morlog.

King Magnus raised a stone from the table that held the corner of a map flat and rapped it hard on the surface to draw the attention of the room in his direction.

"It is a joyful moment, when we share such a revelation, but a greater issue is at hand. Keeper Odemog, you will now step forward to master this plan, uniting all in the protection of our Kingdom."

"Protect the Kingdom we shall, Sire, but we shall first disable Thane-Ra and remove his leverage with the rescue of your Queen and daughter the Princess Annabella." Odemog almost seemed taller now for he exuded a renewed confidence that exceeded his normal state. His heart and will strong, he felt a greater connection to his father than he had ever known. He would serve his Kingdom with all his heart, mind, and strength as never before.

26

"My brothers," Odemog turned immediately to Sam and Dero. "Take a place at table with us." With outstretched arms, Odemog gestured for them to come forward and join the protectors, princes, and arms men at table. Two senior arms men stepped back from the table to clear the way for Samezog and Deronezog. At the same time, pages brought forth fresh water and mint tea for those at table. Odemog waited for them to finish before continuing.

"We lay out our plans again with urgency and clarity. First," he looked for confirmation from Sam, Dero, and Marsdell, "we have urgent word travelling now to Thorandal and MaginTor as well as Sweetbrooke Wren. Aureopiscis is dealing with its own tragedy and we will send others with consolation and offers of aid after the morrow. Siwa is another story, I take it." Odemog looked to Kasreya for details who, in turn, encouraged Juliet to address the table.

"The day before you and your travel companions arrived at Siwa, Odemog, six double pledges departed, at the invitation of King Magnus, making their way to Constantia Glen by way of The Meadows. Barring any difficulties they should, in fact, have arrived today."

"There was a storm along the west coast last night which may have blown inland, Juliet. This may have delayed them," Marsdell interrupted her.

"Thank you, Marsdell. That said, I would estimate they shall arrive by morning, latest."

"This is good news Juliet. We have lost Piralius and his men. Kasell, Marsdell, how do you see this affecting the strength of our forces?" Odemog put the question to the King's first and second arms men. Marsdell gestured to Kasell to speak to the question.

"It will lie in two measures, Keeper Odemog." This reference was strange to Odemog who blinked twice on hearing himself addressed as Keeper for the first time. Kasell continued, "First we must consider whether Thorandal will reach us in time. His fighters are rather ragtag but determined. He will take any willing man residing locally or inbound from a trade ship. The traders know the risks and step forward willingly for they value the riches that are traded in Mazgamor. His force could more than double ours, instantly. The second consideration is in our ability to take Pierce Island by surprise. Should we do so and free those in captivity we will gain another hundred souls. They shall be weary but no doubt willing for all they have suffered at the hands of Morzan and Thane-Ra."

Considering this, Odemog spoke. "I offer you this plan, Magnus, Kasreya, and I welcome your wisdom. We depart before sunrise by boat to Pierce Island. We take half the Constantia arms men and half who arrive from Siwa in time. Prepare for the greater number. The other half, with half the Tsesiwan force, will march the coastline in secret. By taking Pierce first we generate more fighting souls with whom to return to Khordom Palace for our final stand against Thane-Ra. The remaining half from Siwa will begin a march inland to the base of Mid Lake from where they will then travel the boundary of Galdordon Forest to avoid being seen as they head toward Khordom Palace. Now, we hope for Thorandal's men and arms. Word shall be left here, directing them to Khordom Palace, joining the Tsesiwans from an inland position." Odemog gestured along the curves and lines of the geography presented on the map before him. "They, too, may travel the south end of Mid Lake and along the edge of Galdordon Forest. Thus, they will come upon Khordom Palace from a northerly direction and we from the southeast, from Pierce Island." Odemog looked to the leaders for their input.

"There is one other possibility we have not entertained, Odemog, but it cannot be relied upon in any way," Magnus spoke knowledgably.

"MaginTor, too, could come from the northeast by way of Dragho Ocean. If the messenger's intelligence bears true and raiders watch the Point, I know MaginTor to be inventive. Were they being watched or had they been attacked, he would have taken the coastal exit through the caves of Dragho Point. From there, they would travel southbound, knowing us to be on the threshold of attack." King Magnus offered a secret escape plan that had long been known by the Circle, having been established at the Gatherings, should one be required.

"MaginTor would then stop for rest and provisions in Siwa which would guarantee that he would learn of our recent movements. This is a very likely scenario, Magnus." Kasreya agreed.

"MaginTor and his men would be of great benefit to our cause. Still, we cannot be sure of this." Odemog found himself to be very pragmatic in the formation of his plan.

"And what of Sam and me? What of the mordaghas, Moggie… uh, Keeper Odemog?" Dero felt rather out of place in such a formal setting and knew by Sam's expression the thought was shared.

"A wise question, Brother," Odemog drummed the fingers of his right hand on the table as he took a sip from his mug. "A boat, Kasell. The mordaghas shall take the first part of the journey by boat. Upon landing at Pierce Island, they will be guided to a safe and protected area. Fazzog, check your maps please," Odemog was now commanding directions to various people around the table as he found his voice as leader. Fazzog nodded and pulled a map from the pile before him.

"Sam and Dero, and you also, Morlog, will travel by boat. Prepare to fight by land and when we have seized Pierce Island, we shall then take flight. Magnus, we have not spoken of the Queen or Princess. What is their experience of travel by mordagha?"

"You know my Queen is from Sweetbrooke Wren. Her own history is why our children have taken quickly to travel by mordagha. Save for our

Fazzog, they each could one day be master riders. Queen Madelina surely would qualify."

"Then, with your permission, this is how we shall see them safely home, or at very least, safely away from their prison."

"So it shall be, Keeper Odemog," replied the King.

"What of us? Shall we then escort the Queen Madelina and Princess Annabella to safety?" asked Sam.

"I would surely be up to rescuing another princess," added Dero.

"It will be no easy feat. Nothing at all to be made light of, you two." Morlog shook his head as he pondered their readiness for battle. After all, they truly were farm folk. While this was something they shared in common with Odemog, his skills had been stretched further through the Gatherings and his travels for trade. Morlog was uneasy.

"With respect, Morlog, I—we—make light of nothing here," Sam stood up and spoke curtly in reply, sensing Morlog's doubt. "My brother," he gestured to his good friend Dero, "and I have shown our commitment without question or hesitation. You must mark our worthiness in battle by this loyalty. We are sworn to our brother, the Keeper Odemog."

"Enough, all of you," Odemog now stood at table, inadvertently knocking over his chair, which was quickly righted by a nearby page. All eyes were upon him. "We shall determine the travels of the Queen and Princess by what is safest on the day and in the moment. All be ready, awake, and aware, and prepare to change plans at a moment's notice. This is not a Gathering exercise or game we face. It is, and will be, life or death. We face the aggressor within Mazgamor. We face the one who seeks to dominate our Kingdom, which is unacceptable. Come dawn we shall assert ourselves, united and fearless. Know this, all of you, come dawn there shall be a reckoning." Odemog drew in a long slow breath to calm himself, glanced slowly around the table, and once again took his seat. "Let us finish our plans." He continued. "Kasell, in what stage of readiness are your men and boats?"

"Marsdell and his men have been preparing weaponry and transportation for moons now. We can be ready to depart any time." Marsdell nodded at Kasell's statement.

"Then we have what we have and know all we can know, for now. I suggest rest, to be ready to depart in the morning, before first light." Odemog finished his plan and, having heard no suggestions, observed the non-verbal approval from Kasreya, Morlog, and King Magnus.

"Kasell, Mezzog, Fazzog, and I shall review the prison documents at hand for a strategy of attack upon our arrival. Borzog and Marsdell, if you would, please join us. I expect each of you will be leading a boat to landing tomorrow."

All but this select group dispersed. Those who would lead the assault gathered around the table with their leaders and Odemog. For a moment he stood, looking at Morlog. His friends patted him on his back and wordlessly took leave to gain a healthy sleep in preparation for what would come in only a few hours. Sam and Dero felt no bruising to their egos over the previous outbursts, only stronger loyalty to their friend—their brother— the Kingdom Keeper, Odemog.

Odemog returned his focus to the table and planned the final assault with Fazzog's interpretation of access points along the shore, placement of guard towers, and the general layout as he had researched it through archival documents and stolen plans.

When Odemog finally reached his bedchamber, he knew he would sleep only a couple of hours before rising to face the day ahead.

27

Odemog woke, opening his eyes to see Morlog standing over him. He rubbed his eyes and shook his head roughly to try and shake off his sleepy state after a restless night. As he shook his head, Skeeter stirred on the pillow beside him; sleepily, he rolled off and drew himself under the pillow to continue his rest.

"Morlog," Odemog said returning his focus from Skeeter to the man who stood looking down at him. "You look disturbed. Did you not rest well?"

"I slept not a moment, but that is not important now. There are things you must know to protect yourself and others on this day."

"I am sure there is much to know and I can't imagine that I could begin to know everything, Morlog. In truth, this is a mantle put upon me that is far greater than I. Does this not concern even you?"

"It does not. You must lose your self-doubt, Moggie—what lies ahead has no room for doubt. For every moment you may find yourself in battle today, there is a greater battle of evil around you that must also be faced. Last night, you spoke wisely of the one who wishes to dominate and that is Thane-Ra. But his desire and insidious nature is only half of the evil you face. There is another evil in Khordom Palace. This evil goes by one name and that is Morzan."

Morlog took the bedside chair after handing Moggie a mug of tea so hot, he felt his hands burning. Morlog studied him before speaking. "You feel the heat of the beverage in your hands and I feel the burning pain of Morzan's evil in my heart,"

"I don't understand."

"You wouldn't, and now is not the time to interrupt; just listen to me, Moggie."

"Moons ago, Morzan experienced a great pain that blackened his heart beyond repair. What I never understood before was that his heart was already black. The death of his mother—"

"His mother? I am sorry, Morlog, but what are you talking about? How would you know his—Morlog, you are Morzan's father!" Odemog stood in disbelief and took a step closer to Morlog. "I thought your son died with Morzanega at the Gathering?!"

"Sit, Moggie, sit down. Yes, you are correct. A son I claim no more. After Morzanega, his mother, died in the violence, he was gone from me. Far and away, he was gone. In a way, he did die back then. I blamed myself at the time but, on reflection, know the blackness was deeply rooted and only released during the tragedy at the Gathering. But enough reflection; we've no time for this."

"I am very sorry, Morlog, truly, I am." Odemog felt a deep pain for the man he considered his uncle, who treated him more like a son than a student.

"I know, Moggie, thank you. But now, more important than sentiments, heed my words. You may think you outsize and can outfight Morzan, but this may be impossible. He fears nothing. He thrives on the unspoken inner fears of others, on their pain. Morzan feeds on darkness. If pain were food, he would feast upon it. What you must understand, Moggie, is that, in the moment you feel strong and resilient, he will capitalize on something, anything around you that emits the scent of, or even memory of fear. He is a quick study and, once he knows your interests, he will find a way to pierce your armour. Do you understand?"

"What you tell me is very simple. I should be strong and courageous. These are the signs of any good warrior. You taught me well."

"Keeper Odemog, listen well—do not take for granted any weakness you may think you observe in your opponent. It will be a test of your resolve in ways you cannot anticipate. He may not know you are coming to defeat Thane-Ra or himself, but once you are upon him, he will surely know he has nothing to lose and everything to gain. He will find advantage against you—do you hear me? He will test your resolve. Mark my words, Keeper Odemog. I speak to you now not as a student but as a liberator, a warrior, a Keeper of the Kingdom of Mazgamor. Heed what I have said and you will battle well."

Odemog sat quietly, gazing into the eyes of the Teller and teacher who sat before him speaking in a way he had never before spoken. Odemog set his mug on the table at the side of the bed. He straightened his back, cleared his throat, and stood with hand outstretched. Morlog rose and took his hand.

"Teller Morlog, you have shown me throughout my life your infinite wisdom and teachings. I thank you and I assure you that I take all you offer me and hold it here." Odemog touched his left hand to his head then his heart. He gripped Morlog's hand strongly with his right and placed his left hand on Morlog's forearm, holding steady as he cemented the moment to memory.

"I know, Keeper Odemog. May this day be a victory to you and all who, in the interest of Mazgamor, serve at your side."

"I shall dress and arm myself and meet you at table, Morlog. Thank you."

Morlog smiled faintly, turned, and left as quietly as he had arrived. Odemog went to the table on which his chainmail was laid out. He adjusted his shirt and raised the tunic of chainmail over his head. This time, he left his braid covered and drew the hood of the mail over his head. Strapping on his sword he turned to face the bed as he slipped his dagger into the straps of his left boot. He would pick up his bow and quiver in the Royal Hall, where he had left it. Odemog walked back to the bed and slapped the pillow that covered Skeeter. It popped up in the air as he pulled his large hand away—and so did Skeeter.

"You have your hood up, Moggie." Skeeter realized the day of reckoning was now upon them.

"I do, Skeeter. I've no time for games either, my friend. We shall be away in no time. You will wait with Princesses Lily and Tulip until we return." Finishing this statement, Odemog turned to look out the window when he heard the hollow clip-clop sound of the hooves of many horses on the cobblestones below as they maneuvered for their place in line or at troughs outside his window. Muffled voices accompanying the movement of the horses told him that the Tsesiwans had arrived.

A voice called out, "Arms men, take over for these travellers. Rest and feed these horses. Archers, get yourselves indoors for nourishment. Your journey shall begin again soon."

Odemog took these words to heart and returned focus to his own preparations. For a moment, he turned his attention back to Skeeter who was speaking to him.

"No, Moggie, I will not remain in the company of the princesses...." Skeeter was both angry and fearful making this revelation. "Where you go, so go I. Please don't suggest I act a coward and stay behind."

"And in what battles have you fought, Skeeter?"

"Battle, schmattle. What is your point? I am no coward. I know your dagger and no one suspects a great grey squirrel to be armed."

"A great grey squirrel now, is it?" Odemog rolled his eyes.

"It is the perfect protection, Moggie. I shall join Morlog as one of your protectors, Keeper—yes, that's it—I, Skeeter, Great Grey Squirrel of Sweetbrooke Wren, am your protector!" Skeeter stood tall, as tall as a squirrel can stand, and puffed his tail nearly twice his size.

"No, you are not my protector. What you are is ridiculous. Listen to yourself, squirrel, and cease this argument. You will remain here and keep company with the princesses who care deeply for you. You have won their affections."

"And I have lost yours, then?"

"Don't be foolish. And I mean that in more ways than one. You are not travelling with me and that is final. Besides, we are going by boat. You remain here at the castle. This is a battle that is too dangerous. And water is no friend to you Skeeter; you don't swim. Do not press me on this."

"I shall press whomever it pleases me to press. But I shall cease arguing with you right now. You are wasting my time." Skeeter abruptly lifted his chin and turned his back on Odemog.

"I am off to a morning feast and, apparently," Odemog gestured to the window, "to meet with those who now join us. You may come and stay at my side before we say farewell today."

"Fine." Skeeter spoke the word with finality. Odemog momentarily thought the friendship bruised. Before he could say anything, Skeeter leapt up and grabbed hold of the chainmail on Odemog's chest. He landed four paws spread wide and scurried up to Moggie's shoulder.

"I'm hungry, move on now." And off they went, Odemog the giant and his friend marched down the hallways to the Royal Hall where final nourishments awaited those who would journey this day.

28

"What word do you bring me then, Morzan?" asked Thane-Ra, who rose from his bed as Morzan stood nearby stoking the fire in the great fireplace situated at the opposite end of Thane-Ra's bedchamber. It remained dark and still outside and as Morzan turned to reply to Thane-Ra, the flames of the fire, as tall as and taller than he, in the center of the enormous fireplace cast an orange glow that backlit him, casting a long black shadow reaching all the way to Thane-Ra in bed.

"We can count the hours to a very sweet victory, Thane-Ra," Morzan raised the steel poker he held in his hand and touched the fiery hot tip to the palm of his hand. Where another would have cried out; he did not flinch. Observing this grotesque act, Thane-Ra cringed, recalling how Morzan generally created in him a sense of disgust and displeasure. Still, he would never dismiss this vile creature for he knew that the forward movements of his plans were largely the result of much of Morzan's dirty work on his behalf. And, as dark as Thane-Ra took pride in being, he could not stoop to the depths in which Morzan resided. Morzan now smelled the burning flesh of his palm with his eyes closed and smiled.

He continued, "Two messengers were dispatched with your instructions. They should have reached their primary and secondary targets each by sunrise. From there, when the sun reaches the highest place in the sky, your orders will be acted upon." Morzan paused as he turned and hung the steel poker back at the side of the fire. He walked to the table upon which sat a jug of water and poured himself a drink. As he approached, Thane-Ra felt his stomach flip when he drew a breath of air that carried the smell of Morzan's burnt flesh.

Vile creature, thought Thane-Ra. Aloud, he offered support for Morzan's news. "You have done well, then. We move ahead. I will sleep awhile longer. Come see me at breakfast and we shall discuss the fate of the Queen—or should I say, former Queen."

With this joke he laughed and Morzan feigned laughter with him. Morzan knew her fate already. Still, he would humour Thane-Ra and hear out his plan. What Morzan knew already was the intention Thane-Ra had to get rid of the Queen so he could marry, with ease, that supercilious little princess daughter of hers. Morzan had much more torturous ideas for her, too, but he realized he could not be entirely greedy or his other wishes may not be granted by Thane-Ra.

"For now, send a boat to bring them here. I look forward to breaking the news of the success of our advance." Thane-Ra smiled, pulled his covers up to his neck and rolled over, thus dismissing Morzan.

"Right away. They will be here after your noon repast. Until breakfast, Thane-Ra, I wish you continued good sleep and shall see you anon." Morzan bowed and, lifting the edge of his long robe from the ground, he turned and strolled from the room.

Morzan made haste down the dark corridors of Khordom Palace. Torches blazed a path for his every step. From light to shadow to light to shadow he walked in and out as he passed each torch. Hung from a chain, they could be easily raised and lowered to give greater or less light depending upon placement and the amount of oil on the peat baskets that formed each torch light. By its construction, the Palace was dark day and night so the peat was used to burn all hours to aid in both light and warmth. Khordom Palace required large fireplaces and many torch baskets. The use of peat generated much smoke so the construction allowed for many sky openings where smoke may escape. Except in some fireplaces, peat was rarely used in smaller chambers to ensure no one asphyxiated from the dense smoke.

As he made his way down the corridors, Morzan listened to the silence. He hated silence. Morzan preferred the chamber in which he often stayed on Pierce Island where he could listen to the sounds of anguish and suffering. A desperate breath, a cry of sadness, voices dressed in fear or other stages of desperation. This was where Morzan found his satisfaction. Peace, kindness, goodness, or warmth of heart caused him pain; such behaviors or emotions only brought rage and hatred to the surface for Morzan. He longed to be back in the prison where he controlled the sounds and anguish of many.

Suddenly the silence was broken with feet running in every direction. A soldier came quickly upon him, the presence of each startling the other.

"My Lord Morzan, we have been looking everywhere for you."

Morzan stared at the soldier who stood with a spear at his side, vertically with blunt tip to the ground.

"Quit your heavy breath and speak," Morzan spat the words at the man.

"My Lord, the butcher, Dobble, heard a constant thumping sound and called us to investigate. After some time—" Morzan slapped him across the face and shouted.

"Man, get to the point!"

"We found one of the soldiers with a dispatch on his person."

"WHAT? Alive, then?" Morzan was enraged. He looked back down the corridor, determining if he should return to Thane-Ra, and thought better of it. "Take me to him, at once."

Morzan followed the soldier down the corridor to a central grand staircase. Down they went on the outer stairs, then down on a centre staircase. From there they took another corridor to the north side of the Palace. As Morzan followed the soldier, others stood tall, coming to attention. Torch lights ahead of them were illuminated and slaves emerged from dank corners to stoke fires to raise the heat and the light along the way. Inside, Morzan was fuming, his anger burning hotter than any of these freshly stoked fires as he considered which of the messengers had been found and in what condition. How had he come to be this way and for how long?

Obviously, it had been hours and, worse still, the attack had been critically impaired.

Gesturing to the room, the soldier spoke as they arrived, "We, along with Dobble, brought him to this chamber when we broke the door down my Lord." The soldier stood back and away from Morzan as he spoke this time, not wishing to be struck again. A soldier should not fear a strike across the face but Morzan's evil was such that one felt a poison in the sting of such a slap. Morzan swept past the soldier as if he did not exist and came into a brightly lit kitchen preparation chamber. This was more to Morzan's liking. Hanging from various hooks about the room was an assortment of wild birds and game in assorted stages of preparation. Lying across the heavy wooden table, with a chopping block beneath his head for a pillow, was the messenger. Dobble stood over him with a filthy stained rag that had been soaked in cold water. He held it to the head of the man who had been struck from behind, bound and gagged and concealed in the cold storage of a root cellar. On seeing Morzan, Dobble stepped away from the table so quickly that he tripped and bumped into a table of tools of his trade: cleavers, knives, meat tenderizers, and the like. He wished, just for that moment, he were invisible.

Morzan looked around the room quickly as he stepped forward. On seeing Morzan even the semi-conscious messenger wished he were anywhere but lying on that giant butcher block. Morzan smiled. The messenger warily returned the smile.

"Fool! What have you done?" Morzan shouted and walked around the table. He pushed Dobble out of his way and stood inspecting the butcher's tools. He reached over and picked up a large cleaver the butcher might use to take the leg off the corpse of a wild boar. Morzan turned the cleaver over in his hand slowly. He then turned to face the messenger whose face was now whiter than when he was first found bound and gagged on the floor of the root cellar nearby.

"You are well then?" Morzan changed his tone, speaking with concern. The soldier glanced around the room, afraid to answer. "ANSWER ME," Morzan bellowed.

"I, my Lord, I…oh, forgive me, Sire, I was taken down from behind."

"Forgive you. Well, that should be the most you will get. You do know what you have done? Where is the other messenger?"

"We left together. If he has not been found I expect he made it away soundly, my Lord Morzan."

"And to whom were you delivering your dispatch?"

"I was to go North, Sire."

"Well, you failed then, didn't you?" Morzan continued to turn the cleaver over in his hand. He was holding it in one hand and with the sharp corner pressed into the tip of his index finger on the other hand. A small trickle of blood dripped down the blade. He stopped, licked the finger, and looked at the man for a brief moment.

"I can't help but wonder what need you have for this foot, since you are unable to use it to deliver a message. For your failure…" Morzan spoke in a very matter of fact tone as he raised his hand and brought the cleaver down with intention towards the man's ankle and foot. Although a butcher and well experienced in the art of carving up game, Dobble fainted at the *thunk* sound of the cleaver landing in the solid wood of the table so near the foot of the soldier. Morzan enjoyed the terror he perpetrated upon the man as he deliberately came down to the side of the soldier's limb. "Take him to the prison." Morzan felt only a small amount of satisfaction at having delivered the first blow of his own form of fear-inducing justice. But what of Thane-Ra's plan of attack? This was all that now consumed him.

Morzan turned to leave the butcher's hall. He forgot to dispatch the order to bring the Queen and Princess over from the prison and pondered how he would break the news to Thane-Ra. This was not a total defeat, but a partial setback. They still had time to attack the North. He knew that Piralius was gone already and they had an early advantage there. The messenger to the South would soon dispatch the sleeper raiders to their missions and Magnus, Thorandal, and anyone else who even tried to help them would be powerless. Or so he thought for, as he finished processing one thought, another emerged: this would all be true if the messenger to the south had, in fact, departed Khordom Palace without incident.

"Search the Palace!" Morzan had turned on his heel and was back in the room, commanding the soldiers, before both feet had crossed the threshold to leave. "I want every assurance that the other messenger got away. Get me proof. And find the devil traitor who bound and gagged that idiot. He shall never bind anything again." The soldiers scattered and Morzan could no longer hear himself think over the din of shouting and banging of doors echoing all around the Palace.

Soldiers searched everywhere and one young soldier took to the stables. He knew the two messengers and checked the stalls for their horgles. Only one remained. With pride he returned to present his findings to Morzan. The only reward for such good news in Khordom Palace was to keep one's limbs intact and sustain one's breath. It was reward enough.

Morzan found himself in the dining hall where he would meet Thane-Ra within the hour. He sat in his usual seat to the right of the chair Thane-Ra always occupied. He stared blankly at Thane-Ra's seat and pondered how he would break the news of the disruption to their plans…Thane-Ra's plans. Morzan was angry, frustrated, and had no desire to be the bearer of such news. This bad news for Thane-Ra was equally bad for Morzan, who held his own agenda for the acquisition of power and spread of his own brand of evil. At least, he thought to himself, this was only a delay in their immediate goal and not the end.

29

Odemog bade Kasreya farewell as she led the Tsesiwan and Constantian riders south along the coast towards their primary destination of Pierce Island to fulfill the rescue of the Queen and Princess. At the same moment, Juliet departed with Honoreya and the newly arrived archers northeast to ride and wait for others north of the Palace, from where they would join in the final stand against Thane-Ra and his soldiers. Odemog listened to the sounds around him as the horses picked up pace to a trot and gradually came silent when they left the cobblestones and began their ride upon dried and broken twigs and patches of moss. The rhythmic sound was like an orchestra softening into silence as they rode out. The silence gave Odemog pause and confidence. It was an assurance of peace in his mind. No sooner were they gone, however, than he turned quickly and returned to the remaining forces and his fellow travellers.

"All is ready, Keeper Odemog," Kasell joined Odemog in step though he took two for every one of the Keeper's. Together, they walked toward the shore where the Constantian arms men had brought the boats. Mezzog and Fazzog had planned for a channel to be dug from the River Constantia, upon which boats could be more readily transferred to the ocean, but this was in the process of being engineered and would not help this time. A slow process of moving logs had been started in the days previous: parties of eight moved logs that acted as rollers beneath the boats as they were gradually conveyed from a lean-to shelter to a boathouse at the water's edge. Four to six logs, depending on terrain, would be lined parallel with a boat perpendicular on top. Four arms men would push the boat, rolling overtop the logs; once clear, two arms men would grab the exposed rear log and race to the front to place it again, behind them two more arms men would repeat the process and so it would continue. As fatigue set in, the four who pushed would trade places with the four runners and on it went. It was an efficient, albeit tiring, process but rarely would a boat receive damage, except in some of the more trying rough or hilly parts of terrain. This normally was a very simple task. But now dozens of boats were launched into water and this took many dozens of arms men to successfully and safely achieve the goal. The last boat to be rolled out was of broad beam and a unique deck had been added to give extra stability. This was the boat upon which the mordaghas would travel. Save for three boats surrounding it for protection, this would be the last boat in the fleet.

Odemog and Kasell now stood among the remaining travellers, who watched as the arms men gathered under Marsdell's direction at the water's edge. The Royal Family walked together toward the shore.

"Father," said Tulip, "You take with you our hearts. Lily and I wish to be with you but know only our love may travel as you journey to unite our family once again."

"It will be soon over, Father," Lily offered, "I take comfort in this. I can feel my mother's arms around me already. I am certain Annabella can feel your comforting arms too. They know—of this I am certain—they know you are on your way." Lily hugged her father as did Tulip. They then turned to their brothers and, in rather a different tone, Tulip announced to them, "not one of you will let another from his sight and you shall care for our father always. Fools are you, brothers, going to battle. But if asked, I trust few more than you." Tulip smiled as she uttered her words and pinched Fazzog's cheek.

"Tulip, really!" Fazzog pulled away and pushed her hand down. He turned several shades of red, some shades representing anger and others embarrassment. Whose cheeks are pinched before battle? Such a sight caused all to laugh and eased the tension greatly. Of course, this was exactly Tulip's intention and she reached out to hug her brother. The three princes and two princesses were a sight as they stood close, holding one another for a long pause. No attempt at levity could conceal the reality of the danger that lay ahead and what potential loss could befall the princesses.

Odemog observed the King, who stood tearing up and took this as a welcome sign to break up the emotional send-off.

"Enough, enough, these are now warriors, not princely brothers. Back away, Princesses. Time is now, more than ever, of the essence. We must move to the boats and be off."

"Fortune upon you all," Princesses Lily and Tulip cried out in unison while they, fending off fear, watched as their brothers, the King, Morlog, Kasell, and Odemog, who led the group, walked to their place in the solid wooden boats.

Odemog and Fazzog took the lead boat with Morlog, Sam, and Dero aboard. Kasell and Mezzog took second, with the King joining them. Borzog led his own boat which paired along with Marsdell. Odemog observed as Lord Forthrumal glided forward quietly and took a seat in one of the last boats to fill. Odemog wondered if it had been the King or Morlog who had invoked the Healer's presence in the travel party. It was wise to have a gifted healer with them; he wished he had thought of this. Odemog could have no idea in what condition they would find Queen Madelina or Princess Annabella or, for that matter, what would befall those who put themselves in danger's way on this treacherous mission.

Arms men assisted in pushing their boats away from the shore where they held position and turned to watch the mordagha boat. Marsdell called out to them and the mordaghas; Tovar, Bazat, Nassir, Lisan, and Vadim were all seen to fly from the grasses where they now landed, one after another, in the broad-beamed ship. It had been held away from shore using ropes tied tight between the three escort boats and theirs. As each mordagha landed and took a position: forward, aft, port, starboard, and centre; the boat was balanced. They spoke words of encouragement to one another as this was a first experience for all.

"How novel, this contraption!" Tovar was first to land and took easily to the side-to-side movement of the boat.

"Whoa, a bit rough, I think," shouted Bazat as the boat took a long dip back when he took his position.

"Harrumph," said Nassir, who found no dignity in the way the boat seemed to want to tip him out on landing.

"Easy, easy," whispered Vadim who took his place graciously opposite Nassir and stood very still, awaiting Lisan's landing.

"Watch your back end there, my friend," Lisan joked to Tovar as he took the center of the boat and came in for a hard landing. So typical for Lisan to be reckless and show off.

The boat was silenced by Odemog who, standing at the stern of his boat, looked over the waters and called out to all, "Brave Warriors of Mazgamor, today is our day. Victory lies ahead. Songs and stories will be written and performed about this very day. Stand fast, heads, swords, and bows held high." Drawing his sword from its sheath he raised it above his head and shouted, "For Mazgamor!"

Those at oars slapped the flat face of the oar on the surface of the water. Those who were not at oars raised their swords and all voices echoed the Keeper's "FOR MAZGAMOR!" The sound of Odemog's voice rolled over the water like a wave followed by the wave of the hundred strong arms men in surrounding boats. The strength of the cry was uplifting and confident. The echo drifted through the mist across the water, eerie and foreboding. Upon the shore, the echo landed at the feet of Princesses Lily and Tulip who felt their skin tingle with anticipation.

Away from the shore, oars picked up and dipped back into the dark waters in unison as the group followed those who had left on horseback along the shore less than an hour before. The energy among the arms men was raw and ready, causing them to pull the boats through the water at a fast pace. In no time, those in the boats would see and pass the ten score riders along the shoreline. Soon they would slow to enable a change of rowers amongst the arms men of the various boats. By changing places at various points along the way, they would remain strong. Provisions were passed among the men to further sustain them. Forthrumal had ground roots through which the water had been strained when filling the skins. These various roots would give energy, while at the same time calming the arms men— energy to sustain and the calming effect to help them focus in battle. This would be a long day.

* * *

The path Kasreya took with a mixed force of Tsesiwan archers and Constantian arms men was a rocky one. Amara rode beside or behind her cousin changing places with the Constantian arms man known as Leo. As they travelled in silence, riders could hear rocks shifting and breaking away as they fell to the water below. At times, they rode dangerously high above the waters in single file. They tightened ranks to three and four astride when on lower elevations, nearly at sea level. Kasreya's united forces advanced with purpose and maintained a good relationship with those who travelled by boat.

Soon, they would lose sight of one another as those at sea turned south, away from the southern tip of Khordrya. Odemog would lead them further out to sea and deeper into the mists, where they would establish their attack formation.

"May I ask you something, Mistress Kasreya?" The young arms man who rode as her second spoke. Up till that moment, his shyness around Amara had kept him silent.

"Be wise with your questions."

"Tsesiwans are legendary archers in their offensive and defensive tactics." He looked uncomfortable as he prepared to pose his question. "But I see not a man among you. From where does your warrior strength come, if not from your men?" He glanced over at Amara as he spoke, his face tinged a pale berry color.

"You are bold to ask as you do, what name do you go by?"

"I am Leo, named for the lion's heart." He spoke strongly now. "I am told I cried more than my fair share and my father begged my mother to quiet my roar."

"Lion-heart, you have answered your own question." Kasreya smiled at the fortune of having a confident young man at her side, such as one must be to ask this question. "Leo, if you consider the patience required of a mother to gently quiet a boisterous child, more so an infant who lacks comprehension and only makes demands, you will understand that the strength of the Tsesiwan women, both defensively and offensively, comes from the wisdom of our patience. We rush nowhere and neither attack nor defend without cause. We live for peace, and this is the wisest way to thrive in life. Know, too, that there are few fools among us. We hope for but do not expect peace, for there will always be the likes of Thane-Ra and so we prepare well to attack and defend, should there be cause. Does this help you understand?"

"You tell me that your strength is in your wisdom and your wisdom is in your patience. I understand you to say that to bear and raise a child—one like me," he laughed as he put his gloved hand over his chest, "is the core from which your archers draw patience, which begets your skill and strength?"

"Precisely. To know this is to understand the defensive focus of a Tsesiwan archer, Leo."

Leo watched Kasreya as she spoke and stared at her as they rode forward. He observed her relaxed in her saddle, head steady and still, body subtly rocking forward, back, and side-to-side with the natural rhythm of her horse.

"But I have no children and I will fight from my heart to defend Constantia and Mazgamor. How can this be any less, Mistress?"

"Your dedication in battle is not in question, Leo. Neither is your skill in question." She smiled. "You asked me how it was that Tsesiwan Archers, all women, were as accurate and strong as we in fact are. The men of Siwa are equally wise, for they honour our skill. The trades mastered by our men are those that give us advantage to be who we are. They are foresters, who make the bows we use, blacksmiths who hone our arrows, swords, and other tools, even those of our kitchens. We honour our men for their strengths and skill as they honour us. Those of our women without children find the same passion in other devotions. It is innate. Our practices may be less familiar to you, but they are driven and focused to sustain our place as a people of peace. Does this answer now serve you?"

"In many ways. Perhaps I may visit Siwa when all is done?" Leo glanced shyly in Amara's direction. Kasreya observed his glance, feeling slightly amused by the young arms man.

"Those who bring peace are always welcome in Siwa, arms man." She dug her heels into the rib cage of her horse, encouraging her to pick up the pace a bit. With a long line of troops behind him, Leo followed.

Kasreya appreciated the opportunity to teach Leo about Siwa. She was wanting for home and speaking of her beloved Siwa took away some of her yearning. At the same time, it reinforced the importance of her mission. She thought of the many archers with her who had left young families at home. This was neither her nor Juliet's dilemma. She had only once been close to birthing a child but lost the baby during a fever before it could be welcomed into the world. She was told in life this sometimes happens and there is little explanation for it. As a result, Kasreya redirected her maternal instincts and looked upon Siwa as her offspring. Juliet's dedication was to her archers, whose hearts she held close as her own. Not all were mothers in the truest sense of having given birth but, in one way or another, they felt a natural passion, a passion similar to that which a mother naturally lives and breathes. It had been an interesting diversion, this conversation. She refocused her energy now on their journey.

In silence, they travelled on for another hour or more, from time to time catching glimpses of the boats. A light flashed from the water. Kasreya raised her arm to call a stop. Leo copied the gesture and so it went down the line as horses drew up close to those in front of them, coming to a full stop. Leo came directly to Kasreya's side and looked out over the water with her. She had ridden out onto a ragged outcropping of rocks, Leo watched as she counted the flashes of the lantern.

"It is a steady and clear signal, Leo." she continued to stare out at the water as if more would come but there was nothing but darkness. Kasreya gave a signal to Amara who reached in her saddle bag and took out a small bundle.

"Hold this," she passed it to Leo. "When it lights, toss it in the air." Amara clapped two small flints together and the sparks ignited the pouch. Forced more by the heat than the instructions, Leo threw it out and up over the cliff. He shook his gloved hand as a reactive gesture for he had not been burned. They had acknowledged the signal from the boats and prepared to move forward. "They have observed the southern tip. If Fazzog's maps are accurate, we could make our way down from here and we would come upon the point ourselves. Odemog and his crew will head further out to sea now. Send word down the line that we turn northward. Now."

"We do not go to the point?"

"We do not go to the point. We cut across land now to the other side of the point in a northward direction. There is nothing but open sea at the point, Leo. Send word."

"Right away, Mistress. We turn northward." Leo turned and rode toward another, still younger, arms man.

"Ride back four lengths. As you go, give word we journey north across the point. Command others to follow our lead. When you reach four lengths, hold there, and continue to give the word for the passing of ten more lengths and, at that point, rejoin the ranks. Have the word pass orally from there."

Leo asserted himself with a confidence observed and absorbed from Kasreya's leadership. Leo was coming into himself on this journey and he welcomed his newfound confidence with pride. Reins in his left hand, he pulled them about, turning himself and his horse back to follow Kasreya who rode with Amara close by. Leo set his hand upon the hilt of his sword and sat up taller in his saddle as he drew up beside Kasreya.

30

They were not long into the ride into the woods, heading inland, when a scout was stopped as he raced into the rear guard of Tsesiwan riders. This eager scout was brought forward and greeted Juliet with great enthusiasm. Clearly this was no soldier but an eager tradesman sent forth by Thorandal.

"My Queen," he called out to her, bowing deeply, taking his hat in hand and sweeping it across his chest.

"Enough then, man." Juliet couldn't help but burst out laughing. Others around her knew better than to laugh but a few snorts were heard to pass about the group. Juliet sent a strong look to those who rode close.

"There is no queen among us here. I am Juliet of Siwa. Who has sent you and what word do you bring?"

"They call me Swenson. I come here for Thorandal today. We are not far behind you if you are able to call a halt and wait for us. We've ridden long and hard to join you, My Lady. What word may I take back, if you please?" Swenson looked plaintive as he spoke out of breath.

"Swenson, you may rest with us. I shall send a rider back if you can give me an accurate bearing. We shall wait here."

"Perhaps I should ride along. My land bearings are not as good as my bearings at sea."

"We have journeyed this way and can double back with ease. I bid you go with Honoreya; she will make clear your instructions." Juliet gestured to Honoreya, whose horse stepped forward from the others. "Ride out with Swenson here, take word to Thorandal and his forces that we camp here in wait for them to join us."

As Honoreya and Swenson departed, the group set about removing saddles and watering their horses. Some sought water and rest for themselves for they knew well that this may be the last long rest they would take before battle would be upon them. And no sooner had they come to a comfortable place in their hearts and minds, than they were called from this restful state.

A rolling swell vibrated below their collective hooves and feet as Thorandal and his forces came upon them, emerging from the woods. If they had not heard them coming, they would have felt the rumble of the ground.

Juliet, in conversation at the shore of Mid Lake where she watered her horse, had stopped speaking long enough to fully take in the dramatic sight of Thorandal's arrival.

Were he a god of thunder, he could not have arrived more dramatically, she thought privately. With her eyes Juliet handed her horse over to her second, turning wordlessly to walk up and greet Thorandal. From where she stood, he held a commanding position. As she came within feet of him, he swung his leg over the neck of his horse and jumped unceremoniously to the ground. Juliet stepped back with a new appreciation for Thorandal. His presentation was thunderous, but he was a mite of a man, small in stature in every way, except for his belly and his beard. She understood now why she had never really noticed him at the Gatherings for he was small enough to easily miss. His voice redeemed him, yet again, in this comedic presentation for it, too, gave forth as rumbling thunder. Thorandal spoke with a force so powerful one would choose silence over argument.

"Greetings, Juliet. It has been too long since we have met."

"Welcome, Thorandal. You and your men and women are truly welcome in this journey. How was your ride?"

"Long, 'tis true," he twisted his beard, looking around. "But we are a hardy lot. A hardy lot." As he spoke, he turned to wave at the riders behind him who let out a cheer in return, causing Juliet to shake her head.

A hardy lot, indeed. What a ragtag bunch! She kept her thoughts to herself, smiling all the while as they dismounted and took up care for their horses.

"Thorandal, we have enough time for a good rest for your riders. I can brief you on the Keeper's plans."

"Word came there is a new Keeper. Hurrah then. And what say he?"

"Keeper Odemog…"

"Odemog? What? The giant farmer from Sweetbrooke Wren?" Juliet nodded, confirming his query. "Well, I'll be a trader's hammock. This should be good. A giant such as he could take down an entire force, I should imagine."

"Well, that could be so but I do not consider him to be so inclined. How long have you been out to sea, Thorandal?"

"I should say better than five full moons. We left the Gathering and have not returned until now."

"I suspect there is much to brief you on. I will fill in the blanks. But first, let us refresh." She raised her arm and a young archer came forward with water and clean cloths for them to wash away the dirt from their journey. Another brought drinks and fruit forward. There were no words exchanged as they washed away their fatigue.

Later, Juliet and Thorandal went together to a large waiting tent, where she briefed him on recent happenings, including the tragic loss of Piralius over which he briefly wept before regaining his composure. She then went on to elaborate, as instructed by Keeper Odemog, on what was yet to come.

The waiting tent, one where comforts and strategies were both attended to, sat in the central part of their lakeside camp. The camp had been struck quickly once Juliet made the decision to wait for Thorandal and his forces. With the arrival of the trader forces it was further enhanced for, far from being soldiers of any kind, they carried with them a wealth of goods to make this camp one of plenty for the night. The two forces mixed well together as they put on a feast suitable for the occasion, knowing that one should always enter a battle well rested, well nourished, and well prepared in knowledge of the other side. Together, Juliet and Thorandal would spend the evening sharing what each knew of the plans and events that had brought them to this point. This would add to their strength in the days that would follow.

31

Walcod leaned against the pillar as he stood behind Morzan. He had long established Morzan's postures and movements and knew when he should pay more attention to his own presentation. He was loyal to Morzan for he valued his life. The benefits of his place at Morzan's side made his deeper loyalty that much more valuable. At this moment, he watched with a sense of gratitude as Morzan discreetly chewed at his fingernails.

Sitting alone at the table, Morzan waited for Thane-Ra to join him. While he waited, Morzan pored over a map of the Kingdom of Mazgamor. He compared the various villages for size and benefits when he would rule outlying lands on behalf of Thane-Ra. In the back of his mind, he mulled over Thane-Ra's reaction to his failure to implement part of the plan. *Perhaps I should have wakened him,* Morzan considered. What was done was done and he would now face the consequences. A delay of this nature would not weaken Khordrya, only delay settlement of Thane-Ra as the new ruler. Although Morzan was impatient, he could live with this. But could Thane-Ra?

Walcod stood erect and set his back to the pillar, eyes cast down as footsteps approached. Morzan stood and turned to see a long dark red cape billowing behind the frame that approached rapidly.

"Morzan!" What is this I hear of imprisoned messengers?" Thane-Ra's voice boomed louder than Morzan had witnessed before.

"Sire, I had hoped to inform you my—"

"Do you think me a fool? Nothing is withheld from me." Thane-Ra lifted his robe around him to take his seat at the table. Without the benefit of the touch of a hand, the chair curiously repositioned itself behind him as he moved to sit down. Thane-Ra had been studying the dark arts and mind control for some time. He had mastered the art of telekinesis out of boredom. It was strongest when he felt a rage brewing inside.

"Of course not, Thane-Ra. I intended not to keep this from you but to let you rest for the matter has passed. Nothing could be done." Morzan angled for Thane-Ra's approval. "The sniveling waste has been dealt with and will receive his punishment for failure. With your approval, a new messenger will be sent. The failure was travelling north. In the north, we have already defeated Piralius of Aureopiscis. The Siwa women have been distracted by horgles and mounted raiders. Chaos is already rampant in the north. Our attacks in the south will commence in just hours as that messenger, we know, is away."

"The southern message has been delivered?"

"It will be delivered in due course this morning. We wait for word on these attacks at the height of the sun."

"Do not fail me Morzan, you do not wish to know my wrath." As he spoke, Thane-Ra, using his mind as a third hand, lifted a jug and poured pomegranate juice into a carafe. Morzan watched and, thinking of the range of possibilities for Thane-Ra's telekinetic powers, cleared his throat before he again spoke.

"Sire, from here our raiders prepare to assemble and move out to relieve and reinforce fighting raiders currently in field. All is in order and now we wait."

"The Queen then, has she arrived from the prison?"

Morzan froze inside as he realized his grave omission. He looked to Walcod, who nodded and strode quickly away to attend to this detail.

"She will arrive." He considered the timing of her arrival from that moment.

"Bring her to the Great Hall." Thane-Ra spoke abruptly and turned his focus to the breakfast laid out before him. Morzan took this as the message of dismissal that it was and removed himself from the table.

* * *

Once out of sight and hearing distance of Thane-Ra, Morzan hurried to find Walcod. To bring this task about quickly Walcod would have had to send a message by air. Morzan raced to the stables below to find Walcod looking skyward.

"A rider is away, Morzan, as you indicated," Walcod pointed to a horgle outbound from the stable. Morzan looked up and then scanned the stables. He ran to the corner by a gate and picked up a bow. Raising it in the air, Morzan aimed and fired one arrow. A brief second passed; the rider fell away and the horgle flew a circle of panic before continuing on to the Island knowing not to turn back to the stable.

"Master!" cried Walcod, in utter disbelief.

"Ready me a horgle." Morzan dropped the bow and walked away. "I shall bring her myself." He sat on a bale of hay and stared out the arch of the stable gateway.

"Yes, Sire," Walcod replied shaking his head as he thought all sense was now lost. He had never seen Morzan ride a horgle before in his life, but he was just an aide, what did he know about Morzan's skills.

32

The boats continued to cut through the water and the mists that danced over them. Odemog took a seat at the bow of his lead boat. It was here that he temporarily escaped the tension building around him. He leaned forward with a hand cradling the nose of the bow as if to steady himself. Odemog sat still, rising and falling with the hull moving over the blackness that passed below. He looked deep into the water considering what, in darkness, lay ahead and, illuminated in memory, lay behind. Odemog chose to direct his energy inward. He meditated on the commitment of those around him and how readily they had accepted him as their Keeper. *Keeper Odemog.* It still sounded foreign to him, but he had no reason today to question this honour. He straightened himself in the boat as he considered again his responsibility.

Perhaps the tension is a reflection of my own, he asked himself. Looking about the boat, he smiled at the arms men whom he realized had been watching him all along.

"I am proud to serve with you all" Odemog thought words would please them but they just smiled and nodded. Morlog, sitting close by, conveyed his thoughts with nod and smile. 'Relax' was what Odemog read into the gesture. And relax he did, for it soon dawned upon him that it was not his words the arms men were looking to, but his actions. Today, he would have to prove himself beyond his size and his role as Keeper. He would lead today. He was no more a simple farmer chasing rabboo, but a man who held the lives of many in his hands. He brought his hands together now and squeezed them feeling his own flesh and strength awakening him further to the challenge he would soon face. A song would help at home but not here, not now, not in this moment. Only forward movement. Do not look back, only ahead, to the glory that will follow their confident success. And so, Odemog reached over to Morlog and returned the gesture grasping his shoulder and nodding his understanding to his mentor and Protector.

A few moments passed before Odemog felt his dagger move. Thinking it had come loose, he reached down without looking, to tighten the leather straps. He jumped ever so slightly as he found he grasped not his dagger, but a small furry bundle.

"Oh no—that had better not be—Skeeter, what are you doing here?" he whispered loudly. "I forbade you to—"

"What is it, Odemog?" asked Morlog, leaning forward.

Pinching Skeeter's fur and skin between his shoulders, Odemog lifted the squirrel into the air, revealing the stowaway.

"What's done is done," Morlog motioned, his hands rubbing one over the other.

"I should more than wash my hands of you, squirrel. I should pitch you overboard. You are as good as dead now. How did you manage to stow away?"

"I rode the back of Morlog's cape and it was a rough ride. I got my tail wet as he climbed in." Skeeter worked at fluffing his tail to show how he had suffered.

"What did you hope to gain by this distraction?"

"I am one of your protectors, Odemog, or did you miss that?"

"Skeeter the Great—I know, but now you will hear me, and hear me from this moment forward, squirrel. YOU are at great risk in this place, and I make no promises." In truth, Odemog was terrified that the little stowaway was making a one-way trip and feared for his ability to protect him, while leading the others.

"I cannot make you stay in the boats while we fight for I know not what will become of them." Odemog tugged at the hemp pouch concealed beneath his chainmail. "Climb in here. And, no matter what happens. Do not let me see the blacks of your eyes until we return to Constantia. Do you understand me?"

"Yes, and I think we shall all be the better for my presence. I shall offer you a spare—yet hidden—set of eyes as your protector. You will not regret this, Moggie. No, you will surely not!" Proud of himself, entirely too proud, Skeeter squirmed from Odemog's grasp and climbed into the pouch where he was, in no gentle manner, tucked away for the remainder of the journey.

If there was one thing the stowaway accomplished, whether he knew it or not, was that he had protected Odemog already. This simple distraction erased Odemog's angst and returned his full focus to pursuing that which lay ahead.

33

The boats drifted in quietly, one after another, landing along the shore of Pierce Island. There was a distance between each landing as the shore was intermittently rocky. This proved to be in their favour, for it prevented them landing all bunched together where they could easily fall victim to a prison defense from above. Two boats were left at the shore where they could be best hidden. Two additional boats sat offshore, tethered to the one that safely held the mordaghas. Arms men crept up to complete their formations. The other boats rowed away to hold and prepare to bring back Kasreya's archers and their arms men, if needed. A rapid burst of five short horn blasts would invite this return. One long blast and two short would signal both success and safety.

Along the coast, within striking distance, Kasreya, her archers, and the Constantian arms men lay in wait of a signal to barrage the prison with arrows.

Pierce was a barren island. There was no wildlife and the few plants were weeds grown from seeds blown in by the wind. If there were a beauty assigned it, it would be the unique rock formations carved moons ago by the tides and volcanic eruptions. A dark stone covered much of the island with a foundation of sea crags that had erupted from the ocean floor once upon a time. The stones differed, ranging from blade sharp edges in some spots, where one would maneuver with caution, to luxuriously smooth formations that welcome passage. Smoother boulders lined the shore and immense stones provided shelter for the men to move freely. A collection of giant boulders formed a semi-circle at just the right position to allow them to make their camp, while other large sentry stones formed a perimeter nearer the gates of the prison.

Odemog, followed by his forces, raced up to the large perimeter stones that surrounded the prison structure and tower. The tower hovered over the water on the opposite side of the prison. He signaled to Borzog who, with his troop, Sam and Marsdell, raced around the other side of the stones to make their way to the gate. Once they had control of the gate, they held the greatest advantage over an unsuspecting host.

Magnus and Fazzog, along with Morlog and Forthrumal, watched from behind a crescent of stones where Kasell commanded the movements. Moving up slowly were Dero and Mezzog, who would storm the gate behind Odemog on the second horn call, once the passage was cleared. Having now lost cover of darkness, it was no surprise that, just as Borzog's group was about to move in, someone called out from above.

"What ho!" shouted the voice that caused all to stop in their tracks. But there was no weaponry engaged; it appeared they had not been seen. Instead of firing on the advancing troop formations below, guards drew attention above to a horgle that flew in over the prison. It was the second one in a brief space of time. The first had been without a rider and flew frantic circles before disappearing. This one carried none other than Morzan, himself.

"It is the Prison Master, Morzan," a second voice called.

"FOOLS—BELOW YOU!" Morzan pointed as he flew recklessly into the prison courtyard, tossed, as the horgle landed, into a pile of straw. Guards inside the courtyard ran to him from all directions. Accustomed to his yelling, the prison guards did not hear his words as an alarm.

For Odemog and his men, there was a brief lapse of time that allowed the forces to take aggressive advantage. Borzog signaled his immediate advance. Mezzog and Dero moved forward as they watched Borzog's arms men forcibly impair the gate mechanism, causing it to drop by jamming a post through the gap in the wall from which the ropes emanated. This caused the lock to unhinge and break away. The gate dropped.

Odemog roared, "For Mazgamor!" and all with him stormed forward into the prison.

In the moments after their distraction, the prison guards took to formation faster than Odemog anticipated. Boredom on Pierce Island meant many drills pitting guards against each other. Thus, they had literally fought for their lives many times before, purely for Morzan's entertainment and pleasure. They were ready.

On landing, Morzan had raced up the side staircase and stood briefly behind a pillar to witness this unspeakable trespass. He would protect his greatest treasure in the prison if it meant his life. He raced the open stairs up yet another level to reach the entrance to the tower. Odemog witnessed this and followed.

A cadre of nasty fighters swinging spiked balls on chains stood waving them. Odemog reached to his side and picked up a bench. He lifted it to shoulder height and began a little bit of footwork to spur them on, causing the three to reposition with their backs to the stairs from which he had come. Drawing the bench back over his shoulder, Odemog swung it like a bat. One, two, three, he knocked the swinging spiked balls which in turn flew away through the air carrying their wielders. They tumbled down the stairs, weapons and guards still connected, colliding with several more guards who were racing up the stairs. Odemog threw the bench down the stairs to dissuade others considering making chase and turned to follow Morzan up into the tower.

Ahead of him now came a flurry of swordsmen running and jumping down two and three steps at a time towards him. One by one, as they came close, he engaged them with his sword. One by one, he eliminated his opponents. If fairness were considered important to battle, there was none here. Odemog's size and strength outfought all who came towards him. There was no chance for them.

Below, a single short blast from a horn sounded. Odemog glanced around as he continued his climb and observed himself to be in safe cover.

Across the way, the signal had been heard and the Tsesiwan archers with Kasreya raised their bows and fired high into the air.

The King and Morlog, still waiting outside the prison for the first wave of fighters to complete their attack, watched with shields raised to fend off any stray projectiles as the arrows flew high above the channel and came to meet their victims, the Khordrian guards of Pierce Prison. Guards who had made their way out to search the perimeter and further defend their stations fell to the ground as the arrows struck like raindrops from a sudden summer storm, fast and hard. First wave accomplished. A double horn blast sounded.

Mezzog witnessed Odemog's single-handed fight and decided to follow him into the unknown, because it was just that—unknown. As he clambered around and over fallen guards, Mezzog signaled to Borzog who acknowledged his departure and kept an eye out for any who would follow. Borzog reached for his dagger and threw one quick blade into the back of a guard, whose attempt at stealth was quickly foiled. Satisfied, Borzog returned his attention to matters immediately at hand as one of his own arms men dropped from a balcony above at his feet.

"Not acceptable," he muttered to himself. Reaching for the bow of a fallen guard, Borzog grabbed a handful of arrows from the man's quiver and pressed himself up against a wide pillar. He peered around quickly, sighted his target, repositioned, placed an arrow in the bow, and in one smooth motion swung out from the pillar and fired the arrow into the heart of the one who had slain his man. "One down," he asserted and ran to a better location from which to fire his arrows. Jumping and stepping over bodies and around battle debris, Borzog grabbed arrows as he could and found an elevated corner niche from which it was ideal to fire. Borzog's assault began again and, one by one, they fell. He continued for some time until a body fell upon him.

"Sorry about that, chum," said a voice as Borzog struggled to get it off him. "Let me help you there, Prince." Sam jumped down beside him and gave the body a tug at the waist. It rolled off and landed between them. "Just a minute," Sam rolled it again making space beside Borzog and hopped over to look up and face Borzog, noses almost touching. "Seems he was a bit upset about you stopping his friends." With that statement, Sam turned back, pulled his dagger from the man's back and reached under to remove a dagger from the man's belly. Destined for Borzog, the assailant's dagger had turned in upon himself as he fell from Sam's dagger strike.

"My gratitude, Samezog," Borzog seemed none too shaken by these events and returned his focus to his present task. "Where are we at, then?" he asked, trying to regain full focus.

"Call me Sam. Second horn was called as he landed on you, I believe," Sam chuckled.

They looked to the gate, confirming the activity. A fresh storm of arms men came storming through the gates as they looked out. Led by Marsdell and Dero, the arms men came in as the wind in an arrow shaped formation, protecting Fazzog and Morlog in the center. As they fanned out, continuing their offensive, Fazzog and Morlog instructed injured arms men and those who were fatiguing, to fall back with them for care. Arms men assisted their fallen comrades and fought their way out to a safe camp, where Lord Forthrumal addressed their needs.

The King, with Kasell, greeted his men with honour and respect for their efforts and encouraged their healing. All the while, inside, the battle raged on. Kasell stepped away to monitor the progress and prepared to summon the call of third horn.

34

The higher Odemog climbed, the darker the tower became. Fewer and fewer window slots were cut away. Not a single torch was lit, and he dared not use a torch to draw attention to himself. The darkness slowed his pace. He finally hesitated and reached down inside his mail to the pouch.

"Skeeter," he spoke softly, cautious of who might be lurking. "I need your night eyes. The darkness has become my enemy. Help me find my way."

"Moggie," Skeeter's voice was raspy. "Thank goodness, it was getting hard to breathe in there. You sweat a lot in battle, did you know that?"

"Oh, for goodness' sake, just do as I ask." Odemog took the squirrel and placed him on his shoulder. "Now, please, hold fast and, if you need to, climb inside." He pulled the chainmail hood away from his ear and flattened his braid to make room should Skeeter need a place to hide and hold fast if they were found.

Immediately, they heard footsteps creeping up from behind. Odemog pressed himself against the wall, which did nothing to conceal him, considering his size. He breathed slowly from his mouth and waited for Skeeter to whisper what he saw.

"Mezzog!" Skeeter called, in no semblance of a whisper at all. Odemog reached up and gave Skeeter a smart but gentle *swack* with the tips of his fingers. "Hey, what was that for?" Skeeter asked in whisper-like tones.

"Keep your voice down," said Odemog. "Mezzog, where are you?"

"Coming, Keeper. I'm right behind you."

"Alright, Skeeter will be our eyes now. Be cautious with your steps. Let's go."

Mezzog placed his hand on Odemog's back to follow closely as he marked his footing. The three climbed up with Skeeter as their guide, counting steps as they approached a landing he could see.

"Not far now, eight, seven, six more steps. Can you see a faint light ahead?" Skeeter whispered.

"Ah, yes, do you see it, Mezzog?"

"I do now. What is the plan?"

The tower landing was surprisingly large. Where Odemog had expected to find a single cell or two, there were many lining the perimeter of the tower. He glanced around as he got his bearings.

"Morzan is here somewhere. I say we split up and find him."

"Fine with me. You go ahead to the right and I will start here and move left. We'll meet in the middle."

With Skeeter still in position, Odemog crept ahead. The lights began to increase and he found an open door. Cautiously, Odemog peered in. His height again gave advantage as no one expects eyes to peer around from the top of an archway and here, especially, he had to duck to avoid crashing into keystones. The room was empty; on to the next. And so it went until he came full circle and met back at the last door with Mezzog who, to Odemog's surprise, was not alone.

"Storsumal—what are you doing here?" cried Odemog.

"Too long have I been here, lad. I thought a gift of horgles would bring peace for me but it only brought greed and they wanted more. Before long they were not just back for horgles, but for me. I cannot say the moons. I have tried to count but it has been many." The elderly Healer leaned heavily on Mezzog, who was still dumbstruck by his discovery.

"We shall take you to safety. Can you sustain yourself a while longer, Healer Storsumal?"

"I shall do my best; it is all I have left to give."

Odemog nodded and held his hand up to silence them. Their voices had triggered a sound. He listened and heard again more urgently this time: *tap tap tap – tap tap tap.*

"Have you checked this chamber yet, Mezzog?" Mezzog looked at Storsumal and back at Odemog.

"Well, I've been rather busy," he replied.

"Wait here," Odemog commanded.

As Odemog walked to the chamber door, Mezzog moved closer to the wall for Storsumal to lean into it. There was no window at this chamber entrance. He looked down and took Skeeter from his shoulder.

"There's a good friend, make your stowage useful. Stick your head under the door and tell me what you see." No sooner had Skeeter stuck his head under the door, than his whole body disappeared. Odemog, startled to see the whole tail gone in the blink of an eye, waited a moment, then another, and bent over, himself, to peer under the door. There was no sound coming from the other side and he saw nothing. *If that darn squirrel found gabelnuts, I will—* He shook his head to clear his thoughts. The door must go; he tried the latch—nothing. Odemog stood up and backed away from the door, preparing to put his shoulder fully into it. He took two full steps forward and leaned into it, full force. The next thing he knew, he was on the other side of the door, flat on his face. Odemog pushed himself up from the ground using both hands and shook his head as he rose. He snapped up and drew his sword all in one quick motion.

Odemog stood there blinking. Standing before him with her hand on the latch holding the door open was the Princess Annabella. For a moment he was dumbstruck, then he bowed fully as he sheathed his sword.

"I found her tied up with a cloth in her mouth," Skeeter rattled the words quickly. "I chewed through the ropes that bound her hands and she did the rest, honest, Moggie."

"Oh my goodness, thank you," the Princess said.

Mezzog heard his sister's voice and came reeling around the corner, half-carrying Storsumal. Odemog relieved him of his burden to watch the reunion of the brother and sister.

"Annabella, sing praises—you are safe!" Mezzog took hold of his sister and held her tightly. Only two years separated the Princess from her triplet brothers, six from her twin sisters. The joyful reunion was brief as more pressing matters were clearly at hand.

"This is the Keeper Odemog, Sister. He is leading this mission."

"We have a new Keeper?"

"It is my great honour to meet you, Princess. But we must keep moving. We do not know what lies ahead. Are you well to travel?"

"I am quite well, thank you. We must find the Queen."

"Where is Mother?" Mezzog demanded with great emotion.

"Calm yourself, Prince," Odemog spoke to Mezzog, looking him directly in the eyes with hand on his shoulder. "We have done well thus far."

"But what of our mother, the Queen?" she asked.

"In which cell is she held?"

"That's just it. Up until minutes before your arrival, she was with me. That wicked man…"

"Morzan?"

"Yes, Morzan came in screaming and bound me roughly. He bound Mother's hands and tied a rope to her waist, then dragged her away. I don't know where he has taken her."

"He must be trying to get away from Pierce," said Mezzog. "How could he do this? We saw him fly in by horgle but a horgle cannot ride two away."

"But they can, now," came a weak voice from the corner. All turned to listen to Storsumal, whom Odemog had taken to sit on a broken chair.

"Speak, Healer, how can they now carry two?" demanded Odemog.

"It was a breeding program, experimental you see, that Thane-Ra insisted I produce for him. He wanted his raiders to move from horseback to horgle with the ability to carry supplies or double mount to bring about stronger armed invasions. But it has not gone well. It has not gone well at all." His voice began to fade as the sorrow of his work welled up within him.

"Where are these horgles kept?" Odemog looked away from Storsumal and stared inquisitively at Princess Annabella.

"I have never seen them, but I know the path to the torture cells, and I can tell you that there have been some very gamey smells encountered along the way. Follow me!" She beckoned to them to follow her and ran from the cell.

Odemog picked up Storsumal and carried him on his back. Skeeter ran up the front of Mezzog's chainmail and took his place, for the first time, beside the ear of another. Nervous at travelling with an unknown, he longed to be with Odemog but now there was no room. So, with tail twitching in front of Mezzog's nose out of sheer nervousness, Skeeter travelled behind Odemog. Mezzog, on the other hand, found it difficult to see and to concentrate with a flicking length of grey fur flailing frantically in front of his face.

Annabella led the way down a narrow, nearly hidden, set of limestone stairs that Odemog and Mezzog had both missed coming up. The tower was bigger than they had realised. Odemog wondered how this would impact the release of prisoners. After a minute of careful stepping, they followed Annabella off on a new level and down even more steps. Soon they came into a modestly lit chamber. It seemed a chamber of horrors.

All around the chamber lay horgles in various stages of ill-health and needing attention. Odemog set Storsumal down and heard him crying softly to himself.

"What can you tell us here, Healer?" Odemog was firm but gentle as time was not on their side.

Annabella walked to a large stable door, observing it ajar, she called to Odemog.

"Here. He must have left from here!" She pushed the doors open and the light poured in. They all shielded their eyes and looked out to a simple plaza from which anyone could take off or land.

"There is an empty stall here," Mezzog called from the side. "And—oh no—Mother's shoe!"

"Can you see anything Annabella? Look skyward, Princess." As Odemog spoke, the chamber began to flood with guards.

"Mezzog, take the right flank. Annabella, help the Healer to a safe place."

Annabella raced back inside and helped Storsumal to his feet. She walked and dragged him to the empty stall from which Mezzog emerged. Skeeter jumped off Mezzog and ran to Odemog where he climbed to Moggie's waist and hung on.

The fight ensued with a vengeance as the guards believed they would quickly take down the duo. Their assumption was both bold and incorrect. The fighting was arduous and long but, one by one, Odemog or Mezzog vanquished an opponent. Skeeter made note of one guard's moves and watched him closely. Odemog raised his sword again and again, standing beside or back-to-back with Mezzog as they circled the room, swords clanging and bashing against the swords of the guards. The numbers were down to just two opponents and Odemog's battle moved gradually out on to the plaza. Mezzog stayed inside, close by his sister and the Healer, to ensure their protection.

Odemog's final opponent fell to the ground, and he raised his sword to finish him. Just as he placed the last blow, he heard a cry behind him. A guard stood, eyes popping and voice trailing in a surprised scream. The guard dropped his sword and fell to his knees. Odemog swung his sword and completed the task

Looking down, Odemog could not believe what he saw. Just as he had promised, Skeeter had confirmed his place as a Protector of the Keeper.

Standing just a short distance from the calf of the fallen guard was Skeeter, looking astonished. He had been watching this wounded guard move about, attempting to rearm and reposition to strike. When opportunity presented, Skeeter unstrapped Odemog's dagger from his leg and waited. Once the guard was too close for Skeeter's comfort, he leapt onto the man's tunic and swung the dagger down into the man's lower leg.

"Skeeter—I could have struck you with my sword! What were you thinking?" Odemog growled at him.

"And you, Odemog, you knew he was readying to strike? You were prepared?"

"By all that is tiny, Skeeter, you just saved my life!"

35

Amara observed the figures flying out and away from the prison. She saw it was not a mordagha that had taken flight and raised her bow to fire. Kasreya brought her arm up to stop her. She sensed something familiar about a shape riding the beast.

"Let them go. We know where they are headed." Kasreya made her statement without emotion and returned her focus to the matters at hand.

* * *

Morzan looked behind him to see the last of his guards fall at battle with Odemog as he flew away from Pierce Island. Secured to his waist was Queen Madelina, now unconscious, who had fought valiantly to break away from Morzan before he struck her and placed her on the horgle's back. He turned his attention forward and prepared to alert Thane-Ra of the attack on Pierce Island.

No sooner had he landed, than he was greeted by Walcod. Seeing Morzan's disheveled state, Walcod prepared for the worst. He first reached up and took the Queen from Morzan in his arms and laid her down on a pile of straw.

"Clean her up, wake her, and make her presentable to Thane-Ra." Morzan did not look at Walcod as he stormed away.

Morzan stopped long enough to make himself presentable. He quickly washed and changed his robes. Standing at his mirror, he took a moment to catch his breath. There was little time for the latter. He must bring a solid story to Thane-Ra; things were not going as planned. Morzan exited the chamber and walked quickly to the Great Hall.

"Thane-Ra, greetings."

"Where is she? Why do you make me wait?" thundered the man seated at the throne in the far end of the Hall.

"She shall be here presently. I have urgent news and it is not good."

"Speak."

"I do not know why or how; I can't explain it…"

"Confound it man, SPEAK!" roared Thane-Ra.

"Pierce Island—it has been attacked." Morzan gave in to the truth and spoke it simply, now waiting for what would come next. For all the wickedness and power he had wielded to now, he could not know what would come next.

"FOOL. You fake. Your mouth unleashes promises of defense and attack that cannot be kept, and your guards cannot even protect a rocky island? Tell me truthfully that the Queen Madelina is here in Khordom Palace?" His thoughts returned to himself and his plans.

"Oh Sire, she is here and will be in this room presently, I do assure you." Morzan, for the first time, was intimidated.

"SILENCE!" Thane-Ra raised his arm, palm up, pushing it forward. With not a soul standing at arm's reach, Morzan was flung back several feet before falling to the ground. "Send for General Pervan. If they attack the Island, they must also be coming here. Gather border patrol reports. Get moving—now!" Thane-Ra spoke to no one particular soldier, but all scattered like bugs at the fire of a torch.

As word was sent out to gather border reports, Pervan entered the chamber.

"How may I serve you?" offered General Pervan.

"Gather intelligence from your border patrols and put your raiders at the ready. It seems we may soon be under attack," Thane-Ra sneered these last words with a tone of vengefulness mixed with glee. Pervan nodded and withdrew.

"We shall see whose strength prevails at battle. Off with you and bring me the Queen." Thane-Ra dismissed Morzan with a wave. Morzan rushed to meet Walcod and fetch the prize.

36

Odemog led the way back through the prison. Skeeter sat proudly on Odemog's shoulder, now that he was officially a hero. Aware that danger may appear from around any corner, they were attentive as they travelled through the corridors and stairwells. Soon, they were in the open courtyard, where now silence enveloped what remnants of battle remained. As they crossed the courtyard rushing to the gate, a great sound emanated from the archways. Mezzog and Odemog resumed defensive postures on either side of Storsumal who still struggled to walk. Annabella took up position with them as she had picked up an abandoned sword. The three raised their swords at the same gradual rate at which the noise increased.

Suddenly, a swell of men and women emerged from the darkness of the archways. Some were armed. Most were not. As they emerged into the brightness of day, the noise reduced to an awestruck chatter. Here were the prisoners of Thane-Ra, at the mercy of Morzan, released to live again. They gathered, shielding their eyes, adjusting to the light of freedom.

Realizing who it was that they faced, Odemog, Mezzog, and Annabella relaxed. Storsumal managed a weak smile and slipped to the ground, exhausted.

"You there, and you," Odemog beckoned to two of the arms men. "Take this man directly to Lord Forthrumal's care."

"Yes, Keeper,"

Behind and among the throng of prisoners—and there were over a hundred— came the arms men of Magnus. Satisfied with their accomplishment, they took a moment to let out a cheer and the final horn was sounded.

Across the shore, Kasreya looked to Amara and Leo and said: "The job is done. We move on to Khordom Palace." She raised her arm and signaled a forward movement. The archers and arms men together moved out to their next calling.

* * *

Arms men gathered surrendering and injured guards and guided them to the west side of the prison, while the freed prisoners were directed to the east side so their care could be attended to first. Odemog left the prison walls with his charges by his side and went directly to the makeshift camp from where the attack had been overseen. Unobserved thus far, only this foursome and a little four-legged hero knew what joy they would soon impart to the others.

Magnus greeted his warriors and friends one at a time as the leaders returned, having designated senior arms men to secure the guards and attend to the free men and women. In the midst of a great hug with his son, Borzog, Magnus looked out and stopped in amazement.

"By all that is beautiful," he cried. And he did just that—tears filled his eyes as he released his son and guided him to see what he saw. "My joy continues to magnify. What have you done, Odemog?!" As he spoke, his body frozen in place, Annabella ran into his arms nearly knocking him down. A cheer erupted in the camp.

"Annabella," Fazzog and Borzog shouted in unison. They took turns hugging her. Mezzog joined in the reunion as he reached the group.

"My dear brothers, thank you for coming for me. I knew you would; it was just a matter of time."

"Of course you knew," laughed Fazzog. "Ever the optimist!" The others laughed with him.

Odemog watched the King as he observed his children. He knew what Magnus was thinking. Quietly, the Keeper took position at the side of the King. He leaned down and spoke softly to him. Kasell, ever present, stepped forward on Odemog's signal and listened.

"King Magnus, as you see your daughter is safe. We were moments too late to rescue with her the Queen." Magnus looked desolate.

"Do not be discouraged. She is alive and as we know it, she is well. Morzan escaped with her, and I am confident he has taken her hostage to Khordom Palace. It is the only refuge that remains for him."

"We must act immediately," Magnus said.

"We are acting, my Liege," Kasell reminded him. "The last horn signaled Kasreya to turn north to the Palace. The others will flank Khordom Palace and lay siege upon Thane-Ra. We will take this victory with us, adding to our strength."

"Kasell is right, Magnus." Morlog stepped into view. He had been assisting Forthrumal and, on seeing Odemog and Annabella emerge, stepped away. "We must finish here and make our way forward to join them."

"I shall see him burn should he bring harm to Madelina."

All stood in silence to hear such a vengeful pledge from the compassionate King.

"Magnus, you have been strong this long. Keep your faith. We are all at your side," Odemog reassured the King. "Go be with your Princess daughter. Enjoy her beauty, grace, and optimism. She has maintained a strength that can buoy an army. Go now."

Odemog turned to Kasell, who now was joined by the remaining leadership of the attack. Together stood the victors: Marsdell, Sam, Dero, Mezzog, Borzog, and Odemog.

"We must move quickly," Odemog looked to each of the men and began to guide the next phase of their movement. "Dero, I would ask you to fly now, taking the Princess Annabella on Vadim back to Constantia. From there, if you wish, you may rejoin us at Khordom Palace, though I would prefer you to remain and help lead the defense of Constantia. I would think that, while Thane-Ra is defending his palace, he is still enough of a snake that he will have some raiders slither out to wreak havoc on others, and Constantia Glen is the most convenient and the most obvious."

"Keeper, I accept this, but I must be honest and tell you I wish to go with you."

"You are a good man, Dero. This is the plan," Odemog smiled and continued. "For now, Brother, take leave and instruct the arms men to place the guards under arrest and secure them in cells below. Kasell, once all is done at Khordom, you may dispatch men back to see to them suitably." Kasell nodded. Odemog continued, "The boats moored off Kasreya's location will have turned back on hearing the last horn. Marsdell, take command and direct arms men and the freed ones to the shore, where they will take up their places in the boats. I will see to it that the free ones are given the choice to join with us in a moment." Odemog looked around and considered the plan again. "That will be all— to your assignments. And success to each of you."

As each went about their task, Odemog returned to the King's side with Dero. The Royal Family was at the spot where Storsumal rested, having been carefully attended to by Lord Forthrumal.

"Princess Annabella," Odemog addressed her formally. "This good and trustworthy man, Deronezog, will take you safely home now, to be cared for and protected."

"I shall not go home, but with you, to find my mother," Annabella asserted herself strongly.

"My beautiful daughter," the King's voice sounded pained as he responded. "Enough is enough, you cannot take such risk. You will obey and return presently. More than a hundredfold are closing in on the palace to bring about the safe return of your mother."

"But they do not know she is there. You cannot know what may or may not happen. Here we have been in this dank and dangerous prison infested with evil and madness. You go to a palace infested with more evil and madness. It is not unfamiliar to me. I will not be sent away to dresses and perfume when you know I can handle a sword just as the best of my brothers."

"Father, she is right," stated Fazzog.

"She may hold a sword better than you, Brother, but certainly not me," argued Borzog.

"Enough, all of you. You force my decision. As Keeper, it is my wish that you return home. But your argument is solid, and I give you leave to join us. King Magnus, to appease your concern, Dero, here, will not leave her side. A further two arms men will be posted to you, Princess Annabella, and you shall NOT leave their sight. Are you all in agreement?" The sternness of Odemog's voice and the clarity of his command stifled even a King, and all responded affirmatively.

"Yes, Keeper."

"Good. Get yourselves together and to the boats. I have one last thing to do." Odemog walked away from the group and re-entered the prison gate. He observed the guards being led away and nodded silently his approval of the progress. To his right, he observed the newly free being tended to. Odemog went to this group and stood tall as he began to speak.

"Good people, I am the Keeper Odemog. I am sorry for your time spent within the painful grasp of these walls and chains. I wish you health and happiness in your new freedom. Today, we move forward to defeat Thane-Ra." A cheer went up from the group. Odemog raised his hand to quiet them, "I bid you, those of you who are able, join with us. Help to make our numbers strong. We are a strong force, yet face too many unknowns in this quest. We can arm you from the fallen weapons of today's battle." Odemog gestured to the armaments that lay about from the surrendered guards. "I can guarantee your freedom and promise you assistance to regain your lives when we are victorious this day. Will you be one with us, then?"

One by one, as the reality of freedom and retribution dawned on the faces of these previously lost souls, they stood and spoke.

"Keeper, you have my pledge," stated one of the released souls.

"I will join. I am not strong," the man raised a twisted limb, "but I wish to be a part of your strength."

"Count me in!" shouted another as he reached up and was pulled to stand by another.

"Me too."

"You have my pledge too, Keeper."

And on it went as the many voices and bodies came together, out of pain and darkness, to form a united spirit that was a force to be reckoned with. Slowly, they found their strength, drank Forthrumal's herbal waters, and gained energy. Arms men went about finding the sturdiest of tools and weapons and directed them towards the shore.

While Odemog was inside attending to this matter, Sam anticipated his next move and called the mordaghas to shore. This added more transportation on the waters for the new recruits. All progressed seamlessly.

Odemog returned to where the King and his family attended to Storsumal, when he was stopped by Morlog.

"Moggie, I have news."

"Good news I hope," Odemog kept moving and Morlog took him by the sleeve as he finished his statement. "We've no time for any other kind."

"Moggie, it's Storsumal. He has conferred disturbing information upon us."

"Tell me," Odemog stopped dead and looked seriously at Morlog.

"You know of the powers that MaginTor has mastered?"

"Yes—telekinesis. Nothing fancy, just moving things about."

"And there was one more in the Kingdom with such power; that would be Storsumal."

"Well, that's good; I thought you were going to tell me that it was Thane-Ra." He gave a light laugh. "What's your news then?"

"In his time in captivity, Storsumal was tortured greatly and forced to conduct experiments and fulfill demands of both entertainment and training for Thane-Ra."

"Good grief, you are going to tell me what I don't want to hear."

"Listen up! Yes, but not just that. Thane-Ra forced Storsumal to empower his skills further. What Storsumal cannot be clear about, is how. He realized, at a certain point in his imprisonment, that Thane-Ra was using other sources, darker sources, to enhance his powers and skills. He feels that even Morzan fears Thane-Ra on some level."

"Well, that is saying something." Odemog paused to consider the situation. "I have done what I can, what more can I do?"

"If— and I say if— there is any truth to the strength of Thane-Ra, I can only think of one thing you can do—we can do. You and I must embark on a separate journey from this battle, Odemog. And from here, I think I can help you find the way to defeat him."

The thought of separating and attending to other journeys only served to confuse Odemog. For all the confidence he had come to know over these past days, he felt it tremble at his core.

"Then, Morlog, this is what we must do." The two stood for a moment, though it seemed to last much longer. Odemog was off to revise the plan.

"Kasell, Sam, Dero!" He called to each beckoning with his arm for them to gather around him. He stood close to the Royal Family, that they would hear the words he spoke.

"I have news that must take me away from our battle today. You must go on without me," he held up his hand for silence as he observed them about to protest. Odemog went down on one knee to be direct and clear with those he addressed.

"Kasell, you and Borzog," he gestured between them, "must take lead. Sam, stay close to Dero and the Princess and, at all cost, neither of you lose that girl. Mezzog, you shall continue to work with these others to strategize and push forward against our nemesis, Thane-Ra. And, Prince Mezzog," he slapped him on the back, "you are a fine man with a sword; keep yourself circling to know all around you." Odemog turned to where the King, Fazzog, and Princess Annabella were seated. "I will leave with Morlog immediately. I do not know my destination or my return but press forward with faith. I will return." He looked at Fazzog, "You are the map of hope; what you know of the passage and your destination empowers your arms men and weakens your opponent. Know your opponent. Your studies will pay off." He looked around him saying, "Trust this man. You enter a dark place, faith and trust will bring you light."

As he finished his instructions, Keeper Odemog rose and walked away from the group toward the shore where Nassir and Vadim waited. Morlog silently followed him.

As they mounted, Odemog spoke.

"Morlog, lead the way."

"Vadim, away home."

"Well, Nassir, you heard the Teller. Follow them."

In their usual fashion, the mordaghas bounced down, up, down, bellies went side to side as wings lifted them up and, in the blink of an eye, they were away. Those remaining behind watched as they continued to board their boats.

Moments later the convoy of sea vessels began to press northward, led in the air by Sam and Dero. Joining them on Lisan was Borzog who, although young, was a Master Rider.

37

Juliet was very relaxed as she stopped her horse along the path to watch her archers parade past. Beside her, on horseback, was the inimitable Thorandal. He leaned back in his saddle making him that much smaller than her. Proudly he waited for the Tsesiwan archers to pass so that he may show off his own collective forces.

Juliet sensed Thorandal's eagerness and called out, "Ride on, then," encouraging her forces to pass quickly. Pleased by this gesture, Thorandal now called to his mix of riders.

"Forward all, together now," and raised his sword to confirm the command. A few who had never ridden in formation kicked about and fussed but then found their rhythm within the group and sat up proudly as their horses trotted out. The mixed force rear guard drew up behind Juliet and Thorandal as they inserted at the back of the line. Slowly Juliet and Thorandal rode apart, one to the right and the other to the left, outside flanks, and advanced to the front.

It would be a matter of hours before they would take position at the edge of Galdordon Forest, where they would send a scout to the meeting point and exchange communications. Juliet quietly hoped that there would be more than one other scout at the meeting point.

38

Nassir and Vadim traded places high in the air. Nassir moved in front to break the force of the winds and ease travel for his older friend. They flew at a higher elevation over Khordrya to avoid being seen and they flew fast. Odemog called back to Morlog, "Where are we off to then, Morlog?"

"Vadim will show the way, have faith."

"But…"

"Keeper Odemog, do not begin conversations of doubt in the air, where we cannot properly debate." Odemog felt the teacher-student relationship rekindled momentarily.

"I understand, Morlog. No, wait. I am the Keeper. What are we doing? They need me at battle. Mazgamor needs me."

"Mazgamor is getting full use of you here, Moggie. Cease and desist."

Vadim drew up beside Odemog and spoke, which for a mordagha in flight, was highly unusual.

"Odemog, we go north to the falls."

"Trezano Falls? We were just there."

"We go to Great Falls."

"Stop distracting him, Moggie," Morlog rebuked his student.

"Tell him then, Morlog," Vadim instructed Morlog, who relented. At this point they were flying directly over Mid Lake and came to a lower elevation to ease the flight for both mordaghas.

"As you wish, Vadim, as you wish."

"Moggie—Keeper Odemog—you will learn another phase of your journey now."

"We land," asserted Nassir. At the northwest banks of Mid Lake now, it was wise to briefly rest and refresh here, before crossing the mountains. This would be a speedy journey, one not meant for one day. Odemog would miss the commencement of the battle. On landing, both mordaghas found a sweet spot at the edge of the lake to eat lake grasses, drink, and float. As they did so, Skeeter, forgotten in Odemog's pouch, pushed his way out gasping for air. "You would think, Moggie, that your appreciation for having your life saved would be greater." Having scampered up to Odemog's shoulder, Skeeter made a show of fluffing and straightened his fur. "Where are we?"

"Sorry, fur ball, my gratitude does seem inadequate. Have patience. We are heading home. A brief diversion from our current adventure," Odemog pressed a hand to Skeeter with affection.

"Well done, good and faithful servant," imparted Morlog, congratulating Skeeter for his gallantry. "Now you shall be silent for a tale." And so it began as Morlog imparted a story to Keeper Odemog.

"I shall call you Moggie for the first part of this story and then I shall speak to you as the Keeper; and soon you shall know why," Morlog walked with Odemog at his side to relieve the discomforts acquired in legs and buttocks on a long flight.

"Moggie, you now know your father and his father before him were Kingdom Keepers. Their precise missions were brought about by the times. Thane the Strong Heart earned his name as a result of your grandfather's quest as a Keeper. The son of Thane, you know him as Thane-Ra, was and is of equal turpitude in his ways.

It was your father's mission to defeat him and release the citizens of Khordrya from his hold. While in pursuit of his destiny, your father lost his life. It is not known for sure if it was as a result of an act of Thane-Ra or a tragic accident. By careful choice, we have always alluded that it was an accident. This was the safest way to protect you and others.

As your Protectors, we were required to wait until you were at least of age, or until evil again rose in the Kingdom. It seems that we should have addressed this directly when you came of age. But this was when the attack took place on Constantia Glen and, as your Protectors, we felt that you, having lived the life of a farmer, should gain more experience at the Gatherings before charging you with your mantle as Keeper.

Your father and his father before him did well by their responsibility. You will do so, also. These very days have proven the truth of my words. Now listen to me closely, Keeper, for I shall tell you this only once."

They circled back to the shore where Vadim and Nassir were enjoying the fresh water.

"Keeper Odemog, only Vadim knows the location of your father's accident. This has been carefully protected for moons. He was in retirement and not shame, protected and waiting to reveal this to you. As we get close to our destination, you and I shall switch. I shall ride Nassir and you, Vadim. Vadim will take you to your destination. From there, you will be on your own."

"I do not understand," Odemog had listened carefully but still could not filter out the intention of his journey.

"Keeper, you are on a quest for Sanctitoro."

"Sancti-what? I've never heard of such a thing, Morlog."

"It is gold of such purity that it seems to hold an unexplainable power; it absorbs the will of the one who possesses it. The purity of this gold, held by the faithful, those who trust in the truth, gives them power to defeat evil. It was an arrow of Sanctitoro that defeated Thane the Strong Heart. Sanctitoro is highly malleable. But when one sets intention upon it, it becomes forged with the intention. This is the gold that you will fashion into a weapon to defeat Thane-Ra. This is the gold protected by Keepers but lost to your father by tragedy, as he sought to fulfill his mission. This is your mission, Keeper Odemog of the Clan Odem of Sweetbrooke Wren: complete the mission of your father, Zodem, and rid Mazgamor of Thane-Ra."

39

Kasreya dismounted her horse closest to the stream. Leo drew up to her right, while Amara remained back a few feet.

"The map please, Leo," Kasreya walked to him with outstretched hand. Leo reached into his pouch and pulled out a map, passed it to her, and swung his right leg up over the horn of his saddle, sliding to the ground.

"I suspect we have come as far as we can at this point. This is the Mosquito Creek I have heard of," He slapped at the bugs that flew relentlessly at him. "We do not wait here long, I hope."

"Well young Lion-heart, I haven't any good news for you there. We do not make camp but only wait under cover. Feed and water horses but remain ready. Get me a messenger." Kasreya unfolded the map as she spoke. She reached for several small stones as she dropped the map on the ground. Placing a stone at each corner she reviewed their location and destination.

"Amara," she called. Amara's horse moved ahead and stopped beside Kasreya. "I have informed Leo that we stop here and await news. From here, the messenger goes to the meeting spot. Please, ready a parchment."

Amara gestured to another rider who came forth with a rather overburdened saddle. The rider climbed down and dismantled some of his kit. He produced a small table and chair for Kasreya. From a flat bag he withdrew a clean parchment. From still another he brought out a jar of ink and a writing implement. The man set the table neatly while Kasreya studied the map and appeared to measure distances. She squatted close to the ground, considering travel times and contemplated for a while. Soon she came and sat at the table. Kasreya documented instructions, paused in thought, and took another sheet of parchment as this one lay drying. She repeated the exact message a second time.

As she wrote, for only she knew these instructions, a rider came forward. An experienced rider who would move fast on this marvelous creature. She had done this before.

"We wait for return word," Kasreya spoke to no one in particular as she sealed the documents, stood, and carried them to the rider. The rider bent over and took them from her, then brought a document pouch from within her vest and carefully inserted the parchments.

"Take the road north along the coast. Stay among the cover of the trees as much as possible. They likely have horgle patrols along this way. When you reach Fansom Stone Hollows, wait in the shelter of the Hollows until you hear the signal of a falcon twice. Reply with one call. If you hear the same, you have found Juliet's courier and you may reveal yourself on hearing the second signal. Remain concealed until the proper call is exchanged. Should we be blessed, there is another signal to wait and listen for: a double tap rock that is repeated. You reply with the call of an owl and their signal will again be repeated. This is the blessed call of a messenger from MaginTor. I should be very happy that you return with report of his presence, very pleased indeed. The signal must pass at dusk." Kasreya looked skyward, noting the light changing. "Go now, ride hard." She gave a pat to the rump of the horse as the rider dug in her heels and was away.

Kasreya turned to see Leo swatting recklessly at mosquitoes that had elected to feast upon him. She looked around and found a wiklow bush. Running her hands along the branches she stripped them clean. Kasreya walked up to Leo and rubbed his face with the leaves, then took one of his hands, turned it palm up and pressed them to his palm.

"Wiklow. The mosquitoes seem not to like it. Study that leaf and share with others. There is a healthy bush behind me. Find others and get the word about. I need you focused and not swatting at bugs."

Amara sat rather smugly atop her horse, as did other archers who had grabbed at wiklow along the way, avoiding any of the bites the Constantian arms men were falling prey to.

Kasreya mounted her horse again and signaled for Amara and Leo to follow. Other riders dismounted to cool their horses at the water. The three rode together, with Kasreya in the lead, out to the open space that looked to the waters below. They were near the ocean. From this vantage point, Kasreya looked southward. At first, she didn't see it. Soon, Amara called out, "I see them. Look to the sky, there come two mordaghas."

"Down below," Leo pointed. "The boats are close behind."

Kasreya took a dagger sheathed at her side and held it up to catch the light. She reflected the light downward to the boats. Momentarily, a flash of light came back to her.

"They know we have arrived. That is good."

As the boats continued forward, the flight of mordaghas turned their way and closed in to land.

"Welcome, Sam. Hello, Dero. Greetings, Prince," she paused trying to discern which of the triplets she viewed. "Is it you, Prince Borzog?"

"Aye, it is. A good eye you have, Kasreya."

She laughed, "No, a lucky guess."

"Where is Odemog?" Kasreya looked skyward and strained, looking down to the boats. Sam spoke quickly, "In truth, we have no idea. He and Morlog re-commissioned our orders and departed hastily northwest."

"Aha," Kasreya mulled this over. "He has gone for Sanctitoro."

"What do you speak of—Sanctitoro. What is this?" Borzog asked as Dero stepped away, drawing his sword and cutting several sheaths of grass for the mordaghas.

"You will know soon enough. It is an important task that only the Keeper may attend to. Patience, and know we are on course."

"What, then, are your instructions, Kasreya?" asked Sam.

"The courier has departed and now we wait. The exchange will take place at dusk and her return will confirm the placement and timing of our attack."

"Do you know when we attack?" queried Borzog.

"For all to be in place, it should be at dawn."

"Does this not give Thane-Ra time to place a solid defense?"

"Many blocks have been placed in his way. The biggest of which was the deception over his messengers and their external attacks. He, as usual," she laughed, "is overconfident. But we should not be so. Thus, these cautious steps forward now. And so, please notify the boats to stay close together and ready to move forward to the beachhead. It will be cold out there tonight. I don't envy them their wait."

"We could fly the King and family up here," suggested Dero.

"You may ask him, but I am of the mind that it is dangerous to be moving about unnecessarily. We shall prepare hot beverages and food here and you can deliver it to them. Are you many more with the free souls?"

"There are over four score," Sam estimated.

"We shall accommodate," she turned to Leo and spoke, "see to it that the preparations are begun immediately. There are many to care for this night. Now, we wait."

With those words, Sam, Dero, and Borzog were lifted away by their mordaghas, returning with messages to those approaching by boat.

40

It was but a brief stop at the shores of Mid Lake. Rested and refreshed, the two mordaghas and their riders were off again, northwest. The light continued to fade as they rode toward the sunset. The skies took on a golden hue, casting a glow of pure gold on those whose quest was that very thing. It was as if their path forward was being paved in gold, drawing them ever closer to their mission. Odemog considered the beauty his eyes beheld as the Kingdom glowed below him. Everywhere represented his duty. Everything was cast with his intention. The gravity of his cause became further entrenched with each passing mile.

The sun dipped as they passed over the mountains. Darkness would be upon them soon.

"We should stop the night at Sweetbrooke Wren," Odemog called back to Morlog. There was a pause before a response was heard.

"That will do. From there, you may ride out on Vadim in the morning."

Soon the mordaghas brought them down again. They landed at the River Constantia. This would be their last rest before stopping the night at Sweetbrooke Wren. It was just a stretch and water break. When Vadim was younger, he would not take such breaks. He could fly a whole day. He preferred the air, by far, over the ground, or even in water. When he felt strong again, Vadim spoke to the travellers.

"Let us make our last flight, then." On those words, they again lifted to air and flew to Sweetbrooke Wren.

41

Drifting off the coast, north of the beachhead, appeared to be a dense kelp bed. It was not unusual to see this during this season and not a soul took notice of it.

The sun continued to take rest on the west side of Mazgamor and those on the east coast could feel the chill of the evening settling upon them. Concealed in the rocks of Fansom Stone Hollows, there stood the messenger sent by Kasreya. She was shivering as the caves, so close to the ocean, were cold and damp. She watched as the light continued to fade. She was pleased with herself for she made it in time for dusk.

Only a moment passed when she heard a falcon cry, and then again. She returned the call with her single cry. A pause, two more cries; she stepped forward.

"Show yourself," she said.

"What brings you here?" asked the other.

"I represent the south."

"I represent the north."

"So, you are with Juliet then?" asked the rider as she withdrew a parchment, all the while watching the actions of her counterpart.

"Aye, and you? Kasreya?"

"Yes, thank you." She received the document in the exchange and backed away. The two returned to their hideaways hoping for another signal. They waited, cold and hungry. She picked at some seaweed that had attached itself to a rock on a very high tide. Turning it over in her hand, she decided it would do to chew on as she passed the time.

Tap-tap. Tap-tap. The signal— there it was. Each of the riders responded with their owl call and the sounds were heard again. *Tap-tap. Tap-tap.* This time three souls emerged from the rocks, the third looking much more wary of the other two. The same verbal exchange took place as the documents were passed from hand to hand. Nodding to one another, the riders, now each with two dispatches, prepared to return. Two mounted horses and the third dragged a small skiff from behind a rock. The mission was a success.

* * *

In a tree not far away, a young raider had scrambled and watched the exchange. He had heard little but what he saw was enough to ignite fear. He scrambled down to make way to the Palace. He was torn; after all, he was derelict from his duties, having wandered off out of boredom. This news could win him favour with Thane-Ra, perhaps.

He stood tall and began his stroll back to the palace. A branch broke beneath his foot. He gasped and fell to the ground, an arrow in his back.

That was close, the Tsesiwan messenger thought to herself. She stripped off the disguise that concealed her true identity and Stronleya returned to her camp.

* * *

Covered head to toe in a dark flowing robe, the third courier heaved his oars quickly and efficiently, drawing the skiff further and further from shore. He came upon a bed of kelp and disappeared from sight.

42

Odemog waved from his place on Nassir's back. Below in Sweetbrooke, he saw his mother coming in from the fields.

Odemega set her basket down and looked skyward, straining her eyes. Her eyes supported what she knew in her heart. Odemog had returned. Dropping her basket, she began to run toward their cottage as the mordaghas took to ground in the garden near the door.

"Odemog!" she cried. Arms open, she ran to him where he wrapped his around her and lifted her high.

"Oh, how pleased I am to see you, Mother," he smiled.

"Where are the others? You smile but come alone. Where are the others? Please tell me there is no bad news?"

"There is no news, Mother, save that we returned Princess Lily to her home and freed her sister Annabella. Now we attend to more grave matters."

"Set me down, set me down, boy," she slapped his back from her dangling position midair. "Morlog," she turned speaking sternly to him. "Of what does he speak?"

"The time is at hand, Mega."

"Oh no," she looked crestfallen, aware of impending danger for her son.

"Mother, you know full well my duty."

"I do, but you must know a mother would never wish this on her son. You bear a great responsibility. My heart ached for your father and it aches again out of love for you, Moggie."

"Do not let your heart ache, Mother…" Odemog looked around and smiled saying, "just fix me the finest Brussels sprouts in Sweetbrooke Wren!"

"Fool. Morlog, I ask you, how can such a fool be a Keeper?"

Morlog smiled, observing the angst of those who bravely walk into the unknown and of those who love them.

Together they dined quietly. Odemega rose, kissed her son goodnight and left the room. Morlog stared at Odemog and said nothing. Skeeter, who had been given a place at table, was unusually quiet.

"Look you two," Odemog nudged Skeeter and placed his hand over Morlog's. "This is just the beginning and, if you cannot see what lies ahead, then I do not need your company tonight."

"Moggie, I do see the future and it is a good one. You were chosen as Keeper for a reason and tomorrow you will learn why. I bid you good night. Sleep well."

"Thank you Morlog. Good night, then."

Morlog stood up from the table and left the cottage. Odemog sat in silence and stared into the fire. He felt a gentle tap on his finger. He looked at his hand.

"Gabelnut?" Skeeter held up a large gabelnut in one paw, the other behind his back. He smiled with an expression of fondness in his eyes. Odemog shook his head as he accepted the nut. He placed it in the palm of his hand and crushed it. Opening his hand, the bits and pieces spilled out perfectly on the table. Skeeter's mouth watered.

"You go ahead and enjoy it, my friend. Tonight—well perhaps any time— your appreciation for a fine gabelnut is that much greater than mine. I am off to sleep. Good night."

43

Dawn broke over Sweetbrooke Wren before Odemog had had a real opportunity to allow the lids of his eyes to set as the sun had set the previous evening. Still, he felt a calm that usually came with a good night's sleep. Perhaps this was a good omen. He dressed quickly and was outside before anyone else was up in Sweetbrooke. Waiting for him near the door was Vadim.

"Good morning to you, Vadim. You are an early riser."

"I am here for you, Keeper. Let us be away."

"What of Morlog?"

"This is your journey alone, Keeper. Let us not waste time."

With that final comment, Odemog understood and took his place in the saddle. Vadim did not hesitate. He seemed driven, stronger, and perhaps even more confident. Odemog did not know the real reason and would not ask. They were simply away and out over the Great Falls Lake in moments. Vadim was feeling strong; they were flying faster.

Odemog could feel the warmth of the sun on his back as it rose in the east. They continued their journey northwest and soon he could see the falls in the distance. He had never seen them before. As they came closer into view, he admired their magnificent force and beauty.

A halo of fine mist hung over the falls. Interspersed at different points, where the light refracted at various angles were small, brilliant rainbows. He was in awe of the floating colors. They continued to close in and suddenly he wanted to cover his ears. The roar was deafening. Where the water crashed below the U-shaped falls, bursts of water bounced up in the air as if trying to climb back up from where they came.

To get his bearing, for it had been some time, Vadim flew a circle above where the water broke and fell over the edge. He appeared to find his mark and flew down to a slight protrusion from the rocks. He hovered there a moment, then flew above and landed.

"Keeper, I will return you to the cliff below, where you will climb off. Do you understand?"

"You are joking?" he asked with enormous disbelief and an underlying determination to refuse. "I barely fit that little shelf. How do you know it won't break off and cast me into the waters below?"

"I don't. That's just it. I shall stay close for you this time. Your father sent me away to rest. When his cries reached me here, it was too late and I could do nothing. I will not abandon you, Keeper Odemog."

"I understand." He felt defeated yet assured that somehow this was all piecing itself together as it should.

"Let us make haste. Climb up."

Vadim flew up and out over the edge again. Down they went to the little shelf and Vadim moved in as close as he could get. The wind force of the falling water made it difficult to hover with one as big as Odemog on his back. Still, the Keeper focused hard and pushed away from Vadim. Through the air he flew, landing his right foot, then his left on the shelf. But before he could grasp a handhold, the slippery surface, after many moons of water splashing off it discharged his feet and he fell, slipping away from the shelf. As he began to fall away his right hand caught hold of a corner and he hung on for dear life.

Odemog's left arm flailed wildly trying to find a similar handhold, but he found none. Just as he was about to lose his grasp, he felt his weight give way. *Bless him.* Odemog thought, as Vadim flew up beneath him, raising him enough to hold on with both arms and pull himself up slowly. As Odemog clambered up, Vadim flew a short distance off and watched.

The Keeper waved a sign of gratitude to Vadim who, in turn, simply nodded his head. Odemog peered at the falls, wondering what he was to do next. He observed a narrow ridge that led toward the tumbling water.

Oh no, that was meant for a man my father's size, NOT me. He looked out at Vadim, feeling a heavy weight pressing on his heart. All he could hear inside his mind was: *I can't.* He looked down to the bottom of the falls; he looked at Vadim and considered his move. There was but one and it was straight ahead.

As Keeper Odemog reviewed the condition of the narrow shelf, he thought he heard a voice. He shook his head and tried a first step. Slippery. He heard the voice again. This time he was sure it spoke his name: *"Odemog."*

"I am losing my mind," he shook his head and tried the step again.

"Moggie, my son."

"Who is talking to me?" he stared into the falls. "How do you come to be here?"

"My son, do not think of the steps you take. Look ahead and come to your destiny."

"Enough. show yourself!" Odemog cried, frustrated at his position, his anger building. The waters thinned and before him stood his father, Zodem.

"Father!" he cried. Odemog grasped the stone face of the cliff and placed his feet one at a time along the rock ridge. Small pieces broke away and he leaned into the wall.

"Do not make haste. Take easy steps and come to me," called his father. *"Focus. Sanctitoro—the gold is here for you to take."*

Odemog continued to follow his father's voice, his heart swelled with excitement at the chance of fulfilling this mission at his father's side. He thought of the joy Vadim would feel that Zodem was simply trapped all these years, living inside the falls. Of course. It made sense. Once he climbed out on the ledge, there was no way out, up or down. He needed the flight of a mordagha to get to safety. He wondered how his father had survived but thought better of the distraction. These were questions he could ask later.

"Keep moving ahead, son, you will achieve your destiny. The gold is here for you to take." His father called out to him, repeatedly. *"The gold is here for you to take."*

Carefully, he placed one foot in front of the other, staring all the while into his father's eyes. He looked just the same as the last time he had laid eyes on him as a boy. He passed through the water as it rolled over his back and down to the lake. These were the hardest steps as he struggled to maintain a grasp of the wet rock face.

Odemog slipped, he floundered but caught hold of a crag. As he heard his father speak the next words, he looked up from where he studied the ledge to smile at his father.

"My son, Keeper Odemog, I am proud of you."

Odemog stared straight ahead, the smile faded from his face. He looked left and right. His father had stepped away. Seeing how close he was to the cavern floor, he pushed off and leapt through the air, landing on the floor of the cavern in a crouched position.

"Father? Where did you go?" Odemog cast his eyes around the cavern. They were adjusting to the reduced light. He called again, "Father." No answer. Odemog walked around the perimeter of the cavern and realized he was fully and completely alone. He blinked, scratched his head, and shouted again "FAA—THER!"

Odemog's cry was carried right through the deafening roar of the falling waters. Vadim heard the plaintive cry and his heart ached. Still, he knew Odemog was safely on his way. Flying over to the rock protrusion, Vadim took uneasy rest there for a while, his great size hanging over the edge hazardously. He listened and watched the waterfall, waiting to be called into service.

Inside, Odemog heard his voice echo and turned toward the sound. He found a narrow path leading deeper into the cave. As he followed the path, he began to sense light ahead. Soon the path opened out into a larger cavern with stalagmites brilliant from a phosphorous glow. Odemog began to explore. Unsure of what to do next, he found a flat rock and sat down to think.

He sat for some time and began to hum to himself. He pondered the hallucination of his father and remembered his words. *'The gold is there for you to take.'* But where?

"Where is the confounded gold? This is truly a puzzle," he mused out loud. He stared ahead, got up and began to walk around the cave. He began to chant, "The gold is here for me to take, the gold is here for me to take, the gold…" Cocking his head sideways, Odemog squinted his eyes and reached out to the wall.

"Sanctitoro…?" He stepped closer, examining the wall. "By all that is yellow, the gold is there for me to take!" Odemog danced a jig. He stopped and grabbed his dagger from its sheath. He slipped it into the crack he had observed and began to chip away. Chunk after chunk and chip after chip fell away and the gold began to show itself. He missed the next strike at the rock face and hit the gold. The dagger sunk in easily. Sanctitoro, he recalled, a gold so pure, it is highly malleable, Morlog had said.

Odemog withdrew the blade from the wall and began to cut away pieces. First a long, flat strand came away as he tested the blade against the ore. He took the piece and, testing the flexibility, wrapped it around the hilt of his sword in a figure of eight looping around the hilt over each side of the guard. That would do nicely. He continued. As each sliver came away, he became more adept at the task and began to carve it away in shapes. He was on to the solution.

Odemog considered his goal and tried various shapes he could form as a weapon. With purpose in mind, he toiled at his work for some time. Soon, he came to realize that now may not be the time for the conclusive solution for he had yet to know how he would come upon Thane-Ra. So, with his pouch filled with various cuttings of Sanctitoro, Odemog gave one final look about the cave and made his way back out to the open cavern behind the falls.

He stood for a moment, taking in the sights and sounds, then began to consider how he would jump back. The simple fact was that he could not. One cannot leap from a full cavern floor to a sliver of a ledge against a flat wall. It defied all the laws. Odemog fingered the gold in his pocket and thought of his only way out. He closed his eyes for a moment and gave thanks. He bid the illusion of his father farewell and stood facing the falls. He took a deep breath and bellowed at the top of his lungs, "VAA—DIIIIMM!"

No sooner had he finished the call than he took three steps back and made a run at the falls.

Odemog dove straight into the wall of water and began to fall. He turned and somersaulted through the air, hoping he would break free of the water that had caught him and was dragging him downward.

His wish came true as he burst out the other side, whereupon he continued falling down, down, down to meet the lake. Before he could say 'on the wings of a mordagha', Vadim came up from below and swept him away, catching Odemog in mid-tumble.

"Hallelujah!" he bellowed in a state of amazement and gratitude. "Thank you, Vadim, bless you and thank you. That, my friend, is as close as I ever want to come to finding out what it is like to fly like a mordagha!"

"You are most welcome, Keeper. We are away home, then?"

Odemog looked back at the falls, peace in his heart, and smiled. Laying his hand upon the bulging pouch, he turned to look at the brilliance of the morning as he considered the destiny that lay ahead.

"To Sweetbrooke, you blessed creature. Home it is."

44

Morlog rose from the table quickly as he heard Odemega's cry. "They return!" She stood pointing skyward as Morlog emerged from his cottage. He made note of the placement of the sun in the sky, considering the next stage of their journey.

As Odemog and Vadim flew closer, Morlog felt his heart ease. Their journey was brief, and Vadim flew with a youthful air about him; it appeared they had been successful. Still, it was not over, and much in the way of danger and challenge lay ahead of the young Keeper Odemog. Each test presented him had been set aside with success, newly acquired knowledge, and understanding of the weight of the mantle upon him. The truest test was yet to come. After this journey to the Falls, Morlog anticipated that Moggie would return with more questions, though there remained the chance that, perhaps, he would return with even greater clarity.

As Vadim came to ground, it was clear that Odemog was no longer simply a farmer or trader but had gained insight into the depth and breadth of the responsibility of Keeper.

"Mother, I am happy to see you," Odemog was very formal in his greeting and he leaned over to kiss her cheek. He, for the first time, did not pick her up and hug her with his might. Turning quickly, and with a driven focus on his task, he addressed Morlog, "I bring Sanctitoro." As he spoke, he touched the grip of his sword and turned sideways. Morlog looked down at his sword which gleamed from the gold fastened there.

"An interesting accessory, Keeper."

"You said that Sanctitoro absorbs the intention of the one who possesses it?"

"This is truth."

"Will it not then bring purpose to my sword as I wield it for Mazgamor?"

"You will wield your sword with intention, regardless, Keeper. It is possible that the Sanctitoro will ring true of your intention to attack or defend one who threatens us. I cannot argue against this logic." Morlog eyed Odemog's pouch. "You have come prepared?"

"I cannot imagine how I may come upon Thane-Ra. I took enough of the gold to be able to fashion a range of implements. I knew not what to do."

"There is a danger in too much Sanctitoro having been removed. You must give this thought Odemog. Should you be separated from that which you do not use, it may fall into the wrong hands. Carry with you only what you know in your heart you will use. The rest, you must conceal in a place that only you will be able to find. Give this consideration and do so immediately. We shall return to join the others before the highest hour of the sun."

"You continue to challenge me, Morlog. I shall attend to this." Odemog shook his head as he turned and disappeared into the cottage.

Odemog stood inside the cottage and looked around. With himself, he began a dialog, *If I were gold, where would I hide?* His reply, *Fool, gold would not hide.* Back and forth he argued as he emptied his pouch upon the table. *First, consider what you will need, what you can use. Then, remove the rest and set it aside to conceal.* Odemog stood looking down at the contents of the pouch. He pulled out a chair and sat. Drumming his fingers on the table he stared at the Sanctitoro glowing before him. *Too much, too little... what will it be?* An idea struck him, and he divided the amount in half returning half to the pouch. The other half he began to roll into balls between the palms of his hands. Tweaking the ends, Odemog formed them into teardrops as they began to take on the appearance of golden gabelnuts. "Rather authentic looking, these," he said aloud, to no one in particular. Standing up, Odemog walked to the fireplace and withdrew a charred piece of wood. He broke off a piece making it the size of a writing implement and began to colour the new shapes. Soon, not only were they shaped like gabelnuts but they had begun to look, in colour, like Skeeter's favourite nuts. "Now, all I have to do is keep Skeeter's teeth out of them." He laughed out loud.

"Keep Skeeter's teeth out of what?" came the voice from atop the cabinet across from where Odemog sat.

"Skeeter, I might have known you were sleeping up there." Odemog picked up the freshly painted nuts and dropped them carefully into a small bowl on the table. Skeeter, with a remarkable acuity for nuts, spotted them immediately.

"Fresh gabelnuts for me?"

"Not if you want to keep your teeth, squirrel."

"Well, that's not nice to say to a friend who sav…"

"…Saved my life, I know Skeeter, but I am serious. These gabelnuts you will protect with your life and a reward of the juiciest gabelnuts you can imagine will be yours. You are still one of my Protectors?"

"Yes."

"Then, Protector, you have your assignment." Odemog lifted the bowl and set it up on the top of the cabinet beside Skeeter's resting spot.

"Mmmm…they look good."

"Skeeter, have I your word?"

"Yes, Keeper, you have my word." Dejected, Skeeter stared at the nuts then turned and climbed down from the cabinet, jumping to a wall post, and scrambling down with claws tightly grasping hold as he raced down headfirst. Halfway, he pushed off and jumped over to a chair, then launched through the air to the table from where he climbed up to Moggie's shoulder after the Keeper had returned to his seat.

Odemog sat for a moment as he considered again the contents of the pouch, wondering how he would meet Thane-Ra, and what would be the best way to bring an end to his reign of terror. Perhaps the simplicity of grandfather Fazzog's arrow would be best. It had been good enough for Thane the Strong Heart. Odemog shook his head and pushed his chair away from the table. He picked up the pouch and slung it over his shoulder. Looking about the cottage, he took in the familiar smells and sights, turned, and went back out into the light where he joined Morlog, his mother, and the waiting mordaghas. This, again, would be goodbye.

45

As the day had dawned, Leo found himself up and picking wiklow leaves yet again. These mosquitoes were relentless. It confounded him how a bug so small wielded such power and drive. Yet there was nothing mighty about them, for a simple swat flattened them, ending their assault. He thought to himself, how lucky they would be this day, if the battle which lay ahead of them could be as straightforward as the act of swatting a toxic little bug. With that, he flattened another mosquito as he reached out to grab a handful of wiklow. The end was near.

* * *

Sam and Dero were both early risers, for they were always attentive to the needs of their mordaghas. This day was no exception. They rose before the sun and quietly moved about observing the mists over land and sea.

"An eerie morning this, Dero," Sam spoke softly to his friend, not wishing to wake Prince Borzog.

"A good protective cover, this mist, I should think."

"You have a good point, Brother."

It wasn't long before the two were joined by Borzog who, conscious of those who had slept in the cramped and cold refuge of the boats, wanted to get hot teas out to them as soon as possible. "Can we build a fire Sam?"

"I imagine, in this fog, a good and well-tended fire would easily go unnoticed."

"I should like to brew tea and fly it out as soon as we can. I imagine they would be some lot worse for wear, curled up on the planks in the damp."

"A wise idea. I shall go to Kasreya's people for tea, Sam, if you and Borzog get the fire going."

"As you wish, Dero. Perhaps you will find some morsels to chew on, as well."

"Do my best, Brother, do my best!" Dero walked into the brush towards the encampment formed by Kasreya's archers and arms men. He wondered what lay ahead of them, all spread out north, south, and east, and Odemog nowhere to be seen.

* * *

Juliet, Thorandal, and their riders camped concealed inside the edge of Galdordon Forest. Galdordon was a dense and dark forest, rich with wildlife, and a world of its own. Many who feared Thane-Ra took refuge within the towering dark trees. It is said that deep within, there exists an entire community of deserters and escapees from the angry rule of Thane-Ra. To show oneself or return to Khordom Palace was certain death. Every so often, Thane-Ra would send a raiding party into the forest to find those disloyal deserters and make an example of them. Fearful of these attacks, those who sought to live in peace took to the woods to destroy those who entered in order to protect their very existence. And so, while many a man, woman, and child adopted a hidden life within the safety of Galdordon Forest, it was not a safe place in which to take refuge.

The guards posted faced both the direction of Khordom Palace and into the forest, wary of attack from both sides. As the men and women who formed the mixed troops rose to a new dawn, each considered what excitement and challenges lay ahead for each knew this would be a day that would go down in history.

The return of the courier just before dawn sent a wave of optimism through the camp. Greeted by both leaders, the courier presented first the parchment from Kasreya and, to Juliet's relief, then presented the hoped-for document that came from MaginTor.

"We are assured of success with our friend from the north at our service. He is disguised at sea with a small armed fleet."

"A seafaring warrior brings as much as one by land, Juliet."

"True to your own sea calling, Thorandal, you will know this of course from your own experience. I am sure you welcome our friend's contribution."

"As sure as we stand together this day, it is reassuring. I am concerned of the Keeper's departure however."

"We are a strong force coming from three points of attack, such that we almost entirely surround Thane-Ra and his palace. I have faith in the unity of our cause and the plan the Keeper set out for us before his departure. Still, he promised his return and I am confident of this."

"This is true; then let us be ready." Thorandal turned and gestured with both arms as if to push something away. Long having served by his side, Swenson knew this meant, in sea terms—prepare to cast off. For today, Swenson would take it to mean break camp and mount up. As the men and women of the combined forces moved about in careful preparation, an uneasy air descended upon them. Those who encircled the camp as sentries tightened their placements. A wind began to blow through the forest trees, and sentries facing the darkness of the trees took up defensive postures, one after another.

"Call your placement." The lead sentry spoke just loud enough for his voice to carry along the line.

"Fromal, here."

"Baloren, here."

"Wilodor, steady on." One after another, the sentries answered. After a dozen were reported in, the first arrow struck a tree, followed by another and on it went. Each sentry dropped to one knee with bow at the ready but saw no source at which to fire. The arrows stopped just as soon as they had begun, and a single arrow pierced the bark of a tree inches from the lead sentry's left ear. He heard the wind of the arrow as it blew by.

Attached to the arrow was a tri-folded parchment. Desryd, the ranking sentry, carefully removed the parchment and reported immediately to Swenson.

"I would say it was a warning from those Galdordon ghosts."

"Galdordon ghosts?" Swenson shook his head at Desryd.

"Yes, that is what the men are calling the Khordrians who live in the forest. I think it rather amusing."

"Well, whatever you call them, they are demanding to know what we are planning to do. They suggest here," Swenson tapped his finger on the parchment, "that the forest is full of deadly traps and many who will fight to the death if we think we should like to come after them."

"Do they think we are here representing Thane-Ra?"

"Who knows, Desryd. Have the men stay alert, but do not fire into the woods. I will take this to Thorandal. He will, no doubt, attempt to reply."

"As you wish," replied Desryd, and promptly returned to his unnerved sentries, who continued to scan the forest for those who would attack them.

Aware of the passage of time, Swenson now ran to where Thorandal and Juliet discussed the day's movements. He stood waiting impatiently as they looked over a map and reviewed their assault.

"Forgive me, Thorandal, for interrupting," Swenson stepped forward, holding the parchment up at eye level.

"What have you there, my friend?" Thorandal reached out, taking it from Swenson.

"A strange little attack on the sentries facing the forest just occurred."

"What?"

"Not to worry, it was really a feigned attack, perhaps to demonstrate resolve. This message nearly took off Desryd's ear, I gather. I think you might consider an invitation, if they are not too feral, to join with us against Thane-Ra."

"A fine suggestion, Swenson," Juliet nodded approval. "What say you, Thorandal?"

"An interesting proposition. The note reads: *Friend or Foe? If you are of Thane-Ra, be warned death traps surround you...* and other ramblings. I say we take a walk, Juliet. Shall we?" Thorandal crumpled the parchment and dropped it onto the table with the maps. He reached out offering her his arm. "Show us the way Swenson—no time to waste."

The three walked hurriedly over to the line of sentries, who parted for them to pass.

"Ahoy, there!" called Thorandal. "I am Thorandal of Trader's Peninsula. On my arm is Juliet of Siwa. We come as friends. Will you show yourselves, then?" All about them was silence. The sentries behind them stood quietly with bows raised.

"Lay down your arms," came a voice from the trees. Juliet turned and gestured to the line of archers who dropped to one knee and rested their bows across the other knee.

"Show yourselves, please, we mean no harm to you, people of Galdordon Forest," Juliet spoke in a warm voice. Out of the corner of her eye, she spotted movement. It was a sight to behold as people of all shapes and sizes began to appear from hollows in the ground, covered by twigs and leaves. They slipped down from vines that hung from trees and emerged from bushes as they dropped woven cloaks of brush. It was as if a giant blanket had lifted to reveal a whole village of people.

"Well, I'll be a harvester, look what turns up when you talk nice, Juliet."

"Don't be rude, Thorandal." Juliet let go of his arm, giving it a shake. She turned to the older man who stepped forward wearing a worn armour chest plate and gripping the hilt of his sheathed sword.

"I am Jackman of Galdordon, former blacksmith within the walls of Khordom Palace. Free leader to our people." He raised both his hands to include those who stood behind and around him.

"I am pleased to meet you, Jackman. Please call me Juliet, and this is Thorandal. We mean no harm to you or your people. We are on a journey against Thane-Ra. His push to destroy Mazgamor as a Kingdom is about to end. We, the peoples of Siwa, Trader's Peninsula, Constantia—from all over the Kingdom—are united in a retaliation against his attacks. Today, we battle from all fronts to stop Thane-Ra from achieving his goal. There is a new Keeper in the Kingdom…"

As she spoke these words, a swell of murmuring rose from the group. Jackman raised his hands to silence them.

"Since when has there been a new Keeper?"

"Keeper Odemog of the Clan of Odem only recently received his calling. It is he who has set our course of action to rescue Queen Madelina and the Princess Annabella from Pierce Island. The rescue occurred yesterday and our courier brought news of the rescue of nearly a hundred souls from the prison as well."

A cheer erupted from the forest people. Many friends and family members of these very individuals were amongst those who suffered the fates of Pierce Island.

"You have our gratitude, as you can see. My own brother was a prisoner of Morzan. I was fortunate to escape when they came to arrest us." Jackman continued, "Perhaps we can repay your people for saving our own?"

"We welcome your assistance. What do you suggest?" Juliet remained diplomatic throughout the exchange.

"Over the years, we have dug many tunnels and hiding caverns to help people escape as well as to steal our way back inside to loot the Palace for needed supplies and equipment. We know it well—this should be of great value to you."

"What ho!" Thorandal let out a laugh. "Great value? This is a treasure trove of value, friend Jackman. Pure as gold, I would have to say, my friend."

"We leave within the hour to converge at the same time as MaginTor from the east and Kasreya who comes from the south. Can your people be ready?" asked Juliet.

"We must always be ready. However, we travel on foot—quickly, but still on foot." Jackman looked around at his people. "Fully arm yourselves, my friends, and prepare to vanquish the lair of Thane-Ra." As quickly as they had appeared, the people of Galdordon Forest vanished, leaving Jackman standing alone before Thorandal and Juliet. Thorandal turned to Swenson who stood with the sentry, Desryd, and instructed them.

"Gentlemen, withdraw your sentries from within the forest and allow them to refresh before our departure. We will be joined by these fine people in our adventure this day. Swenson, please make them feel welcome as they assemble. Away with you now." Desryd nodded and turned to dismiss the sentries. Swenson stood waiting for Jackman's people to return. He took out his dagger and began to clean his nails.

"So, Jackman," Thorandal struck him on the back twice as he led the Khordrian toward their station. "Tunnels and caverns. Brilliant. I think we should be able to manage some fine trickery with your assistance. What seemed like it would be a routine attack is shaping up into a fine adventure, I should think. A fine adventure, yes."

"Jackman, Thorandal's enthusiasm is shared. But practically speaking, we should be clear. This attack must move forward quickly to converge on the Palace with our east and south flanks. We cannot give them a chance to escape and, more to the point, it is the intention of our assault to come upon them from all sides to deplete their stronghold quickly."

"I understand, Juliet. Our own survival has meant that we move quickly. It is true, we will be slower than your mounts, but I think we bring to you yet another advantage by way of our tunnels. You converge by the north…"

"We will spread out to cover north and west, to be true," interrupted Thorandal.

"That's fine. You also come from south and east, so all directions are covered. What if we add another access for assault? One they cannot even begin to anticipate?"

"You are suggesting a tunnel assault?"

"Precisely, Juliet, precisely. You tell me when and how you would like us to proceed and we shall oblige you with all our hearts." Jackman pressed a clenched fist to his chest, raised it and tapped twice over his heart as he smiled. She knew what this meant to those who would return to the home from which they were banished.

46

Odemog stood scratching behind Nassir's ear just the way he liked it. The mordagha was crunching on an apple. They stood waiting for Morlog to emerge from his cottage. It was a beautiful, sunny day in Sweetbrooke Wren. Odemog hoped that, across the Kingdom, his friends and fellow warriors were sharing in the same comfort. A turn of the weather could cause great challenges to warriors coming from the sea or on land. He thought of the coastal fogs, the rains, and the cold.

Morlog emerged with his burlap kit, preparing to bring it to Odemega to fill with her usual feasts for travel. Right away he observed the distracted expression on Odemog's face.

"Moggie, really, I should say Keeper—something disturbs you?"

"Morlog, I was appreciating our beautiful weather when it occurred to me that those who face battle this day will face dire conditions should the weather not be in their favour."

"You know Keeper, of all the things you could be concerned about at this time, this is the least of your worries. Your concern is a safe return in battle-ready mindset. Can you do this?"

"But of course, Morlog, of course."

"Then brighten your face and say your goodbyes. We must be away." Odemog walked to the cottage and met Mega as she emerged, carrying his kit.

"I have a surprise for you, Moggie."

"I could use a good surprise, Mother." She set down his kit and handed him a pouch. It was larger than the hemp pouch he had carried for years in his travels, but not by much. It was actually a bit deeper with what appeared to be a burlap window as a central band around the bag. It was as if the burlap had been stretched, or alternate strands had been removed for greater breathability. Odemog held it up and turned it over several times in his hands before looking at Odemega, puzzled.

"Well, Moggie, Keeper Moggie, what do you think?" came a voice from below. Odemog looked to the ground beside Mega.

"Aw Skeeter, you can't be serious? Mother? This is for Skeeter?"

"Well, my son, he is your Protector."

"I don't know what this squirrel has told you…"

"I saved your life, Moggie."

"He saved your life, Keeper," Morlog added.

"He did save your precious life, my son," Odemega smiled and took the bag from his hands, beckoned for him to bend forward, and draped it over his neck and right shoulder. She draped it to his left side and bent down to pick up Skeeter. Odemog released the flap and held the bag open. Skeeter hopped into the bag, turned around several times, peering out the burlap screen as he did, and poked his head back out.

"Oh Mega, it is perfect. Just perfect…I can breathe in here and I will be able to see clearly to protect Moggie. It is perfect."

"Well then, I am happy for you all. I, on the other hand, have one more thing to worry about: a squirrel," Odemog complained and Morlog, who had come up beside him, reached over and hit him hard on the arm.

"Ouch."

"Keeper Odemog, may I remind you again that there are far more important things to concern yourself with. But I shall ask a more practical question about this bag and your travel companion. Where will you carry the Sanctitoro?"

"I made sure there was room," offered Odemega quietly. "There is a second pocket within so that it cannot easily fall out and it will not be uncomfortable for Skeeter."

"You think of everything," Skeeter piped up.

Odemog shook his head, trying to conceal his smile. "Mother, you are a grand woman. I thank you. Now we must be away, for many lives are at stake today, and I owe each a debt of gratitude for their commitment to our Kingdom. We must make haste to join with them."

"Travel well and safe, my son, Morlog, Skeeter. Travel well and safe." Mega backed away as she spoke, fearing for her son, all the while hoping for the best.

Odemog, Morlog, and Skeeter took to their mounts and Vadim and Nassir lifted them skyward on their journey back to Khordom Palace. This day they would fly non-stop. It would be a hard-pressed journey, though a possible one. The mordaghas would rest on arrival, this they knew, so they pushed themselves to their limit to return the Keeper to his cause.

47

Atop the perimeter of Khordom Palace, guards passed by one another in pairs as they paced the wall-walk, shielded by the protective battlement. Standing in an enclosed turret at each corner of the castle, stood vigilant guards. They carefully scanned the terrain surrounding Khordom Palace, looking for movement or change.

General Pervan stood within the keep below, commanding a second general alarm calling all soldiers of Khordom Palace to arms. They had been on guard all night and, with the change of shift at dawn, many went to quarters for rest. By Pervan's standards, this was unacceptable. Exhausted, armed guards appeared from dormitory halls and residents of the Palace keep, too, came forward, carrying rough implements they could use to fight off attack. While not everyone was loyal to Thane-Ra, there were those in business who were in his favour and benefited from his wealth.

"Place a double guard at the gate and reinforce the couplings to secure the mechanism." He thought of the manner of attack on Pierce as reported by Morzan. *They will not so easily overrun us this time,* he thought to himself. "You there, take that hay wagon away from the guard house. It is an easy target for fire arrows." Pervan commanded the soldiers and citizens swiftly and curtly. They would be under attack soon, though he knew not when.

Morzan stood in an archway two tiers above the keep, where Pervan busied himself. He watched, feeling confident that Khordom Palace was reinforced well, both structurally and by the strength and determination of the guard. This would be a much easier battle to win.

"Well, Morzan, what do you make of all this?" Thane-Ra had quietly slipped in beside Morzan at the rail.

"Today is a day of bravery for your men below. It is a good day to die, I would say."

"A good day to die—hmm, I like that, Morzan. But let it be them and not us, yes?"

"So it shall be, Thane-Ra, so it shall be. Are you in need of anything?"

"Just be sure that the Queen is by my side today. Whatever happens, she will die before she has any chance of escape or rescue. I will have this assurance with her close that I may inflict the certain death myself, should it come to that."

"Should it come to that. I shall see to it at once." Morzan bowed and walked away, thinking that he would prefer the privilege of making her suffer, but Thane-Ra ruled Khordom Palace and Morzan would not have this type of power until he took control of the north. "Patience, Morzan, patience," he muttered to himself as he strolled the dark passage to his chambers.

48

The hour was upon them. From the south, Kasreya, followed by her mixed force of Constantian arms men and Tsesiwan archers, advanced along the coast to Fansom Stone Hollows. At the same time, the boats with the additional Constantian arms men, the free souls, and the King, Princess, Mezzog, and Fazzog were guided up the coast by the trio on mordaghas: Sam, Dero, and Borzog. The two groups would gather at the Hollows and begin their journey inland, cutting south and west to take up position nearest the main gate of Khordom Palace.

From the east, MaginTor and his crew made their way to shore under the cover of the mists. They turned several degrees north as they closed in on the shore, coming to a rocky beach, north of Fansom Stone Hollows. Men jumped out before the boats hit bottom and dragged them to shore. They lifted the boats over the rocks, so as not to damage their hulls. Others ran to cut brush and covered the boats as best they could to conceal them from scouts. Once done, they armed themselves and began their march inland. They would make formation amongst the rolling hills looking at Khordom Palace from the east and wait for the final signal to advance.

From the north, the newly revised assortment of warriors pressed forward. There were only a quarter the number of Galdordon people, perhaps only fifty in all, walking the distance behind the many mounted troops. But they were driven and they walked at a quick pace, not tiring in the least. Juliet felt confident they would not hold the group back from achieving their goal.

A supply horse from Thorandal's travellers was relieved of heavy packs and a spare saddle was unpacked so Jackman could ride alongside Juliet and Thorandal.

"I am not much in favour of riding when my people must walk," protested Jackman.

"Your protest has been heard, Jackman. It is imperative we travel together to discuss how we may unite our efforts. This you understand?"

"I do, Juliet, I do. Lead the way; we shall follow." Jackman turned in his saddle to look back upon his people, whose drive was evident by their swift pace and determined faces. He waved a sign of solidarity and many returned the salute.

49

Both Nassir and Vadim flew like very young mordaghas, without a care to speed, testing their endurance and throwing full caution to the wind. Odemog had never flown so fast. In truth, he did not know a mordagha could travel at such a speed. He found it unnerving yet invigorating at the same time. They had long passed the Trezano Mountain Range and were in view of Mid Lake. It would not be long before they would be upon Juliet and Thorandal if all was timed right. There was no point in flying further south or east, he had informed them. He would join the first group he could come upon and that would be those in the north.

Odemog considered the placement of the sun and where each of his flanking warrior groups would be at the moment. They should make their first move very soon. He adjusted his position in the saddle, leaning forward. It was as if this movement would help Nassir to fly even faster. He was eager to lead his friends and allies. Nassir sensed the Keeper's intent and pressed himself just a bit harder, jumping ahead in the sky.

50

United now with Magnus, Morlog, and the rest of the ocean travellers, Kasreya looked across the stretch of trees that formed the line at the edge of a meadow. Ruts, bumps, and hills gave the appearance of waves that, if they were not so green, one might confuse them with the ocean. The geography presented both benefits and challenges for, where in places it would hide them, in others it would reveal them.

Still inside the cover of the trees, she rode the edge, passing before the line of archers and arms men on her way to consult with Borzog.

"What is your plan for Lisan and the other mordaghas?" she asked.

"They shall remain back until we breech the palace, for both safety and surprise. We do not wish to give away our position by flying overhead." Borzog looked to Mezzog, who nodded in agreement.

"Dero and I shall stay with Princess Annabella until the first wave of attack has broken through, then we three shall fly forward and join you," added Sam confidently.

"Magnus, you are in agreement on this?"

"I support the Keeper's endorsement of Annabella's skills and those with whom he has entrusted her. Keeper wanted additional men with her and I heartily agree. Kasell has made his choice, and they are with her now. There is no more I can say or do, Kasreya."

"You should know, Magnus, that I endorse her participation as well. With such a guard accompanying her, a wise head on her shoulders, and the skills she will have learned from the masters at your castle, I have faith in this young woman. So should you also give her your trust."

"I have much faith in my children and those with whom they travel and battle today, I assure you." He turned and looked at the faces of those near him. "I have faith in you all."

"Mezzog, illuminate us on your plan for the advance, now that you have the free souls with you?"

"Kasreya, although they are strong of spirit, many are weak physically and so they shall form second wave to allow them to advance with greater ease. Our men and women are as eager as these free souls of Khordrya to defeat Thane-Ra. They shall prove themselves worthy."

"Alright then, prepare yourselves." Kasreya turned to Leo and instructed him.

"Leo, call forward your strongest climber," Leo dropped back to instruct another, then turned and met Kasreya as she returned to her followers. A rider came forth and saluted Leo who, in turn, introduced August, a stone mason by trade, who became an arms man in quest of greater adventure.

"August is a capable man, Mistress Kasreya; it seems he knows the stones well. Both cutting and splitting as well as climbing. He should be up to your task."

"Fine then, August." Kasreya dismounted and rolled out the map again. This time, she offered one side to August to hold, freeing the other hand to show her plan. As she pointed to markings on the map, she walked away from the trees a short distance with August at her side and pointed toward Khordom Palace. "The southeast corner of the castle houses a watchtower, a turret that must be breached silently. The guard must be removed and a signal sent to confirm your actions. There will be others from our northern and eastern flanks who will fulfill the same task." Kasreya turned to speak to those closest, who would lead the troops forward. "Once this is accomplished, Amara will fire an arrow skyward with flash powder sending the signal to advance on the castle. Do you have any questions?"

"Those who wait north of us will not see her arrow."

"That is not your concern. All has been attended to amongst your leaders. Have faith, stay true, and give your best for Mazgamor. August, we await your signal."

"It is my honour to serve," August replied, as he draped a coil of rope over his head and shoulders. In his pouch, he placed a flint and smaller bag of fire powder. Finally, he withdrew several daggers and placed them on his person, one in the leg of each boot, and two in the drape of his tunic. He unbuckled his long sword and traded it for one half its size. This would be easier to climb with. Finally, August took a three-pronged hook that resembled a giant fishhook and carefully secured it to the end of the rope he had draped over himself. Smiling, he took a couple of quick steps and began to run low from the trees and out into the short brush. August darted from bush to bush and around rocks, in an effort to reach the wall of Khordom Palace without being seen.

As August came closer, he observed a two-man foot patrol. Dropping flat to the ground, August lay still as he waited for them to pass. Slowly, he began to creep along the earth, hoping to gain even an inch more to reduce his distance to the wall he would soon climb. Once they turned the corner, he knew he had just enough time before they would make their way along the perimeter and return.

August stole his way to the base of Khordom Palace, where he stood and leaned flat against the wall to catch his breath. He lifted the rope over his head and felt the weight of the anchor at the end. He closed his eyes for just a moment to visualize it flying through the air and catching just the right hold to bear his weight. August's only concern would be the patrols along the wall-walk. If he timed it right again, he could make his throw when they were marching the other way. He listened and marked the voices.

Tossing the bulk of the rope down, August took three lengths in his hands and then took two generous steps out from the wall. He only hoped his placement was adequate for the height of the wall. Both speed and accuracy were required and he likely had only one shot. Quickly now, August began to twirl the anchor end of the rope, letting it out bit by bit and then, in one strong swing of his arm, he set it flying up into the air as he watched the coils of rope race up after the hook. A quiet *thunk*, and he waited—no cries. Pulling the rope taught, August began to raise himself up hand over hand. He wore his riding gloves, which gave him a tighter grip on the heavy twisted rope. August moved well up the stone face. It was constructed at enough of an angle with rough mortar and stone to grip with his boots as he sped up his climb.

It could not have been easier. August lifted himself into the low segment of the battlement. He peered around to see where the guards were. Quickly, on seeing he was clear, August jumped down. He turned and rapidly pulled the rope up from where it hung, just in time to see the pair of guards return around the corner. Dropping the rope beside him, August peered around the wall of the turret. The soldiers seemed to be distracted along the wall as they now stood together over the top of the gate, talking amongst themselves. He spotted the turret door and made a quick dash and pushed it open, landing inside.

"It's about time, Balthazar, I've been waiting…"

"Hate to disappoint," replied August as he drew a dagger on the now-startled watch guard and put him to rest forever, "but I am not Balthazar." Quickly, he retrieved his rope and tossed it aside within the turret. August then dragged the still guard in front of the closed door to create a barrier and rooted around in his pouch to find the flints and fire powder bag. "Aha, there you are, rascals."

August set the pouch on the ledge of the loophole, a narrow window from which the watch guard had observed his viewpoint. He set one flint down and picked up the bag. August struck one flint against the other—nothing. Again and again, he tried as sweat began to drip down his back. Finally, a large spark bounced from the flint onto the pouch and August flung it up into the air as it caught light. He prayed it had been seen by those for whom it was intended.

Safely ensconced in all four corners of Khordom Palace were men from each of the forces who, like August, had successfully taken control of the turrets. One after another, they lit their powder to signal control of their watchtower. This gave each leader the confidence to send their signal without fear of detection. And so they did.

* * *

"Did you see it?" called Amara.

"Just as you did, cousin," replied Kasreya. "You know what to do."

"Leo, I need you to light my arrow while I protect the flash pocket."

"Like this?" he asked as he held the flame over the tip of the arrow.

"Perfect. Now we carefully raise up and…" Amara raised her bow, directing the flaming arrow skyward. Her movements were entirely graceful as she leaned back, her long hair falling away from her back. "Release," she said, as she let loose the grip of her right hand and the arrow slipped away through the air. With the force of air against the flame, it blew back on the small pocket of flash powder. This concentrated powder would illuminate quickly and could be missed easily. It flashed a brilliant blue for a mere second or two, with such force it caused a small shock wave. It was a dangerous powder and not one to be used for any purpose beyond such an airborne signal.

All looked to Kasreya for direction after witnessing the flash. "Patience," was all she said as she turned her horse to face the east.

51

"Now that is what I want to see, right…there," MaginTor raised his arm and pointed a gloved hand, as if to touch the flash of blue that appeared briefly in the sky. One would have to be expecting it to happen or, purely by accident, to glance in its direction to have caught sight of the perfect signal.

"Launch your signal," MaginTor directed. A young archer, in the identical manner of Amara, held out an arrow to be lit, leaned back and fired into the air above. The effect was the same and MaginTor walked to the young man to give him a firm slap on the back. "Very good, very good. Ready, then."

"Sir, Lord MaginTor, there's the reply from the north now."

"Confirm." MaginTor watched as the soldier repeated his previous action.

"All ready, then. We march forward." MaginTor drew his sword slowly as he began to march toward Khordom Palace, flanked by a driven force of warriors eager to defeat Thane-Ra, to remove the fear from Mazgamor.

* * *

Kasreya observed a blue flash in the east. *One away,* she thought to herself. Her horse was becoming restless, but she was eternally calm. All were silent, waiting for her to respond or react to the flash they, too, observed in the distance. But it was not this flash she waited for—it was the next flash that moved her to action.

"There it is." Kasreya nodded in the direction of the blue flash. "MaginTor has heard from Juliet. Khordom Palace is surrounded. All flanks will now close in." Kasreya raised her arm and waved her hand forward. She gave her horse a nudge and the advance on Khordom Palace began.

Like a wave rolling in from all directions, forces moved upon the Palace; a dark sea of men, women and horses converged to swallow Thane-Ra and all those who followed him. Keeper Odemog's plan was alive and in action.

52

Jackman pulled back on the reins of his horse that was startled briefly by an overhead shadow. Observing his hesitation, Juliet looked around and up, in time to see Odemog on Nassir as they circled to land with the travellers.

As Nassir took to ground, Odemog leapt off and beat a quick step to the mounted riders.

"Friends, you are safe and advancing. Good news!" he called cheerily. "We've no time to lose. Don't stop; I shall walk beside as you ride." Odemog turned as he spoke and gestured to Nassir to rest. They had agreed while in flight, that Nassir would wait and rest where they landed, watch until the group marched from sight and then advance again to meet them. This would allow the mordagha some respite and keep him from view in the air.

"Odemog, we are pleased and relieved to have you join us." Thorandal punched the air enthusiastically with a clenched fist as he spoke.

"Pleased to see you and be with you, Thorandal, Juliet. And who have we here?" asked Odemog noting the unfamiliar face of Jackman and the unusual collection of foot soldiers following the group.

"These are the Galdordon people, with whom we have aligned," she replied.

"I am Jackman of Galdordon Forest," he said as he leaned forward to shake hands with Odemog. "And, this is my cousin, Mikael." He gestured to Mikael who now walked beside him. Odemog reached out to grasp Jackman's hand with his right while squeezing his forearm with the left.

"Welcome, friends. Galdordon, eh? Formerly of Khordrya, I suspect?"

"Long ago, 'tis true. Free now to go as we please in a forest we now call home," added Mikael.

"Perhaps this may change for you and many others this day," Odemog smiled as he looked at the surrounding faces.

"Sir Odemog,"

"Please, just Odemog."

"Odemog, I think we may offer you an advantage in this charge for we know the Palace well."

"I— we— welcome any and all advantage, friend. Speak freely, please."

"I was preparing to show Juliet and Thorandal what lies ahead when you came to land." Jackman prodded his horse forward and turned to the west as the others followed. Jumping down from the horse, he beckoned to several of the men of Galdordon. The group moved toward a triangle of trees and rocks. One of the taller men took hold of a sturdy branch that lay between two large boulders. He stepped back and handed it to a burly fellow who raised and planted it with force into the ground on an angle. The others came forward to help. All hands on the branch, they applied pressure until all those around saw movement. A boulder shuddered and rolled out of the way. The process was repeated, and the second boulder was moved to reveal a burm. Next, they began to clear away leaves, branches, and other coverage.

Odemog stared at what was revealed and turned to Jackman for an explanation. Thorandal had ridden forward and slipped down from his horse, approaching the group cautiously.

"I present to you," Jackman said, smiling, "the keys to the kingdom!" He stepped forward with Mikael and both tugged hard on the handle, together they opened a door built into the sloped side of the burm. Thorandal stepped forward to inspect the gaping doorway.

"Certainly not your home in there, Jackman," he mused. "You speak in riddles, lad."

"This, Thorandal, Odemog," and, looking up to where she remained on her horse, he added, "and Juliet, was our tunnel to freedom. It was through here that we escaped from Khordom Palace when no other way was possible. It remains a secret and now serves a greater purpose, should you wish to take advantage." Jackman looked directly at Odemog as he made his point. "Through this tunnel you enter, unseen, into the core of Khordom Palace itself."

A smile crept across Odemog's face, as he fingered the sheathed dagger at his side with one hand and felt the bag concealing the gold with the other. "Jackman, I can think of no greater gift to receive at this time than that which you have just presented. Tell me the condition of the tunnel."

"If you are considering entering, Odemog, it will not be a comfortable distance, for at times, it narrows greatly, and the ceiling drops to only four feet in height. There are torches to light along the way and the tunnel always remains dry, though it has not been used in moons. Many moons, in fact. I would suggest that I lead my people through on your behalf."

Odemog looked between Jackman, the tunnel entrance, and the other leaders, as he pondered this happy turn of events. He strode forward and entered the opening, took in a deep breath, paused, and turned around, emerging with a look of utter determination.

"Juliet, you and Thorandal shall lead the arms men forward as planned. I think I shall delight in following Jackman and the Galdordon people into the heart of Khordrya. Key to the Kingdom, indeed." He reached out and slapped Jackman on the back.

"Sir, uh, Odemog, your stature, that is, you are—well—a giant…"

"My stature, as you put it, has not stopped me yet, my friend. Where necessary, I can put hands and knees to the earth and crawl through. There is no shame in being accommodating of the situation. Why, it is the very best of oneself who can adapt and flex. Listen to me. Time is wasting. You have seen the signals?"

"Moments before your arrival," Thorandal replied.

"We have fallen behind, then," raising his arm to wave all forward, Odemog stood at the doorway as he watched Thorandal mount, while Juliet recommenced the advance. As the horses moved forward, so did the

Galdordon people, who now came to the doorway and, one by one, disappeared into the tunnel.

"It's dark in there."

"Skeeter, you have been quiet. I nearly forgot you were there."

"Do you really think it wise to enter such a small, dark space?"

"I think trust is in order here, my friend. This is nothing to what we face ahead." Odemog reached up and gently took Skeeter's tail in his grip at the base. With fingers wrapped around it, he slowly pulled his hand away, stroking the tail, a caring gesture that reassured them both.

"I am with you all the way, Moggie."

"Let us join them now, Skeeter." And with those words, Odemog turned to enter the tunnel, pulling the door closed behind him.

53

From the north, the south, and the east, arms men on foot and on horseback closed in on the Palace which, until this moment, was entirely in its own world of confusion. And then it happened: "Sound the alert," a voice shouted. "Alarm! Alarm!" called a second voice. Kasreya's movement and MaginTor's offense were spotted as they emerged from the last of the sheltered ravines and pastures. Into open fields they all marched as the Khordrian soldiers raced to their posts to defend the Palace.

In moments, the sky filled with waves of dark slivers that grew to perilous arrows as they met with their targets. The arrows emerged from the field and were returned by those who took to their posts along the palace structure.

Word quickly reached Morzan through Walcod, who nearly bumped into him as he raced around a corner.

"My Lord, we are under attack!" He shouted, out of breath.

"What gibberish are you uttering, fool?" Morzan shook his head, his heart knowing the battle was finally afoot.

"Movement was spotted emerging from the outskirts. All are at station and ordered to fire first."

"Out of my way," Morzan brushed Walcod aside and stepped up his pace to a run as he burst through the passage to emerge into the center court grounds. Looking up, he saw men fall from the wall as they grasped at arrows embedded in their chests and necks. "Move in," he called up to them. "Close the gaps!" Troops moved across the grounds and raced up stairs and ladders to take position along the wall-walk.

Morzan looked to the turret to see a sword fight in play. He was puzzled to see his ranks fighting amongst themselves when it dawned on him that they had been infiltrated.

"Sword," Morzan called as he raised his arm. Through the air vertically, came a long sword which he sidestepped in a manner that enabled him to grasp hold the grip as it passed in front of him. Gathering momentum, he raced to the stairs, taking them two at a time. Looking about, he began to run towards the stairs to the wall-walk. He called down to Walcod "Double the guard on Thane-Ra. Hurry, man."

From the turrets now emerged the remaining signal men who had been first to move on the Palace. Seeing one who came from the east, Morzan refocused as he raced toward the infiltrator who never saw him coming. In fact, all he saw of Morzan, who raced up behind him, was the tip of the long sword as it emerged, bloody, from his back through his chest.

"You shall NOT trespass upon Khordom Palace!" shouted Morzan, whose roar was that of an insane and violated man. August, seeing his turret-invading comrade fall, let out a cry from across the structure, drew his sword and advanced to join the fight.

Morzan turned and watched as men fought and fell where they stood. Picking up a bow and arrows from one who lay twisting on the earth, Morzan ran back down the stairs to a protected vantage point and began firing recklessly. His aim was erratic for his rage disabled him. Recognizing his own distress, Morzan dropped his head for a moment. It was enough to change his position, whereby he saw rapid movement from the corner of his eye. He looked to the corner of the grounds below in time to see a ragtag bunch emerge from a milliner's shack and break off in small, fast-moving groups. Seeing the same as he followed Morzan, August slipped by to join the others and strengthen their resolve.

Hunched over to avoid injury, Morzan crept back to the stairs, watching the movement all the while. He slipped behind the stairwell and into a hidden passage that led to the Great Hall.

54

Odemog emerged from the tunnel soon after shutting the door behind him, having raced through tunnels with the determined Galdordon people. It had been a tight space; indeed, his hemp shirt was torn in numerous places in spite of his mail. Skeeter gasped for air as he blinked, adjusting to the light of the milliner's shack. Jackman greeted them with a smile.

"You are a trooper. I imagine that was no easy feat for you, sir?"

"Shall we say, all in a day's work? Where to next, Jackman?"

"Such a tight space, this," he gestured about the shack, "the others broke off in groups as they arrived. Be assured they have gone to work. My people will release the gate as quickly as they can to allow the others entrance to the Palace."

"We should waste no time waiting and go directly to Thane-Ra. Will you know where to find him?"

"I expect him so vain as to lie wait in his lair within the Great Hall. Win or lose, he shall expect an intruder to come to him."

"Away then; my mission waits," commanded Odemog, beckoning Jackman to show him the way to Thane-Ra's throne within the Great Hall. Jackman gestured to Mikael and they moved forward together.

＊＊＊

Confusion broke out in all directions as the attack continued and grew on three sides of the Palace. The people of Galdordon compounded the confusion as they began to strike down the unsuspecting soldiers of Thane-Ra from within their own safety. Gradually, they fought a path through to their main target: the gates of the Palace. And, in no time, the guard that held the gates was eliminated one by one.

A rush of troops came at the Galdordon fighters, but such was their determination that they would not release control of the gate back to the soldiers. The gate was opened and a cheer erupted as they watched Kasreya and her troops press forward. Shields raised to fend off arrows, the first flank narrowed to enter through the gate and the battle continued on both sides of the walls that were erected to protect Khordrya.

Morzan moved quickly down the darkened passage, feeling the walls as he ran. It had been some time since he inspected this secret passage and then it was with a torch. This was no easy race. He counted doors as he stumbled along.

Outside the wall, running cautiously, was Odemog, led back by Jackman. They moved so as not to be seen but with speed, hoping to find Thane-Ra quickly. Khordom Palace was known for its many passages and rooms. A dark structure, the lighting was bad even on a bright day.

Neck and neck, the two parties turned corners and moved through the maze of the structure and then it happened—Morzan burst through a door and into the chamber in which Thane-Ra stood receiving counsel on the battle outside. A guard quickly tackled him, forcing Morzan to the floor with a spear pressed flat across his chest. "Fool, get off me!" he shouted. Walcod ran to his side and helped him to rise from the floor.

Hearing the shout, Jackman and Mikael attempted to stop dead in their tracks as they were about to emerge round the corner, but it was too late. Odemog barreled into them knocking Jackman and Mikael directly into the room. Following behind Odemog, Jackman, and Mikael were seven Galdordon men who had observed their trek. They had sufficient time to see what was happening and stop in good time.

"Behold, we have visitors," called Thane-Ra. The guards advanced on the hapless two. But quicker than they, Odemog reached down to his daggers and heaved them quickly to drop two men preparing to strike Jackman. Recovering, Jackman drew his sword and took on the next guard, allowing enough time for Mikael and the seven followers to come to their aid. Odemog regarded Thane-Ra and stood still with his hands at his sides.

"Enough, enough," called Thane-Ra to his guards who gradually withdrew leaving the casualties on the ground. Jackman held up his hand and stepped back with Mikael and the seven.

"Who is this giant before me, then?" asked Thane-Ra.

"I can tell you the name of the fool before you, Thane-Ra." Morzan, recovered from his narrow brush with the guard, glared at Odemog.

"Is it you, son of Morlog?" Odemog looked shocked as he studied Morzan.

"Shut up, you oversized fool," Morzan spit the words out; he was so filled with venom.

"Until recently, I thought you were dead."

"I was dead until I came here and received the sponsorship of Thane-Ra."

"You left a loving family to chase an evil dragon, Morzan," replied Odemog.

"And you will die by this dragon," Thane-Ra laughed.

Skeeter observed the movement of Odemog's hand as it slowly reached into the bag at his side. As discreetly as he slipped his hand in, he withdrew it and began clenching and releasing his fist. Skeeter, sitting on Odemog's shoulder, tucked behind his braid and grasped the chainmail with all four paws.

"It is not I who shall die this day."

"What makes you think you can defeat the great Thane-Ra?" Morzan demanded.

"Meet the Keeper of the Kingdom," interjected Jackman.

"Did he say 'kingdom keeper? Is that what I heard?" laughed Thane-Ra, staring at Odemog. "Do not stand before me and pretend that the fairy tale of kingdom keepers has been bestowed upon your imagination? Perhaps you are a fool as Morzan suggests."

"There is not a fool in all of Mazgamor, save yourself, Thane-Ra, and perhaps now as I see him, Morzan. You cannot believe that you will continue to rage upon the Kingdom with your brutality and evil!"

"You are the fool who comes to MY kingdom," hissed Thane-Ra.

"I am the Keeper, Thane-Ra," Odemog spoke softly. Thane-Ra blanched as he was unsettled by the voice.

"Kingdom Keepers are but a legend, fool," Morzan blurted, as if his boyhood had returned.

The sounds of battle grew stronger outside of the room as swords were heard clashing and bouncing off one another. Shouts echoed through the halls. Thane-Ra glanced about the room at his dozen guards and waved his right hand in a semi-circle. The guards took up their positions around Thane-Ra in an offensive stance. Jackman, Mikael, and the others stepped forward but Odemog shook his head slowly. Jackman waved off the men, who stood down.

"You have but one fear Thane-Ra, is this not true?" asked Odemog.

"Thane-Ra is fearless," asserted Morzan.

"Will you shut up, you useless flap!" Thane-Ra bellowed at Morzan, who shook in his boots.

"My Lord?"

"You guaranteed me, Morzan, your plan would be executed flawlessly. Victory would be ours. Fool." Thane-Ra, in a moment of distraction, unloaded his anger, humiliating Morzan.

"Yours is a divided house, Thane-Ra. But worse, as Keeper, I know of one fear you hold. Through this, you will know I am Keeper and shall fulfill my mission for Mazgamor."

"I see no evidence and still I stand before you." Thane-Ra inspected Odemog where he stood. "One nod and the guards will strike you down where you stand."

Gesturing broadly with his right hand, Odemog rested his left hand on his hip with fingers pointing down. His right hand touched his sword. "If you must, but there is one thing I should say before your men strike me down." While he spoke, Skeeter clambered down his back to where the fingers pointed.

All eyes were on Thane-Ra to see if he would grant Odemog this wish.

"There is not a word you might utter."

"Sanctitoro," whispered Odemog.

"What say you?" Thane-Ra leaned forward to hear more clearly.

"Gold, and not just any precious metal. Sanctitoro."

"Impossible!" Thane-Ra called out. It was as if an entire conversation had occurred between the two men as the looks on their faces told a great story.

"For Mazgamor!" Odemog shouted as he raised up his arm and launched a small gold dagger directly at Thane-Ra's heart. With his other hand he drew his long sword and swung out at the guards who lunged toward him.

"Attack," shouted Jackman as he drew his sword and joined the fight.

Bewildered, Morzan stepped back and slipped behind a drape, working his way towards yet another passage, through which he escaped.

* * *

Juliet signaled to MaginTor as she and Thorandal fought their way around the perimeter of the building. MaginTor had a grin on his face as he watched them approach.

"Should you not be focused on fighting, friend?" asked Juliet as she came within earshot.

Laughing, he replied, "you have but to enter the keep and see for yourself. This lot fights without direction. Ride on and you shall see." MaginTor directed them to enter the palace gates.

There, before Juliet, the torrid battle they had anticipated had all but fizzled. For these were truly not warriors but an enslaved group of craftspeople and farmers. A sad loss of life lay crumpled about as in any battle, while others dropped their weapons and wandered aimlessly amidst the carnage. The battle consumed itself from within, ending almost as quickly as it had begun.

"There can be no battle worth such loss." Juliet spoke to no one in particular as she scanned the scene.

"These lives sacrificed for the many, Juliet. Without these lost souls, the Kingdom of Mazgamor would have suffered greater defeat." Morlog rode up behind her, joined by King Magnus and the others. The Royal Family had been kept at a distance for safety. Juliet observed the sadness on their faces.

"Who has seen Odemog?" called Kasreya from her position across the center court.

"Search the palace," commanded Morlog.

Several search parties led by the princes, Kasell, and allies spread out in all directions to locate Odemog and the few Galdordon people with whom he had travelled. Arms men and women moved about the grounds tending to the wounded and collecting weapons, then guided those who surrendered readily to another part of the grounds. Energy began to build as all realized the victory at hand.

"This is a day for history, my sister," Kasreya greeted Juliet with a hug as they oversaw the work of the arms men.

"Indeed, it is, Reya. Indeed, it is."

* * *

With eyes bulging in disbelief, Thane-Ra quickly raised his hand, mustering his telekinetic powers and stopping the golden dagger mid-air. It fell to the ground. He leapt from his throne, rage and shock boiling, causing furniture and curtains to blow violently from his path. Safe inside Odemog's pouch of gold, Skeeter watched the turn of events. He pushed pieces forward as Odemog grabbed for more gold strips from within the pouch.

Taking two giant steps forward, Odemog advanced on the fleeing man. With one hand he burnished sword, with the other he fashioned a tip of gold molding it to the blade. Thane-Ra stopped in his tracks, spun about, and raised his arms with force. Decorative armaments flew from the walls and launched themselves at the Keeper. Wielding his sword fluidly with grace, one by one, Odemog knocked them from the air. Thane-Ra continued to back up as Odemog advanced. He stumbled, turned, and picked up the sword over which he had tripped. Odemog was upon him as he raised the sword in defense. The two clashed blades and moved about the room. Thane-Ra's words were cutting as he called out "You, giant, cannot defeat the evil I have set about this land for, if I die, wrath will be unleashed that will poison the lands for generations to come."

"You know not of what you speak, old man." Odemog withdrew his blade for just a moment as he considered the meaning of these words. Thane-Ra saw advantage and turned to escape.

Watching as he fought, Jackman spun around and caught a sword across his blade that reverberated up his arms. He fell back against Odemog, whose life he was protecting.

"Thank you, friend," Odemog exclaimed as he realized what had happened.

"Think nothing of it, Keeper!" Jackman called as he lunged at the soldier.

Refocusing, Odemog watched Thane-Ra attempt to leave. His size his advantage, the Keeper lunged forward, leaping over fallen furniture and landing in front of Thane-Ra. Their swords met again but Odemog was bigger and stronger. This time, he used his advantage. The Keeper swung strong and knocked the sword loose from Thane-Ra's grip. Raising his gold-tipped sword high, he plunged it through the heart of the disbelieving tyrant. Standing over the fallen man, Odemog briefly took pause as he watched the life fade from Thane-Ra's face. He looked around the room of battling men.

Odemog saw a sturdy table and bounded for it. He leapt in the air and landed solidly upon it. Poised atop the table this giant was even larger and commanded the attention of all in the room. "Soldiers of Khordom Palace, men of Galdordon, lay down your swords! Before you lies the end of your agony." He gestured to where Thane-Ra lay. "On the ground, defeated, is the carcass of the dragon that enslaved you. End your battle for the fight is over. You are all free." One by one they lowered their arms. Some dropped their swords and fell to their knees at the thought of freedom. Many fought for fear—and fear alone—that their lives and those of their families would end, should they not stand by Thane-Ra. They looked on in disbelief.

For legend held that, as in generations before, Thane-Ra could only die by the golden tip of an arrow. This was the power that only a Keeper could wield. And on this day, Keeper Odemog did just that.

The room filled with familiar faces as the King, Morlog, and the princes entered the large chamber. Morlog, on seeing Thane-Ra on the ground, went straight to him. Observing the sword in his chest he turned to Odemog who jumped from the tabletop.

"Well done, Keeper," nodded Morlog. Odemog nodded back.

"Keeper Odemog, you have the blessings of the Kingdom of Mazgamor for what you have done here this day," said King Magnus as he rushed to Odemog and wrapped his arms around him in a generous embrace. Standing tall over the King, Odemog blushed at this reception.

"I don't understand how you did it?" asked Jackman as he came around in front. "Thane-Ra stopped your gold dagger mid-air."

"I helped," called Skeeter, who now stood tall again on Odemog's shoulder.

"That you did, Skeeter," Odemog reached up and scratched him under the chin. Skeeter turned his head from side to side to be sure both cheeks were scratched.

"What did that scruffy little fellow do this time, Odemog?"

"Well, Morlog, I sensed the gold on the hilt of my sword was inadequate. I had to work the gold into the tip to achieve the desired result."

"The death of Thane-Ra."

"That's right, Fazzog." Odemog turned to acknowledge the prince. "Skeeter crept into my pouch when the first attempt failed."

"I used my noggin!" called Skeeter.

"I guess you did," Odemog brushed his hand over Skeeter's back. "Skeeter used his fine set of incisors to pinch away at a sliver of Sanctitoro, giving it a point—a better point than I could with my fingertips. As I gave chase, I melded it to the tip of my sword, giving it greater power."

"So, it seems that the legend rings true," Said Morlog with a smile.

"For this, Morlog, I am very grateful!" sighed Odemog.

"As are we all," added the King.

"As are we all," came a chorus of voices followed by laughter save for one. Odemog looked over at Annabella, who had entered with Sam and Dero.

"But I see only one lying there," she said.

"What do you mean Princess?"

"Odemog, you promised to stop Morzan." He looked from the princess to the King who was looking at Morlog. Odemog turned and asked "Jackman, did you see him?"

"Keeper, I was watching you and Thane-Ra. I did not see him. I am so sorry."

"He must be stopped," Morlog shouted. "Borzog, take after him immediately. He must be found."

55

Morzan emerged from the passage through the trunk of an ancient hollow gabelnut tree west of the palace. Wheezing, he leaned against the trunk to catch his breath. He had detoured and stopped long enough to gather some possessions and rope a horgle that had fought and struggled against his pull all along the passage. Morzan could not fly out from the palace for he surely would be seen and shot down. He gave a long hard tug and the horgle now emerged from the trunk thrashing at him. Morzan mounted the horgle and with a makeshift whip in hand urged him into the air. They flew low and fast over the trees as Morzan escaped north and east, toward Galdordon Forest.

56

Magnus stood proudly watching as the allies worked together to aid the injured and fallen. Kasell, Thorandal, Juliet, and a selection of their men and women worked tirelessly in the keep to identify and aid the Khordrians, who had been freed with the death of their dictator. The mood was light but, in truth, Magnus' heart was heavy.

"My friend, I read your thoughts," Morlog laid a hand on the King's shoulder. "We shall find her."

"I fear the worst, Morlog."

"The Keeper and Galdordon people search as we speak."

"And what of Morzan? Perhaps he stole away with her captive."

"You must cease your imaginings; a great defeat has been achieved today. Here, take rest." Morlog took the King by the elbow and guided him to a table where nourishments had been set out. Weary from worry, Magnus sat without argument. Princess Annabella emerged with a pitcher of pomegranate juice. "Drink this, Father," she said as she poured for him.

"My daughter, you are always there with what we need—a good word, a story, or as you have now, refreshment. Body, mind, spirit, you have a caring way about you."

"It is only what you have taught me, Father, nothing more. Drink up." She handed him the mug.

A rumbling of racing feet grew louder and Borzog, with Mezzog and a party of searchers steps behind, emerged through the doorway. "Morzan is nowhere to be found. There are passages everywhere and we continue to search. It will take the day, Father, but we will find him."

"Morzan knows this palace better than anyone, Borzog. There will be secrets we cannot find in a day. We will make our way home to Constantia as soon as..." the King's voice trailed off as he saw what approached from behind the column across the room.

There, emerging from darkness, was Kasreya with a beaming smile. She stopped and turned her head to look behind. The King set down his mug and rose from his seat. A long shadow first emerged, bringing with it the Keeper of the Kingdom. Odemog stepped out from behind the pillar and looked directly at the King. In his arms, he carried a large, seemingly lifeless bundle. Princess Annabella leapt to her feet and raced past her father. "Mother!" she cried.

Morlog cleared off the table as Odemog approached. Borzog slashed a long drape with his sword and ran over with the heavy curtain to make comfortable the table. Annabella stroked her mother's hair as she walked, two steps to Odemog's one, with him to the table.

"Send for Forthrumal," Mezzog called out.

"Gently now, Keeper, set her down here," Morlog directed Odemog.

"Where...?" Magnus was almost speechless as he took Madelina's hand in his.

"She was not far, but the chamber in which she was bound was well concealed. It was Skeeter who found it."

"Oh, Skeeter —thank you!" cried Annabella. Kasreya came forward with a bowl of warm water and Amara brought clean linen. They gently washed Madelina's face, neck, and hands. Kasreya took a small cloth and soaked it with wine. She squeezed it gently over the loosely parted lips of the Queen, slowly allowing drops to seep into her mouth. Annabella continued to stroke her mother's auburn hair. All eyes were on the King and Queen as Forthrumal strode into the Great Hall. Morlog placed his hand on the King's shoulder; Magnus looked up and saw Forthrumal standing by.

"Lord Forthrumal, please, do what you can for your Queen." He stepped away, taking Annabella in his arms as Forthrumal moved to the

Queen's side. Forthrumal nodded at the King, then placed a hand over her heart and closed his eyes to count her heartbeat.

Forthrumal beckoned to the page who carried his bag. "Heart is weak, my King, but the beat is steady—confident." He did not look up as he dug about in his bag, pulling out various powders and plants. "Water," he commanded. The page ran to the fire, knowing this meant hot water. He returned with a bucket and bowl. Thus began Forthrumal's alchemy. He treated cuts while a potion brewed. "Dagger," he held out his hand for the page to rest a dagger across his palm. Forthrumal mixed and scooped a blend from the bowl and placed the laden tip of the blade to the lips of the Queen. With fingertip, he dabbed more potion between her lip and nose. The page dabbed the Queen's forehead with a warm cloth and all about her watched and waited.

The light grew dim in the Great Hall. Magnus sat close by, holding Annabella in his arms. The three princes stood attentively, unmoving, at the feet of their mother. Odemog stood at a distance while the other members of The Circle, Kasreya, Thorandal, MaginTor, and Morlog stood behind the King, waiting.

Odemog puzzled over the escape of Morzan and wondered to what end he had come, if at all. Where in this great Kingdom would such a traitor go to hide, had he survived? And what poisons would unleash with Thane-Ra's demise if there were any truth to his threat? As he drifted deeper and deeper into thought, he did not notice Morlog join him at his side.

"Keeper, you have fulfilled your mission this day. Be proud."

"Only a part Morlog, I fear I have let you down."

"No son, your mission was to defeat Thane-Ra, who kept this Kingdom in a state of fear and despair. Your leadership—this battle today—has freed the people of Khordrya. The threat to the Kingdom is gone. Peace shall be upon us who reside in Mazgamor."

"But what of Morzan?" There was a long pause before Morlog softly spoke. "His evil, too, shall come to an end. Mark my words, Keeper Odemog. Mark my words."

Across the room there was a stirring. Morlog and Odemog moved forward to watch as the King rose from his seat, Annabella now at her mother's side. The princes smiled as they saw Queen Madelina blink open her eyes. She cast her gaze upon her daughter and smiled weakly. "You are safe, my child."

"Mother, do not speak."

"Save your strength, my Queen," instructed Forthrumal, who took her wrist and counted the pulse. Tears rolled down her face as Magnus moved into her view. Disregarding Forthrumal, the King reached out and took his Queen in his arms holding her close. "My darling Madelina. Maddie, how I feared for you. Praise be, you are safe again."

"Always safe in your arms, Magnus," she whispered and closed her eyes, drifting off again.

"My King, she must rest," Forthrumal placed a hand on the King's shoulder, then took the Queen from his grasp to lay her back down. He nodded to the page, who brought forth a hot drink for the King to ease his heart and mind.

As Magnus turned to sit, his fellow Circle members surrounded him with praise and warm wishes. "Ah, my friend," Thorandal thumped the King on the back. "We are a force to be reckoned with, are we not?"

"Gently now, Thor," Kasreya shook her head. "MaginTor, we are dearly grateful for your arrival."

"It was a close escape from the Point, I must say, but the journey to join you worthwhile. I agree Thor, we are a force, we certainly are." He looked around and cast eyes upon Odemog.

"What say you now, Keeper? We of the Circle accept your guidance." Odemog looked at Morlog quizzically. "Who gives guidance to the Circle? Not I?"

"Keeper, this is not done. You have only just begun in your safeguard of this great Kingdom. Of this I am certain."

"If this is so, I propose safe return to Constantia to unite this family," he glanced at the relieved Royal Family. "Let us leave Kasell, Marsdell, and those they choose to aid the Khordrians in recovery of a renewed community. We shall regroup anon at the Gathering." The Circle agreed that a Gathering was called for as they must consider the needs of Aureopiscis and Khordrya both with their loss of leadership.

"The Kingdom shall be renewed. We gather at the next moon, then," directed Morlog.

"The next moon," replied The Circle.

57

And so it was that Kasell and his arms men, with support of a Tsesiwan presence led by Stronleya, aided in the restoration of a united and peaceful Khordrya. The gates were bolted open; the keep was renewed with tents of an open market and grounds to freely travel. Children emerged as the Galdordon people were reunited with families, and laughter filled the air.

* * *

The King, with his healing Queen and their children, emerged from Khordom Palace to travel westward to Constantia Glen, escorted by a relaxed and merry troop of arms men. They would return to Constantia to be welcomed by a happy village and two small Princesses, Lily and Tulip. Joy was restored to Magnus' Kingdom as the Royal Family welcomed their people to the celebration of joy upon their return.

* * *

Followed by Sam and Dero, who had quietly watched the dynamics unfold after battle, Morlog and Odemog went with Kasreya, accompanied by Amara, to see MaginTor and his people off at the ocean shore, while Juliet and Thorandal prepared their own for the journey back home to western and northern destinations.

As MaginTor's fleet cast off from shore, Odemog turned to Kasreya and Morlog. "We go to Constantia?"

"Agreed," replied Kasreya. "Morlog, we must prepare a plan for pursuit of Morzan."

"Leave it to the Keeper, Kasreya," he was abrupt in this matter. She nodded. Odemog frowned. "We go to Constantia to celebrate. This we shall do first." Turning to his friends he said "Sam, Dero, I have a request of you," Odemog put a hand on each of their shoulders.

"Of course, Brother," Dero responded.

"Anything, Keeper," said Sam, nudging Dero.

"Return to our beloved Sweetbrooke Wren and give my mother word. All is right and well in the Kingdom. The greater threat has been vanquished. We shall return home to celebrate soon."

"Joyful words, Odemog," Morlog nodded in approval.

"Let us be on our way, friends," Kasreya returned to her mount.

"We meet at the castle within Constantia." Odemog settled on Nassir as the others took to their mounts with him.

"Safe travels, Keeper," Amara called out as the group took to air. She nudged her horse forward, following Kasreya on the path that would lead them to Constantia Glen.

EPILOGUE

From the air, everything looked fresher, newer, brighter, and freer than ever before. Odemog felt a deep sense of peace as he relaxed, leaning forward on his elbow upon Nassir's back. Skeeter sat upon his shoulder, holding tight the thick braid as he whispered, "lucky I stowed away," in Odemog's ear. Odemog smiled and nodded thanks.

Morlog and Vadim eased forward in the air to fly side by side with Odemog as Sam and Dero cut away in the air to head northwest to Sweetbrooke. "Keeper, your peace is well earned but do not let it distract you from your renewed mission."

"I wish not to think of this until after the celebration, Morlog."

"I understand, Moggie, but remember as you relax, the evil one continues to posture and plot. We know not what he is truly capable of. For all the time spent with Thane-Ra, we do not know what else he learned or amassed, or where the coward Morzan now hides."

"I wonder if it was cowardice or cunning that he stole away as he did, Morlog."

"You pose a good question that validates my point, Keeper," tired, Vadim began to fall back away from Nassir as Morlog called out, "Do not let your thoughts rest long, Keeper Odemog."

* * *

Music drifted up through the air and the smell of a delicious feast caught in Odemog's nostrils. He took a long breath causing his mouth to salivate. *Rabboo...* he thought.

Nassir and Vadim turned and began to head to ground. Below they could see the celebration under way.

Cheering erupted as a horn sounded, announcing their arrival. King Magnus and Queen Madelina, accompanied by their six reunited children, greeted them in the Queen's Meadow where Lisan tore at grass as he stood waiting for his fellow mordaghas to arrive. Lisan had taken to Kasell and returned to Constantia with him, following the settlement of Khordrya, having left Jackman in charge as interim magistrate.

Odemog jumped from Nassir almost before he touched ground. He strode forward to greet the royal family with great enthusiasm. "How pleased I am to see you together, well, and happy," he cried. Lily rushed forward with a flower garland. He dropped to one knee and bent forward for her to drape it over his head and neck. Picking her up, Odemog rose tall and gave her a gentle squeeze. "You are a sight for sore eyes, little one. Thank you for this sweet welcome. Do I smell rabboo?" She laughed, "Put me down Odemog, or should I say, Keeper," she squirmed from his arms as he set her down. "I told the kitchen all your favourites and the sweetest of Brussels sprouts are to be cooked to your liking as well."

"You, my sweet Princess Lily, are a peach!"

The King and Queen laughed, delighting in the exchange. "Welcome," said Magnus "join us at table. Tonight, we dine together, then rest. Tomorrow, Kasreya should arrive, and the real celebration will begin." Lily and Tulip each took a hand and walked Odemog forward as the rest of the family, accompanied by Morlog, followed.

* * *

The celebration began early with the welcoming of Kasreya and Amara. Juliet had decided to rest the archers in Constantia and await Kasreya's return. The reunion was joyful. The young Constantian arms man, Leo, was the first forward to greet Amara and take the reins of her horse. Kasreya, as usual, observed his blush.

Music filled the air and swept joyful energy throughout Constantia Glen. As the day went on, a further surprise was in store for Odemog. The sun began to dip in the sky to rest for the night, and soon a horn sounded. Odemog, Morlog and others gathered with the Royals to observe the alert. There in the sky came Leevon of Twin Ponds followed by three mordaghas. Upon them were riders Sam, Dero, and, to Odemog's great happiness and surprise, the third rider was his mother, Odemega Mary. Odemog turned to the King quizzically.

"On our return, Keeper, we sent word by way of Leevon to your mother that all was well. We invited her to join us in celebration. It appears your brothers, as you call them, have escorted her along."

"What joy! My deepest gratitude to you, King Magnus." Odemog ran to greet their arrival as Leevon touched down each of the mordaghas followed, one by one. He touched foreheads with Leevon in gratitude and strode to his mother. The reunion was nothing but joyful, to be sure.

The day carried on with games, a feast to beat all others and stories of battle and conquest. All was right and good in the Kingdom of Mazgamor. As the evening settled in, everyone gathered to hear Master Teller Morlog present the story of the royal rescue. He began slowly with a traditional opening.

"Listen as I share with you, what will become a legend from the old. Hear the story well, as it is one that must be told…"

With everyone focused intently on Morlog, Keeper Odemog stepped out of the great chamber onto a balcony to look up at the stars. He listened to Morlog's distant voice. As his mind drifted, his peace began to fade; a question forming.

He looked out to the distant forest and spoke aloud. "What made you run, Morzan, cowardice…or cunning?"

ACKNOWLEDGEMENTS

This journey has been a long, patient one with many rests along the way. I am grateful to be at this point on the pathway to share Odemog's story with you. Odemog is a gentle giant with a huge heart and a kind soul. I hope he becomes an inspiration to many.

He came to life in a conversation with my, then 4-year-old, niece who so casually revealed him as her imaginary friend. My response was "he sounds like a lovely character for a story." The rest is history. Thank you for the inspiration, Juliet!

Along every pathway there are twists and turns and there have been many here. To keep it simple I will say thank you so much to Donna Millar for your wisdom in guiding the editing and proofreading process, a journey all unto itself!

To Marilyn, thank you always for standing by me to help me stay on the path forward and not to withdraw when things stalled or detoured along the way. Love is a wonderful thing.

To Jo-Anne Harrison, how is that I should be so blessed to have such an encouraging friend always there at all the right moments along my life journey? Thanks pal!

Forever alive in my heart – I thank my parents for always believing in me and giving me the inspiration and courage to face adventure head on.

A special thanks to Maureen and Gerald for your generosity in sharing your magical cottage with us so I could truly find Mazgamor! It does exist!

Always inspiring my life – to my eleven – as you grow, you inspire me to be my best self to support the wonderful people you have become. I love you all.

To my family and dearest friends – you inspire and support me. My life is blessed as a result. May you all feel the strength and kindness of Odemog and his friends in your lives. And may a little of Skeeter's mischief brighten your days!

Thank you all.

Photo Credits: Mary Simchuk

R.A. Dunne makes her fiction debut with *Kingdom Keeper*—a sweeping tale of courage, friendship, and the triumph of light over darkness. Before stepping into the world of fantasy adventure, Dunne's writing focused on therapeutic recreation, including the 2020 publication *Moments: From Extravagant Programs to Extraordinary Moments*. Now, she's thrilled to introduce readers to **Odemog, Skeeter,** and a loyal band of allies whose adventures in Mazgamor celebrate the power of unity and hope. Dunne lives along the **Fraser River** in **New Westminster, British Columbia**, a little corner of paradise that continues to inspire reflection, imagination, and the occasional mischievous squirrel.

Stay Tuned for Book Two of

KINGDOM KEEPER

Follow R.A. Dunne for updates and upcoming releases:
https://radunne-author.com
@radunne_author on Instagram and
Facebook at https://www.facebook.com/radunne.author/

Printed in Dunstable, United Kingdom